Other Titles By Angie Daniels

A WILL TO LOVE

DESTINY IN DISGUISE

ENDLESS ENCHANTMENT

HART & SOUL

INTIMATE INTENTIONS

IN THE COMPANY OF MY SISTAHS

LOVE UNCOVERED

TIME IS OF THE ESSENCE

WHEN I FIRST SAW YOU

WHEN IT RAINS

A Delight Before Christmas

Angie Daniels

Parker Publishing, LLC

Noire Passion is an imprint of Parker Publishing, LLC.

Copyright © 2006 by Angie Daniels

Published by Parker Publishing, LLC
12523 Limonite Avenue, Suite #440-245
Mira Loma, California 91752
www.parker-publishing.com

ISBN 10:   1-60043-000-7
ISBN 13:   978-1-60043-000-8

First Edition

Manufactured in the United States of America

Dedication

This book is dedicated to the wonderful staff at Parker Publishing.
Wish y'all years of success.

Acknowledgements

To my girls Katherine D. Jones and Maureen Smith for trusting me enough to jump on board and become a part of the fun. Thanks ladies.

To Deatri King-Bey for doing a fabulous job of editing this story and making me dig a little deeper even when I didn't feel like it.

To my girl Angelique Justin for just being you.

Chapter One

Reginald Hodges stepped into the country club with a wide grin on his face. Tonight he would hang with the crème de la crème of the pediatric medical community.

He strolled across the floor and either bobbed his head or mouthed "whassup" as he moved toward a reserved seat at the center of the room. Yep, tonight he got to see how the rich folks act. Halting in front of the large recliner, he frowned. Too bad he was dressed in a Santa Claus suit.

Tonight was St. Louis Children's Hospital's annual holiday party. It was invitation only. Because he was a general contractor, he definitely had not been invited, regardless of how many offices he was responsible for renovating. The banquet hall was flooded with physicians, directors and other medical staff of the hospital and its surrounding pediatric facilities. The only reason Reginald attended the party was because of Dr. Cameron Clarke.

An hour ago, his homeboy had dropped by his place begging him to stand in for him tonight as Santa Claus. Apparently, some honey he'd been trying to get with for weeks had finally agreed to make him dinner, and there was no way in the world Cameron was missing out on the possibility of sampling a little sumptin' sumptin' for dessert. At the thought of a long bourgeois evening, Reginald had quickly declined. That is…before Cameron handed him three fifty-dollar bills with a promise to match it if he stayed until ten.

So here he was prepared to shout, "Ho Ho Ho," while handing out Christmas gifts—toys for the children, and a small gold pin with CARING FOR KIDS engraved in fine script for the adults—courtesy of Children's.

"Heeeyy, Santa," sang a tall red-boned woman. She smiled as she swayed her succulent hips past his chair.

Reginald lowered his gaze to her fine backside in a spandex green dress and shook his head. "Yo-Yo-Yo, sexy mama," he called after her. "Make sure you come back and tell Santa if you've been naughty or nice."

Leigh giggled playfully. "Ask Mark, I guarantee he'll tell you I've been a very bad girl." She winked and disappeared inside the ladies room.

Tossing his head back, Reginald chuckled. Leigh was a trip. Her husband Markeith Montgomery was the medical director of the Wellston Pediatric Center, and one of his homies from back in the day. The two had been together since college. He smiled and took a moment to reminisce on the good old days. Reginald, Markeith and Cameron were once known as the "three musketeers." Chuckling lightly, he remembered how they stayed in trouble. If you found one, you were bound to find the other two knee-deep in doo-doo.

Reginald rested the black bag on the seat of the chair just as his stomach growled. Noticing that people were already eating, he decided to scope out the buffet table before taking a seat. In order to arrive on time, he had rushed out the door, and hadn't had a chance to stop and grab dinner. He strolled to the table, then slapped his palms together while he gazed down at a meal fit for a king. Roast, ham and a turkey with all the trimmings were at one end, desserts at the other.

"Yeaaah, boy," Reginald murmured, then reached for a plate and loaded it with food. At the end of the table, he spotted a dish generously filled with caviar. He reached for a cracker and spooned a little on top. Five seconds later, he was spitting it in the trash. *Yuck! Don't believe the hype*, he thought as he wiped his mouth. He carried his plate over near a nine foot tall Christmas tree, leaned against the wall, and reached for his fork.

Reginald ate quietly as his eyes traveled around the room, looking for any familiar faces. He spotted Markeith on the other side of the room in a gray Armani suit, talking to a distinguished-looking gray-haired man. He would holla at him later. There was a time and a place for everything. Tonight was all about business. Glancing around, he couldn't think of anyone else he knew that would be in attendance, except for one particular golden-eyed beauty he was hoping would show up. Berlin Dupree. The woman had a body that screamed the words M-A-K-E L-O-V-E T-O-M-E. She was fine. She had curves made for holding onto. Breasts so perky and round he was certain they would fit perfectly in the palms of his hands. And big, pretty legs meant for wrapping around a man's waist as he thrust all ten inches in and out of her sweet, hot, juicy…Swallowing hard, he didn't dare allow himself to finish the fantasy. *Too late.* An erection sprung to life.

"Down boy," Reginald mumbled. He was grateful for the oversized Santa Suit that hid a serious hard-on.

Man quit fooling yourself. That's one honey who ain't interested.

If she did show up, the chances of Berlin noticing him were few and far between. But he couldn't help thinking of her. Even while Reginald chewed a juicy piece of turkey, he wondered how she'd taste. The vixen was everything he dreamed of in a woman rolled up into one delectable package. Whenever she looked at him, he felt this strong temptation to walk over, remove her clothes and lick her like a lollipop. He was certain she tasted like candy. Feeling increased movement in his boxers, Reginald decided he better quit while he was ahead and pushed Berlin to the back of his mind.

All around him swirled the sounds and activities of the party. Waiters bearing silver trays of champagne and punch circulated among the throng of guests. Rich perfume scented the air, and at the far end of the room, a band played music appropriate for any holiday party. Several couples moved out onto the dance floor to slow dance to Christina Aguilera's rendition of "Silent Night." While watching, he wondered if Berlin danced. He would give anything to hold on to her nice round ass while they swayed together on the dance floor. As far as he was concerned, dancing was a form of foreplay. He would hold Berlin's hips firmly to his body, and grind against her juncture and have her so wet she'd be whispering in his ear to go home with him. *Oh, yeah, and I'd give the lady what she wants.*

As he chewed on a dinner roll, Reginald scowled at the way he was allowing his mind to run wild. Berlin was not that type of woman and this was definitely not the place. There was no way he could bump and grind to "…round young virgin, mother and child…"

Reginald chuckled and shook his head as he watched an older couple sway offbeat. This was nothing like the holiday parties his boy used to throw. Deejay spinning Motown Christmas jams in the corner. Hips gyrating on the dance floor. Air thick with cigarette smoke.

Oh, well. For three hundred dollars, he could bear it for the next couple of hours.

Taking one final bite, Reginald wiped his mouth with a napkin and tossed the plate into the trash. Time to go play Santa Claus.

Tonight, I'm going to kiss Santa Claus.

Berlin Dupree smoothed down the front of her red satin blouse, and short, black leather skirt. After one final deep breath, she sauntered across the room. For the first time in her life, she stood out from the crowd. Wearing the outfit, she felt as good as she looked. Sexy, and most importantly, naughty. Wearing no panties, and with her feminine folds rubbing together with each step, she felt horny as hell. That Brazilian bikini wax was well worth the money.

A woman on a mission, she had been watching Santa for the last hour. Handing out gifts. Laughing. Talking. Even in that silly red costume she knew what was underneath. A dark, rock-hard body she couldn't wait to get her hands on. For some reason, tonight he was even sexier than she'd remembered. Something was different about him, more appealing.

Berlin maneuvered through the crowd of folks like a tiger fixed on her prey. Adults. Children. Food. None of that mattered. All she cared about was getting to Dr. Cameron Clarke while he was still standing underneath a piece of mistletoe. With each step, anticipation heightened, and she could feel a tendril of heat curling between her thighs.

Ever since the resident physician started working at the clinic, she had been trying unsuccessfully to get his attention. Well, there was no way of avoiding her this time.

Tonight he's mine.

Butterflies whirled in her stomach, but she couldn't stop now. Big Mama always said, "The only thing to fear is fear itself."

She stopped a few feet away and waited. Each of the children already had their turn on Santa's lap. For the last half hour, Santa had been moving around the room, passing out gifts. Standing behind him, she watched him reached inside a black bag, then he handed Dr. Elizabeth Coolidge a small red box with a pretty gold ribbon. As soon as the pediatric cardiologist thanked him and walked away, Berlin stepped forward and lightly tapped Santa on his shoulder. He swung around, and before he could utter a word, she reached out and grabbed him by the neck and crushed her mouth into his. Boldly, she pushed her tongue between his lips, and to her excitement, he took what she offered greedily. Even with the full white beard, kissing him was everything she had hoped for, but not at all what she had imagined. It was better. He even smelled sweeter than she remembered.

Without breaking the kiss, he grabbed her waist and slowly walked her backward through the door, away from the crowd. Berlin was too wrapped up in his mouth, pressed against hers, to notice or care where he was taking her. All she could think about was his thick juicy lips, the feel of his strong arms holding her and that intoxicating scent. *Is it new cologne?*

He led her into a large coatroom where he kicked the door shut. He pressed her back against the feel of mink and leather, and brought her legs up around his waist. Berlin could feel his length, hardening between her legs, and couldn't wait to feel him buried deep inside of her.

Closing her eyes, Berlin allowed him to take control, and she did not object when he unfastened the top buttons of her satin blouse and reached inside. The heat of his hand seared the skin at her shoulder. He traveled lower, and she sucked in a ragged breath when he filled his hand with her lace-covered breast. He squeezed, and she let out a sensual moan. She knew it was not the time or the place, but her body was on fire. And for once in her life, she didn't care. All that mattered was how good his hand felt.

His fingertips teased her lace-covered breasts until both nipples puckered. As another moan erupted from her chest, Berlin leaned in closer and could feel the head of his dick. She rocked her hips against him, wanting to feel his erection where she needed it most.

A Delight Before Christmas

This is insane, utterly crazy. Yet she refused to stop. As far as Berlin was concerned, there was no reality for the moment. All that mattered was Cameron seducing her in ways she had never before been seduced.

He slipped a thumb inside her bra. The callous pad grazed her hardened nipple and sent waves of heat from her breasts down to her dampened crotch. She was dripping wet and on fire. She wanted him and she wanted him bad. With each caress her breasts tingled, and every kiss sent an ache through her body to the slick nub of her clit.

A twirling sensation spun through her, and she had a strong urge to touch him. She lowered her feet to the floor, and then quickly slid open his belt buckle and slipped a trembling hand inside the front of his red suit pants. He groaned when she grasped the base of his engorged dick and squeezed gently. *Nice.* Within seconds, she had him moaning in appreciation while she quivered with delight. The brotha was hung. Long, thick and hard. Everything about Dr. Clarke was perfect, she thought as she continued to stroke him, traveling up to the tip, then down again.

His mouth devoured hers hungrily, while his talented fingers continued to play with her nipples. With every brush, every squeeze, desire tore through her and pushed her closer to the edge. Nothing came close to what she was feeling. Taking a deep breath, she forced herself to breath normally, but found the feat impossible.

Finally breaking off the kiss, he lowered his head and took one nipple in his mouth while he continued to play with the other. She inhaled sharply as his tongue swirled around the hardened bud, licking, then sucking. His lips were as warm as his touch. She rolled her head to the side while her body quaked with every movement of his tongue. She arched against him, feeling the heat of his mouth on one breast while his hand continued to torment the other. Never had she known her body to feel like this, aching and alive, begging for a man's touch.

Burning with desire, Berlin managed to slide her hand up and down the length of him, speeding the motion, then slowing down. She loved the way he felt in her palm and she grew wetter by the second as she imagined how he would feel inside of her. As if he had read her mind, he slid a hand down her hip and up under her skirt. She spread her legs, yearning for his touch. Even through the hosiery, when he stroked her juncture, then parted her folds with his middle finger, she cried out with pleasure. Her body was on fire.

"Oh, yes! That feels good," she cried, her breath becoming shallow as she rocked against his hand. She was so wet and ready for him. "Please," she begged.

"Please what?"

"Touch me!"

Before she could catch her breath, he pushed a hole through her pantyhose and plunged two fingers deep inside of her.

"That's it, don't stop, please," she whimpered while he worked his magic. Lost in a trance, Berlin removed her hand from his pants and braced herself against the wall. Her knees threatened to buckle. Powerless to do anything except enjoy it, she arched against his hand, meeting each deep penetrating thrust. After several mind-boggling strokes, he withdrew his fingers. He rubbed her clit with her juices, slowly at first, then increased the rhythm with rapid circular motion. She was breathing heavily. By the time he dipped back into her well, he had her entire body yearning for release.

"Yes!" she screamed.

He covered her mouth with his, her cries drowning in his throat. The entire time his fingers moved deeper and much faster, his thumb pressed against her clit. Each deep thrust brought her closer to climaxing.

"I'm getting ready to come!" she cried against his shoulder.

"Let it go." Berlin heard him say, and then she rode his fingers until ecstasy blossomed and burst. The orgasm was so powerful she forgot to breathe. She forgot everything except he was inside her. Panting and trembling, she squeezed her internal muscles around his fingers until the spasms stopped. Moments later, Berlin dropped her head to his shoulder, and he held her tightly in his arms until her body began to relax.

"Yo, baby, check this out," he whispered, his breath hot against her neck. "How about we go back to my place so I can finish making love to you?"

The deep cords of his voice vibrated through her, and then her body stilled. Something wasn't right. She swallowed hard. "What did you just say?"

"I said let's take this to the bedroom."

7

A Delight Before Christmas

Oh. My. God. The rich timbre snapped Berlin to her senses. Why hadn't she heard it before? Her head flew up and her eyelids opened, and for the first time she noticed his eyes were darker than she remembered them. *No, it had to be some kind of mistake.*

He chuckled. "Yo, don't look so disappointed. You besta believe I plan to finish what you started up in *here*."

Oh, no! Her breath rushed in and out of her lungs so fast it made her dizzy. She shook her head. It couldn't possibly be…"Cameron?"

His jaw tensed. "Nah, baby." He reached up and removed the white curly wig, revealing ten straight back cornrows. "Do I look like my boy Ron?"

Reginald! Suddenly, she felt sick to her stomach. The harder Berlin tried to catch her breath, the faster it seemed to whoosh away from her. What the hell was he doing here? She couldn't catch her breath long enough to even demand answers. The room started to spin, and she cursed herself for trying to do something daring tonight of all nights. She'd been so stupid to walk up to Santa Claus and kiss him without first making sure she had the right man. Although, if she had been thinking clearly, she would have lost the nerve. *Too late now.* Instead of dwelling on woulda, shoulda, coulda, she concentrated on taking slow, deep breaths and tried not to look at his delicious mouth. Her eyes traveled down to his open zipper, which revealed a pair of striped boxers. Big mistake. At the waist she could see the head of his dick peeking out from the waistband. It throbbed as if saying, "Whassup?"

Good Lord, Reginald was fine. Why hadn't she noticed how sexy he was before?

Because he's so wrong for you.

"So are we going back to my place or what?" he asked with a smile tugging at the corner of his mouth.

Too stunned for words, Berlin tried to step back, to put space between her and him in the small cramped room. But his large hands remained fixed to her waist, as did the pressure of his masculine form against her most delicate spot.

"Let me go!" she finally managed to say. She spun away from him, then begun to angrily button her blouse. "How dare you trick me?"

Reginald gave her a puzzled look. "Trick you? Yo, baby, you grabbed me, not the other way around."

Berlin breathed deeply, knowing he was right. She had grabbed him and was now humiliated by the entire situation. As she reached for the last button, she stared over at his relaxed stance. Remembering what she had allowed him to do, she grew heavy with embarrassment.

She glared up at him while she straightened her skirt. "What are you doing here? Dr. Clarke was supposed to be Santa tonight."

"My boy had a house call to make and asked me to fill in," he said, then gave her a long considering glance. "So you saying you didn't mean to kiss me?" A look of disappointment made her hesitate admitting the truth.

Their eyes met, held and clashed for several seconds before she stuttered, "I, um…" She didn't mind insulting him. Admitting that she had intended to kiss Dr. Clarke was another story all together. "Of course I wasn't trying to kiss you!" she snapped and his jaw tensed.

"Yeah, but now that you have…" Reginald gave her a suggestive smirk that made him look too doggone sexy for his own good. "So, shorty, whassup? We going back to my place or what?"

Anger brewed inside her, chasing away any self-conscious feelings she might have had for allowing Reginald to feed on her breasts, to rub her…It took all she had to focus on the matter at hand and not allow her thoughts to dwell on how good his hands had felt. Despite her resolve, her nipples tingled against the satin fabric. Goodness! Her body stirred, craving his touch again. What in the world was wrong with her?

Ignoring him, she reached over to the coat rack and retrieved a long, wool camel-colored coat she had hung there earlier. After draping it over her arm, she iced him with a look of contempt, then spat, "Do me a favor and stay the hell away from me!" With nothing else to say, Berlin hurried out the closet.

Reginald shook his head as he watched her leave. Berlin had mistaken him for his boy Cameron. He tossed his head back and couldn't stop laughing.

Standing outside the closet, his eyes followed the short leather mini skirt clinging to her slender hips as she stormed across the banquet room.

He chuckled again, and then rested his hip on the doorframe. Berlin typically dressed well, choosing tasteful and conservative outfits for the office. While others wore business casual, she always kept her attire professional. But the skirt and blouse with the plunging neckline she had worn tonight were far from conservative. Watching her retreating back as she slipped into her coat, Reginald drew in a slow, deep breath to counter the effect she'd had on him.

He was at a loss for words. Either this was a dream or someone had slipped something in his food. He had been thinking about Berlin all day. Hell, he'd been thinking about her since the first time he laid eyes on her. And tonight when she had walked up to him and kissed him, he had gone with the flow. Only to discover she had mistaken him for Cameron. He didn't know if he should laugh again or feel insulted. Hell, he wasn't going to lie; her rejection stung.

He'd been watching Berlin for the last two weeks. She had barely said three words to him, beyond the initial formalities. He, on the other hand, had tried and failed to engage her in a conversation about something other than the shade of paint he was using in the waiting area. Unfortunately, paint was the only thing she seemed interested in discussing. So he took advantage of the opportunity to gaze into her gorgeous eyes. They were more golden than brown with long thick lashes that could persuade a man to do just about anything. Not to mention, from day one he had been caught off guard by the feminine quality of a voice that enticed him. What was it about the soft raspy tone that made him want to bend her over the nearest chair?

"I see Santa's been naughty," Leigh cooed.

Snapping out of his daydream, Reginald found his friend's wife standing in front of him with one hand on her hip. Her eyes danced with amusement as she gazed down at his crotch.

"Oops, my bad." Reginald quickly dipped back into the closet and adjusted the suit. He was so caught up in the moment it hadn't even occurred to him that he had been standing in the doorway with his pants open. He groaned inwardly. The last thing he needed was to jeopardize his contract with the clinic because he had been thinking with the wrong head. With a deep heavy sigh, he tucked his T-shirt in his pants.

As he zipped his pants, he decided that it was probably for the best that she had stormed out of the building. Berlin might look and feel soft, but the lady was a piranha, slanted eyes, cascade curls and all. He still wanted her despite knowing that. Since the first day he met her, he'd been laying awake at night with a rock-hard dick while fantasizing about making love to her.

As he straightened the fake beard, Reginald found himself grinning again. Even with her bad attitude, Berlin was a dime piece with dark honey-colored skin and thick auburn curls that framed a heart-shaped face. And he couldn't forget the slanted eyes. Even when she glared at him with icy contempt, he'd felt as if he'd been sucker punched in the gut.

But she ain't feeling you, dude.

He scowled. As much as he hated it, no matter how attracted he was to her, not once had she shown him a hint of interest. She seemed to be intrigued by his boy Cameron.

His homeboy from the Murphy Blair Housing Projects had spent two years after high school bouncing from one job to the next before he had finally decided to attend college and become a doctor. Now single women everywhere pursued the playboy resident physician, including Berlin Dupree. What the sistahs didn't know was that Cameron threw himself into love affairs, sampling women like fine wine. He flirted and chased anything in a skirt, and as soon as he was done, he tossed them aside like an old pair of shoes.

Nah, not this time.

As much as he loved and respected his boy, this was one time Reginald would have to intervene. Folding his arms, Reginald took a deep breath and thought about what he was going to do. Berlin was a mission. She was his challenge. It had been a long time since a woman had affected him the way she had. All he had to do was think about her, and his hormones raged while his dick stood at attention.

Something was happening. He could feel it. Regardless if Berlin was willing to admit it or not, after holding her in his arms, he had a strong feeling the chemistry was mutual. When she had tried to wiggle out of his arms, she was trembling. Not to mention, she was soaking wet when he had touched between her legs. That wouldn't have been the case if she hadn't been aroused. Even when she had realized who he was, the pulse at her throat had hammered so that he had almost grabbed her in his arms and kissed her again. What stopped him was that if he had tasted her once more, he would have said to hell with the three hundred dollars. He would have tossed Berlin over his shoulder, and carried her kicking and screaming home to his bed. While shifting the weight to his other leg, he wished he had acted on impulse. Now that she was gone, he wanted her, and he wanted her bad.

They'll be plenty of time for that later.

Glancing down at the watch on his arm, he released a heavy sigh. It was time to quit hiding in the closet and get back to work. As he adjusted the curly wig and hat on his head, Reginald knew one thing for sure. He planned to be knocking boots with Ms. Berlin Dupree before the end of the holiday season.

Chapter Two

Damn him!

Berlin entered the laundry room by way of the garage and slammed the steel door behind her. She hung her coat on a hook, then while bracing her weight against the washing machine, tugged the boots from her feet. *That man!* She scowled as she flung one, and then the other over into the corner. If Reginald were still in her presence, she would have tossed her boots at his big head instead.

Tonight she had made the biggest fool of herself. Berlin still couldn't believe it. She had been seen lip-locking with a blue-collar worker. The idea was almost hilarious. That is…if it had happened to someone else.

Angrily, she padded into the kitchen, dropped her Louis Vuitton purse on the table, then moved over to the refrigerator and flung the door open. While she tried to decide on something to drink, the last several hours started to run through her mind. Dang, she wished that she could go back to bed and start the day all over again.

For the last week she had been anticipating the night when she would finally show Dr. Cameron Clarke what she had to offer. And just like *that* it was all ruined. She groaned as she retrieved a bottle of water from the bottom shelf, then pushed the door shut with her knee.

Berlin moved straight for a chair, her thoughts spinning so quickly she literally felt dizzy. Or was it the excitement of what had occurred? The whole incident had been so off the wall and totally unlike her. Now what was she gonna do?

"Just wait until I see Arianna," she mumbled as she twisted off the cap. Her good friend had talked her into doing something so daring in the first doggone place. As she took several large swallows, she thought about all the time and money that had gone into preparing for today.

A Delight Before Christmas

After lunch, Arianna decided that the two of them would call off for the rest of the day, then she dragged her into a store that specialized in hoochie mama gear. Before getting out of the car, Berlin checked both ways to ensure no one would see her, and then she dashed inside the building. While inside, hiding behind dark shades, Berlin was appalled and tried to sneak out the back door.

When her feisty friend caught her by the arm, Berlin tickled her armpit and had managed to wiggle free. Arianna called after her and got her attention just as she stepped out door.

"You're not going to get Dr. Clarke's attention wearing a Donna Karan suit."

As much as she hated to admit it, she was right. Once a month, Berlin hit the clearance racks at both Neiman Marcus and Saks Fifth Avenue for bargains. She even had clothes from every upscale consignment shop in town. Donna Karan, Prada, you name it, she had it, yet Cameron Clarke still hadn't noticed her yet.

"Girl, what you gotta do is show that brotha what you're working with," her friend insisted as she looped her arm through Berlin's and dragged her to a rack of clothes at the back of the store.

Feeling slightly flushed, Berlin bent over and breathed deeply before taking another sip from the bottle. She had to be crazy for listening to her. She was even crazier for allowing Arianna to select the outfit. Within minutes, she had suggested a short, leather mini skirt and a revealing red satin blouse. Then Arianna ordered her to go try it on. As she dragged her feet toward the dressing room, Berlin resigned to allowing Arianna to run the show.

Sure enough, her friend dragged her from one shop to the next. High-heeled leather boots, eyebrows plucked, bikini wax and finally to Arianna's cousin Rolesta's beauty salon to get her hair and nails done. Hours later, tired and anxious for a nap, Arianna dropped Berlin off at her car. Then before Berlin could stop her, Arianna snatched the glasses from her eyes, and left the parking lot. Berlin had no other choice but to wear the contact lenses she despised so much.

Berlin rested her elbow on the table and took a deep breath, trying again to calm her nerves. That was easier said than done when she thought about all the time and money that she spent for nothing. She had even considered taking everything back to the store, but five o'clock rolled around and Arianna had appeared on her doorstep ready to transform her into what she had called, "sexy and irresistible." An hour later, Berlin was speechless as she stared in the mirror. With confidence she had climbed into her car and headed to the party while Arianna returned home to pick up her husband. It wasn't until she spotted Santa Claus working the room that she lost her nerve again. She was seconds away from fleeing the building when Arianna had arrived. Berlin raced over to her in those three-inch high-heel boots. "I can't do this," she had insisted.

"Don't think about it, be about it," Arianna had encouraged only seconds before Berlin had found the guts to stroll across the room and get Cameron's attention. Only it wasn't Cameron who had been wearing that Santa suit. It had been Reginald Hodges. Closing her eyes, she vividly remembered taking everything that man had to offer and then some.

And you loved every second of it.

She rose from the chair and paced heavily around the room. It wasn't possible. There was no way she would ever be interested in someone like him. Reginald represented things she no longer wanted in her life.

Then why are you still thinking about the kiss?

Angrily, she brought the bottle to her lips and took several swallows while she tried to catch her breath. The only logical explanation for what she was feeling was that she hadn't had any for much too long. Why else would she have done something so bold?

So stupid!

She took another drink, and then moved to stand in front of the sliding glass door that led to a thirty-foot long deck. Outside, the night brewed a winter storm, predicted to bring a mix of rain, sleet and possibly more snow. Lightning skimmed over the tops of clouds and water slashed the house. She loved snow, yet hated the bitter cold weather. Growing up in the Windy City was a legitimate enough reason, which is why she couldn't understand how she had moved from one cold state to another. Except to say it was job related. But all that would change in time, she told herself as she took a deep breath. She had a ten-step plan, and the last agenda item was retiring in Florida. And it would happen, she reassured herself confidently. So far everything in her life had been going according to plan.

Until tonight.

It took years of college and working dead-end jobs before Berlin had landed a management position at the Dellwood Pediatric Clinic. She worked hard to get where she was and was proud of her achievements. She had pinched pennies, and after years of saving, was now driving a three-year-old Lexus she paid for with cash. Her greatest accomplishment was the two-story, four-bedroom house she purchased last winter. Now the only thing left was finding a wealthy husband and settling down. After dating countless rejects, she now had her eyes set on Dr. Cameron Clarke. The sexy new doctor—with the medium build and thick curly hair—was single and everything she wanted. His looks were average, but she didn't mind. She preferred a kind and intelligent man with a bankroll to match. Not someone like Reginald.

Then why are you still thinking about him?

Oh, damn! In an ill attempt to free her thoughts, she took another thirsty drink and nearly choked. Quickly, she reached for a paper towel. Okay, so maybe Reginald was attractive. He wasn't all that, but he did look good, no doubt. However, if she had a type, it definitely wouldn't be him. She had dated his type before, and even thought the two of them were going to have a life together. Whatever she had seen in her first love didn't last beyond her freshman year in college. A few years later she had gotten herself mixed up with some smooth talking wannabe rapper who wanted her to support him while he pursued his career. The only thing they had in common was raging hormones. Once that died down, there wasn't anything left to sustain a relationship.

Looking back, she could truthfully say that neither of them was as fine as Reginald. What was it about white T-shirts, low riding blue jeans and Timberland boots that turned a sistah on? She shook her head disappointedly. With a man like that she would never get anywhere in life.

Nevertheless, she continued to stare out the window with her arms crossed beneath her breasts, wishing she could free her mind. Even knowing he was all-wrong, she couldn't help thinking about Reginald's big hands caressing her body. He would be an excellent lover. Tonight definitely proved that. Berlin frowned. She had too many disappointments when it came to men and sex. Bottom line, the men who had mastered the craft were few and far between, and usually broke as hell.

She shook her head at the logic. It was a toss-up. You got either a nice man with money or a dog who was awesome in bed. There was no medium, which sucked. She would give anything to find a man who not only looked good, but was also the bomb in bed. After years of rejects, she'd finally decided to give up on being sexually satisfied and settle for a kind, rich man.

She pursed her lips for a long thoughtful moment. Maybe she might get lucky. Who's to say Cameron wasn't good in bed?

The muscles in her face relaxed. She liked Cameron because he represented everything she wanted; yet so far she hadn't felt one beating heart for him. She told herself it didn't matter. All that mattered was that he was a nice guy who had a reputation for being kind to his patients.

Finishing her water, she tossed the bottle in the trash, then glanced over at the kitchen counter and noticed the red light on her answering machine was blinking. She moved over and pressed PLAY.

"Berlin this is your mother. As soon as you get in, give me a call. I've got some exciting news to tell you."

To her mother, exciting news was finding a sale on ground beef. She hit DELETE.

"Hey, this is Gary. Call—"

DELETE. *Damn psycho.* She'd had one date with the lawyer who during dinner confessed he'd gotten his degree while in prison.

"Berlin, where are you? Oh my goodness! Guess what? That was not Dr. Clarke wearing that Santa Claus suit that was—"

She hit the button. *Reginald. Yes, Arianna, I know.* With renewed humiliation, Berlin moved down the long wooden foyer, and then slowly climbed the stairs.

How in the world would she live down what happened tonight? It wasn't like she could hide for the next eighteen days until Christmas break. Instead, she would have to face him in the office again tomorrow. Reaching the top step, she groaned. Whose idea was it anyway to have a holiday party in the middle of a workweek?

She strolled into the master suite that began with a small sitting room. It opened to a spacious sleeping area with dual walk-in closets. She brushed past her queen size bed, and moved into a bathroom designed to serve as a soothing getaway: champagne pink ceramic tile, a step-in shower and a raised whirlpool tub. It was her haven for days like today. And after tonight's fiasco, a long hot bath was just what the doctor ordered. Reaching over, she poured a bath and moved back to her room. Along the way, she stopped to stare at the paint cracking on the wall and shook her head. The old fixer-upper had a lot of potential but was in desperate need of a fresh coat of paint. She couldn't afford to do any work on the house until spring. Last spring she had finally saved enough to replace the stucco exterior with yellow aluminum siding and had hired a landscaper. The view was breathtaking.

Nestled in a charming niche of Landenberg Heights, the large colonial, set off by a great circular driveway, was one of ten historical homes on a secluded street. From the outside her two-story house was as beautiful as the rest of the block, but appearances were deceiving. The inside was like walking through a time warp. She had been slowly working on upgrades, but had a long haul ahead of her. So far the only rooms completed were at the front of the house. Last summer she had hired a painter to paint the walls in the living room and dining area with soft pastel blue and had covered the floors with plush royal blue carpeting. The colors complemented rose-colored furniture she had found at Ethan Allen. It had been worth every penny of the two months salary she'd had to pay. A sixty-day diet of Ramen noodles and scrambled eggs had been her sign of sacrifice. "Only the best" was the motto she governed her life by. And she wouldn't have it any other way. However, with the prices he charged, she couldn't afford to do more than two rooms a year.

Pulling off her clothes, she was shivering long before she slipped into a flannel robe. Whenever she left the house, she dropped the thermostat down to sixty-nine degrees, and barely cranked it up to seventy-two when she was home. The house was too big to heat for just her.

Besides, if she wanted the house completed by summer, she couldn't afford to waste money.

Reaching down, she clicked on a small space heater in the corner, and then closed her door to seal in the heat. The unit kept her room quite comfortable.

It was just a tiny sacrifice. She had put almost everything she'd saved into buying the house she wanted. Eventually it would all pay off, and she would have everything she had always dreamed of having. *Almost everything.* Thoughts of Cameron filled her mind, yet to her annoyance, the face vanished and was replaced by Reginald's dark face with dimples so deep one was tempted to stick a finger inside.

Closing her eyes, she groaned as her body continued to betray her. Her nipples beaded. The mere thought of him caused a heated tension in the depths of her stomach. This couldn't possibly be happening to her. She had an agenda to stick to, and being attracted to someone like Reginald wasn't part of the plan.

Restless with her thoughts, she rose from the bed and went to take a bubble bath.

She had a ten-step plan with ten objects. Eight was marrying a doctor and nine was starting a family, and finally, ten was retiring and relocating to Florida. She was too close to let it all slip away.

Removing her robe, Berlin carefully lowered into the steaming hot bubbles. Leaning back against a small-inflated pillow, she lowered her eyelids and released a deep sigh as she tried to clear her mind. But she could not.

What have I done?

She slid lower in the tub and went over every single kiss. Every touch. And even though she was still shocked at her wild behavior, her body was still responding to the memories. Goodness. That was the first time a man had made her…well, she couldn't allow herself to think about how her juices had flowed freely around his fingers. Even thinking about it made her damp.

Nope, she could not pursue that relationship. Not when she wanted a life better than the one she left.

Berlin had grown up poor on the west side of Chicago. Although, back then, she had no idea she was different from anyone else. They all lived in the same old row houses with little to no grass in their front yards. She and her friends grew up jumping double-dutch with a clothesline, roller skating down gangways with one skate apiece and playing kickball. They looked forward to the summer block parties when everyone made a dish and came together as a neighborhood. Barbecue, potato salad, baked beans, iced tea and snow cones. There had been music and dancing. Nobody appeared to have a worry in the world. Everyone appeared to be in the same economic class—poor but happy.

The Dupree's decided they wanted Berlin to have a quality education during her high school years. And after getting her a partial scholarship, they sent her all the way to the south side to attend Academy of Our Lady, a Catholic, all-girls school. Green plaid skirts and cream tops, uniforms were supposed to hide student's poverty levels, make everyone appear equal, or so they thought. She soon found out her classmates were from different social classes by simply looking at their shoes. Berlin was still wearing Buster Brown while many were wearing penny loafers and the latest fashion at Baker's Shoes. After school they changed into Levi jeans and polo shirts that actually had a man sitting on a horse, or that little alligator, while her clothes were whatever had been on sale that season at Kmart. Within the first year, Berlin's eyes were wide open, and suddenly she was ashamed of her background. She started spending weekends with her friends on the south side. When her best friend next door asked to join her, she quickly declined. She pretended to be something she wasn't and didn't want anyone from the neighborhood to ruin it for her. She was determined to have a life like she saw her new friends living.

Berlin studied hard at school and got a full scholarship that took her away from Chicago. Every passing grade got her that much closer to her degree and dream of having something in life. During that time, she had made a list of ten accomplishments, and now she had three more to go. Dr. Clarke was next on her list, and she was certain she would have him wrapped around her finger before Valentine's Day. And engaged by summer.

She frowned slightly as cold rain began to hit the window in the bathroom. The water slid down the glass just as her brain flooded with thoughts of being in Reginald's arms. She had felt things she couldn't even begin to imagine. She also remembered the hot coil of desire that had grown inside of her when she gazed into his eyes. He was fine; there was no denying that. He was coffee without the cream, with straight back cornrows and an irresistible goatee that accentuated thick, succulent lips. Sepia colored eyes draped with long lashes. A strong nose and well-defined cheekbones and dimples on both side. It was no wonder every woman in the clinic had been drooling over the new painter. But not her. Oh, no. She had better things to do with her life than mess with the hired help. But Reginald wasn't apart of her agenda.

They were literally as different as day and night.

Angry with herself as well as with him for placing her in such a predicament, she took a deep calming breath. There was no way she was giving her dreams up for a painter—no matter how good he made her feel.

As she splashed water across her chest, Berlin tried to figure out how she had confused the two men. Yes, the Santa Claus suit made it difficult to determine who was underneath it. But still, she should have known. With the wig on there had been no way to see Reginald's cornrows. Since Cameron had short cropped curls it would have been a dead giveaway. And the calluses on his hands when he grazed her nipple should have given it away. Reginald used his hands for a living. She felt a flush of heat as she remembered how well he knew how to use his hands. He almost sent her over the edge when he was caressing her clit. A few seconds longer and it wouldn't have mattered who was touching her. All that would have mattered was bringing her long overdue pleasure.

Quit thinking about him!

Yet, she couldn't stop thinking about Reginald. Berlin shifted in the tub, disappointed in herself, because she had been doing so well ignoring him.

From the first day he'd set foot in the clinic, she didn't care for his street slang. He represented a past and a way of life she no longer wanted. She shook her head and tried to further convince herself there was no way she was attracted to him. She had barely said more than three sentences because she didn't want him to even think for a moment she was interested in him. She saw him strutting down the hall like a peacock with his chest stuck out while wearing that cocky grin. And every time it infuriated her. Yet, tonight she had liked everything about him. Berlin drew her knees to her chest and pondered over the ridiculous idea. No matter how much she tried to deny it, tonight none of it seemed to matter. All she could think about was his lips pressed against hers. His hand inside her blouse. Her nipples hardened as she relived the moment Reginald punched a hole in her pantyhose and slid his fingers inside her—

Abruptly, Berlin reached for her washcloth. There was no way she would waste another second thinking about that man. The only reason why it even happened was because she had mistaken him for Cameron. The second she had realized who Santa Claus was, she had ended the game. It angered her that he had known who she was all along. He had known who he was kissing, sucking and licking. Oh, dang, she was getting turned on again just thinking about it. She refused to waste anymore time thinking about him. She quickly lathered her body, rinsed off and climbed out of the bathtub.

Within minutes she had dried off and slipped a gown over her head. She turned off her light and climbed under the warm down comforter, ready for sleep.

An hour later, she was still awake and couldn't help thinking about Reginald's hands on her breasts. Her nipple between his callused fingertips. She loved a man who used his hands, and the way they felt touching the area around her nipples. Her hands slid underneath her gown and across the belly to her breasts. She flicked an index finger over one nipple, gasping as pleasure rushed through her veins. Putting another pillow behind her head, she continued to think about Reginald as she concentrated on her breasts, flicking first one, and then the other until they were hard and sensitized. Her right hand slid down over her belly button, and she imagined his large hands, touching her as she touched herself. With a moan, she traveled even further until she reached her moist fold. Masturbating was nothing new to her. She'd been pleasing herself using her own fingers long before she had lost her virginity. But tonight those fingers weren't hers. They belonged to Reginald.

Her fingers worked along the slit as she remembered the way his lips had felt against her skin. Stroking her fingers in a firm motion, she grew wetter with each hot memory. As she parted her fold and slipped a finger inside, she imagined it was Reginald's long hard manhood. He was blessed. The head had been slick and wet to the touch. She remembered the hard thrust in her palm while she stroked him. Hand trembling, she slipped another finger inside. She took several deep breaths as her fingers plunged deep inside. Building, she spread her legs wider and moved her fingers in and out in a steady rhythm like he was making love to her. With her other hand, she moved down to her clit and stroked firmly. Her pleasure rose, and she found herself drawing near an orgasm. Bucking her hips, she imagined him slamming into her as a spasm tore through her. Heat sped through her vein and she sucked in a deep breath, and then released a loud scream. She began panting as her body shuttered one last time. Easing her fingers from her body, she reached for a pillow and hugged it close to her body. Finally, her breathing slowed and she eventually drifted off to sleep.

Berlin tossed and turned all night, dreaming about Reginald kissing and touching her in all the right places. She woke feeling as she had barely slept. Rolling onto her back, she stared up at the ceiling, and realized it was time to go to work and face him.

Chapter Three

Berlin arrived at work a half hour early, hoping to make it safely to her office before the rest of the staff arrived. Okay, who was she trying to fool? She was hoping to avoid Reginald, as well. She was a coward. She admitted it.

Her heart, beating twice as fast as it should have, slammed against her rib cage when she climbed out of her car. Walking heavily in high-heeled Jimmy Choos, she moved across the parking lot and stepped through the side door of the Dellwood Pediatric Clinic. Berlin took a shaky breath as her pace quickened. She would know, any minute now, if anyone had seen what happened last night. She would also know if Reginald had arrived. The last several days he had come into the clinic early. On the way into the office, she hadn't seen the beat-up Toyota truck in the lot. Although, that necessarily didn't mean anything. For all she knew he had parked around the corner just to rattle her nerves. *Goodness, how could I have possibly been so stupid?* She didn't want to face him this morning. Not when she had practically jumped his bones. She had wanted him to take her, and wouldn't have said no if he had.

As she neared the registration desk, she spotted Celeste behind the desk and her heart did a double take. *Okay, here we go.*

"Good morning, Berlin."

She jumped at the sound of the twenty-something's chirpy voice. "Hello, Celeste." She gave her a brief, uneasy smile, then pushed through the double doors and moved down the hall. It was still quiet, which was a good sign. At the end near the supply cabinet were cans of paint, but no sign of Reginald. *Thank goodness.* Her steps slowed as she passed the clinic, then turned left and moved down a small narrow hallway to a suite of administrative offices. Berlin stepped inside her office, turned the light on, then removed her coat and hung it on the back of her door. While smoothing down the front of her skirt, she moved behind her desk and took a seat.

Maybe no one saw me trying to suck out Reginald's tonsils.

Berlin convinced herself she had done all the worrying for nothing. A small smile curled her lips as she removed her purse from her arm and put it in the desk drawer beside her. Then she leaned back in the chair and allowed her shoulders to sag with relief.

Closing her eyes, she allowed herself a second to remember what happened last night and told herself it wasn't as bad as she had thought. There had been too many people to have noticed. Everyone was having too much fun to have paid her or Reginald any attention.

As she leaned back in her chair, Berlin couldn't help thinking about last night's events and scowled. She lowered her eyelids. As soon as she did, Reginald's dimpled smile came into view with his sexy ass. *Too bad he was born in the wrong social class.*

She looked up and glanced across her small office. He probably wasn't any more interested in her than she was with him. After her haste departure last night, Reginald probably hadn't given her a second thought.

But what if he did?

The thought caused her lips to curl upward. If she were as daring and bold as the outfit she had worn last night, she would have eagerly gone home with him and finished what they had started. Kissing, licking, touching, stroking, a few moments longer and she would have dropped to her knees and swallowed all of him. She loved oral sex. Giving more than receiving because most of the guys she had known never could seem to get it right, and she usually asked them to stop. A dick as inviting as his; she would have welcomed in her mouth. And she would have sucked and licked and teased until he begged her to ride him. Quickly, she would have raised her skirt, slipped out of her torn pantyhose and would have welcomed him home. Legs wrapped around his waist with him pulling and pushing—

Enough!

She hadn't had any in so long it appeared she was starting to lose her mind. Squeezing her legs firmly together, she took a few seconds to try and get herself together. Work was not the time and definitely not the place to be thinking about sex.

Swinging around in her chair, she reached for the top folder in her inbox and told herself to get to work.

"Good morning, girlfriend. And how was your evening?"

Her head flew up from the report, and she gazed over at the door where a small, dimpled smile spread across her coworker's face. In her hands were a cup holder with two Styrofoam cups of coffee and a small bag she knew contained doughnuts.

Berlin steeple her hands on top of the desk, then shrugged. "Like every evening—boring."

Arianna Philips waltzed into the room, batting her fake eyelashes. "The way you were lip locking with Reggie, I thought maybe the two of y'all went back to his place to finish what y'all started."

She jerked upright in her chair. "*Oh my god.* You saw that?"

Arianna nodded as she placed the coffee followed by the bag at the center of the large oak desk. "Me and half the department," she said. Her eyes sparkled.

Berlin groaned, shaking her head of spiral curls with frustration. It was worse than she had suspected. She loved Arianna. Truly she did. In the three years they'd worked together, she'd had her back on numerous occasions. She had even had the pleasure of being the maid of honor at her wedding last winter. But one thing she knew, Arianna was a romantic with a big mouth. If only half the department witnessed her and Reginald making out in the coatroom, by lunch the other half would know. She hoped Dr. Clarke didn't hear about it. If he did, her chances of winning the resident were over.

"So, is he as good as he looks?" Arianna asked with her hip propped on the end of her desk.

Oh, God! It took everything she had not to reveal just how good Reginald was. Just thinking about his big juicy lips wrapped around a nipple was enough to make her vaginal walls contract. *And let's not forget the brotha is packing more than eight inches in his pants.* She had to bite down on her bottom lip to keep from moaning aloud. His tool was long, fat and felt fabulous in her hand.

"I'm waiting," she heard Arianna say impatiently.

Waiting? Waiting for what? She thought. For her to confess that she had masturbated last night while thinking about him. Afraid that Arianna might be able to see it in her eyes; she lowered her lids and reached for a doughnut.

While she chewed, she tried to push the memories to the back of her mind. Remembering was not a smart move while at work. Her breast already ached in the confines of her black lacy bra. Her center pulsed in her low-cut matching panties. She was stunned at how quickly thoughts of Reginald aroused her. She smiled and brought her coffee to her lips.

"I guess I can take your silence as a yes. I told you he was wonderful."

Ever since Reginald started painting the clinic, Arianna had made it her business to befriend him and find out everything she could about Reginald, then share it with her regardless if she wanted to hear it or not. Pretty teeth. Long eyelashes. Dangerously deep dimples. Everything she knew about him was enough reason to justify all the reasons why someone like him was not what she needed in her life.

Berlin rolled her eyes as she reached for the Styrofoam cup. "No, you can take my silence as I don't have any idea what you're talking about."

Arianna gave her a dismissive wave. "Oh please, you're trying to tell me that man can't kiss."

Oh my god! He's a fabulous kisser. Dropping her eyes to the black coffee, Berlin cleared her throat and her mind of the dangerous thought before speaking. "He was okay." She had to force a look of disinterest while she tried to ignore the throbbing increasing down below in her panties. Crossing her legs wasn't helping the matter at all. Regardless of how good he kissed, she wanted one thing and one thing only, and that was Dr. Clarke.

"Oh come off it," Arianna said as she reached for the other cup and lowered herself in a chair across from her desk. "The way you stuck your tongue down his throat, I thought maybe you were trying to take his tonsils out."

Berlin had to bite her bottom lip to keep from groaning out loud. If the situation weren't so serious, she would have tossed her head back and shared a good laugh.

"So what happened once y'all disappeared in the coatroom? Did you give him some?"

Her eyes grew round. "Of course not. We kissed, and when I realized my mistake I stormed out of the room."

"Well that's good to know. The way you waltzed out of there, I thought maybe my boy was a minute-man. I was gonna have to talk about him."

"You are too much."

"Girl, I'm just keeping it real. It's a shame for a brotha to look that good and be a big joke in bed," she added between sips.

Berlin doubted that was the case. She didn't even have to sleep with Reggie to know he was no joke, especially not with all that he was working with. Not to mention, his lips were lethal. She would love for Reggie to go down on her. If his lips felt anywhere near as good as they had felt wrapped around her nipple, she was in a world of trouble. A shock raced straight down to the part in question, causing her to squirm in her seat.

"You all right?"

"Never felt better."

"Uh-huh…"

"The only reason why I kissed him was because I thought he was Dr. Clarke."

Why Berlin felt compelled to share with her friend the juicy yet embarrassing details while chewing on a doughnut, she didn't have a clue. Especially since telling Arianna anything was like taking out an advertisement in the *St. Louis Post Dispatch*. At least this way Arianna would know what really happened inside the coatroom and get the story right. Besides, Berlin realized that talking about it seemed to help make some sense of what happened and reminded her of what her ultimate goal was—becoming Mrs. Cameron Clarke.

Arianna started laughing and splashed coffee on the desk. "Oops! My bad," she giggled as she reached for several napkins from the bag and mopped up the mess from her desk. "So you're telling me at no point you knew you were humping Reggie?"

Berlin handed her another napkin, then frowned with annoyance. "I wasn't *humping* Reginald. We were kissing and things got carried away." The five-foot-one-inch staffing coordinator was getting ready to work her nerves.

"So it seems," she mumbled, eyes sparkling with amusement. "You know I'm not one to gossip."

Since when? Berlin wondered as Arianna rose from the chair and moved over to the trashcan to discard the soiled napkins.

"I heard that seconds after you stormed out of the coatroom, Reggie came out with his fly open."

She took a deep breath as memories of her hand down in his pants reaching for his—

Arianna flopped back down in the chair, startling her. "So what's really going on?"

Goodness gracious, if she only knew. She reached for her coffee and took a sip. *Yuck!* It was cold.

"Are you sure he didn't follow you home? I tried catching you, but you were moving too fast, and the next thing I know Santa was exiting the building obviously not on his way back to the North Pole. So naturally I assumed..." she allowed her voice to trail off, then leaned back in the chair and met her gaze.

"Well, you assumed wrong. As soon as I realized my mistake, I went home."

Arianna shook her head. "Girlfriend, since when is kissing a man that looks like Reggie a mistake? Mmmm, if I wasn't married, I'd be all over his fine tail." She licked the chocolate from her fingers, showing off her two-inch long red nails and three-carat diamond wedding ring.

"You can have him."

"Look at you trying to give me your leftovers." Arianna looked at her as if she had lost her mind. "I can't understand why you would want to pass up on an opportunity like that to be with Dr. Clarke. That brotha walks like his drawers are stuck in his butt."

"Arianna!"

"I'm serious. He's too pretty for his own good, and he knows it, too." She rolled her eyes. "You know I can't stand that type. Now Reggie, that brotha is in a class all of his own. Body. Personality. Beautiful smile. Did I mention his body? *Good God Almighty!*"

"Uh-huh. I'll admit he isn't bad looking."

"Isn't bad looking?" She shook her head. "I don't know what's wrong with you. Reggie is a sweetheart."

Berlin snorted rudely. Though he was polite, Reginald exuded arrogance, as if he was used to getting his way. Well, not this time. No matter how much he made her juices flow, he wasn't getting that close to her again.

Tired of the conversation, she reached inside her inbox. "Don't you have work to do?"

"Whatever. This conversation isn't over." Arianna rose from the chair. "I'll see you at lunchtime."

"I can hardly wait," she mumbled without bothering to look up at her.

Long after Arianna had gone, Berlin sat at her desk with her head back in her chair. She placed her hands on her stomach as her mind went over every touch, every kiss, and found her body once again responding to the memories. She blew out a breath of air and tried to stay angry with Reginald for taking advantage of her, during an opportunity that would have never happened, if she had known who was behind that white beard. Only she couldn't blame him, not completely, especially since she had been a more than willing participant. She would just have to find a way to push the memories aside and make sure that it never happened again. Satisfied that she had wasted more than enough time thinking about Reginald, she leaned forward in her chair and logged onto her computer.

She prepared the payroll, glad to have something to take him off her mind. As the fiscal manager, she was responsible for the department budget, payroll, as well as insuring insurance claims had been submitted correctly for payment. With a degree in accounting and a love for numbers, she found the job to be quite challenging. She loved her job because her days were always filled crunching numbers.

Especially when she needed to get something—or in this case, someone—off her mind.

It wasn't long before the smell of fresh paint lingered to her nostrils. She needed to go to the bathroom, but there was no way she was walking down the hall. Instead, she crossed her legs and forced herself to hold it for as long as she could.

Berlin was avoiding him.

Reginald was sure of it. He had been waiting to catch her in the hall. Usually Berlin was up and down the hallway brushing past him with barely a "good morning" to talk with the staff or visiting the employee break room for coffee. Today, however, she had been taking the long way around the office. He frowned. She was determined to pretend yesterday had never happened. Too bad. There was no way he could forget about it. He had spent most of the night lying across his bed staring up at the ceiling thinking about how good she had felt while holding his dick in his hand. A cold shower this morning did nothing to counter the effect she had on his lower region.

He was still pissed off that she didn't want him. He didn't believe that. Especially not after yesterday.

Sensing her presence, he looked down at the end of the hall, and sure enough, there she was. Berlin was leaning against a medical records cart talking to the nursing supervisor, Terri Carmichael.

The thigh-high split in her skirt revealed gleaming smooth legs before it fell to those expensive strappy high-heeled shoes. As his gaze moved upward, he found a neat waist and only two tiny straps holding up the low-cut bodice to her blouse. He felt disappointed.

Dude, did you really expect her to be still wearing the short leather skirt?

He shook his head at the ridiculous notion. Of course, the outfit was inappropriate for work. Only seeing her back in her conservative clothes made yesterday seem almost like it had all just been a dream. He would have thought that maybe he had imagined the entire event if it weren't for her hair. He was glad she hadn't put her hair back up in that severe bun or wore those Urkel-looking glasses. The new style made her look sensual and youthful. Yesterday was the first time he'd seen her hair down. He didn't realize it hung to her shoulders. He had always been attracted to a woman with long hair. Large auburn curls bounced around her face that he could see clearly now that the librarian glasses were gone.

Ms. Dupree had transformed from classy to sexy. Why had she waited until the night of the department Christmas party?

She was trying to impress your boy Cameron.

The reason hit him. She had gone to all the trouble for someone else. Cameron was his boy and all, but Reginald couldn't help being jealous.

Something told him to quit staring, and he reached down and dipped a small paintbrush in white semi-gloss he was using to paint the trim along the hallway.

He counted his strokes in an effort to keep his eyes off Berlin. Yet he could not stop himself. His gaze returned to Berlin who was looking directly at him, and he smiled. Their eyes locked for one long hypnotic moment before she blinked, then turned and walked away. He chuckled. Berlin had told him to stay away from her. She tried to act as if she weren't interested in him. But just now, the eye contact told him otherwise. If it had been one second less, then it would have been a different story.

Reginald chuckled as he leaned down and dipped his brush in the paint.

Baby, it's on now.

By noon her stomach growled, and Berlin decided she'd been hiding long enough. She moved across the hall to Arianna's office and knocked lightly on the door. "You ready to go get lunch?"

"Give me a minute, and I'll be right there."

"I'll meet you out front." She returned to her office long enough to reach for her coat and purse. She slipped into her coat and strolled toward the side entrance. As she rounded the corner, she ran into something solid. She would have stumbled if not for the hands that grasped her waist. *Reginald.* Her cheek landed against his spattered T-shirt. For a startled moment, she stood jammed against him, unable to move. The heat from his firm chest invaded her senses. *Good Lord, I'm on fire! Someone bring me a glass of water.* Then she reared back and stared into his piercing eyes. In defiance of all her common sense, she felt a yearning to be pressed up against his hard body again. To feel his strong hands down between her thighs and his mouth against hers once more. Startled by her ludicrous thoughts, she jerked free of his hold and took a small step back. Hoping he hadn't noticed she was slightly shaking from the encounter, she refrained from rubbing away the goose bumps on her arms.

"Oops. My bad, sexy," Reginald said. A grin that literally left her breathless stole across his chiseled features. *Breathe, girl.*

"Watch where you're going!" she snapped.

"Yo, if you had been looking where you were going, you wouldn't have bumped into me," he said, his breath warm on her brow. He smelled like Double mint. She loved a man with fresh breath.

Berlin frowned and narrowed her eyes at him. "Me, bump into you? You're the one who bumped into me." She crossed her arms defiantly across her chest. She knew she was behaving childishly, only she didn't have time to care.

"Whatever, I'm not going to argue with you." He stared down at her, and his lips curled upward. "Although as angry as you are, you must have been thinking about me," he said in that arrogant manner she despised.

Reginald obviously expected every woman to bow down and kiss his big feet. Regardless of how attracted she was to him, he'd never know it. She would do whatever it took not to fall for a man like him.

She rolled her eyes upward. "Why would I want to do something stupid like that?"

"Cause I couldn't get you off my mind. All I could think about is how sweet your lips tasted. How warm your breasts felt in my hand."

"Whatever," she uttered with disgust. Although despite her best attempt, her body instinctively responded to his tired rap. "Can you please get out of my way?" she said as she tried to step around him, but Reginald moved in front of her, grabbed her wrists and moved her with him to a corner where anyone coming down the hall would really have to be looking to notice.

Her eyes grew wide, panicky. "What are you doing?"

Reginald's hands slid down and cupped her butt, pressing her firmly against his arousal. He gazed down at her with desire burning from their depths. "I just want a minute to talk to you in private."

Think fast! She felt a tingle in her stomach. The first thought that came to her mind was that she had to resist him. But a second thought came to her—that she was dying to feel his lips again—and she felt herself move even closer to him. Shamefully, she felt a deep yearning that she knew would take everything in her power to ignore.

Berlin pursed her lips and tried to put on a brave front. "Well hurry up. I don't have all day. What do you want to talk about?"

Reginald looked stunned by her harsh tone. Good, because it was nothing compared to what she was feeling. He gazed down at her for several long seconds before his smile returned.

"Why do you dislike me so much?" At her silence he continued, his hot breath caressing her nose. "I've been trying to get your attention since I started here. Yet, every chance you get, you blow me off. What have I done to piss you off?"

She tried to stay angry and unaffected by his presence, his touch, but it sure as heck wasn't easy to do when he smelled so good. Weren't painters supposed to smell like turpentine? And to make matters worse, it didn't help for him to look at her with such a warm inviting smile. Especially since she knew how his lips tasted.

"Well?" he asked, breaking into her thoughts.

"Well what?"

"Whassup? Why have you been giving me such a hard time?"

Slowly, she shook her head. "Because I'm just not interested," she somehow managed to say in one shaky breath.

Reginald tossed his head back and chuckled as if her answer was ridiculous. "That's not what your mouth said last night. You were interested last night. In fact, you were all over a brotha."

The memory sent heat flowing between her legs. "That's because I thought you were someone else." She tried to break free, but he held her firmly against him. She had no choice but to feel his erection—hard and long—against her belly. Closing her eyes, she remembered how *it* had felt in her hand, and had to bite her lip to stifle a whimper.

Leaning forward, he whispered next to her ear. "That's what your mouth says, but your lips were saying something entirely different last night."

Before she could think of a quick response, his hand left her waist and moved over her blouse and skimmed across the fabric to the swell of her breast, where he captured a nipple and squeezed. Berlin nearly cried out. She held it, knowing if she made any noise, someone was likely to find them.

"I think you like me." He continued to fondle her breast while his lips moved away from her ear. "In fact, I know you like me." He trailed his tongue along her neck and up to her cheek. Berlin turned her head just before he reached her lips. One kiss and she would have been dragging him to the nearest closet.

"Well, you're wrong," she said, sounding out of breath. "Now move," she ordered with as much conviction as she could muster, considering she was ready to tear his clothes off. "If you don't I'll scream."

He paused, then must have realized she was serious because he raised his hands in surrender and stepped aside. Berlin brushed past him and made a serious effort not to move her hips anymore than she had to. Nevertheless, she felt the heat of his gaze on her backside. Glancing over her shoulder, sure enough, he was standing there watching. She stopped in her tracks, growing angrier by the second.

"Can I help you with something?" she asked with a shaky hand planted at her waist.

Ignoring her deep frown, he answered, "Yeah, Berlin you can. Want to go grab a bite?"

35

Something indefinable hummed in the air between them that she felt each and every time she was around him, and she didn't like it. "Not with you. And if you bother me again, I'll call your boss and have you fired." She wouldn't really. The last thing she would ever do is take food from his table, but he didn't need to know that.

"Dang girl, you're tough." Reginald didn't sound frightened, rather amused.

She rolled her eyes, and then spun on her heels.

Once around the corner, she stopped and leaned against the wall, catching her breath. She was relieved to put some distance between them. At twenty-eight she wasn't so naïve that she didn't recognize her reaction to him for what it was—lust in the most dangerous form. Damn she wanted his fingers between her legs again, penetrating her. She reminded herself that she had once reacted the same way to her ex. *Never again.* The next man in her life would be based on choice, not hormones.

Reginald watched her leave, loving the way her generous hips moved with each step. He couldn't help chuckling. By the widening of her golden eyes and the thin lines of her lips, Reginald knew he had pissed Berlin off.

Good, cause the woman was definitely a trip.

He rounded the corner and resumed painting the wall peanut butter with a satin finish. One of his favorite colors, it would look fabulous along the wing of administrative office. Last week he had completed the pediatric clinic, which was on the right side of the building.

He dipped his brush again and looked up as Arianna came around the corner.

"Hey, Reggie."

"Whassup, Ree-Ree?" he greeted, causing her to smile at the way he comfortably used her nickname. "Where you off to?" He noticed she was wearing her coat.

"Lunch, want to join me?" she asked as she swung her purse over her shoulder.

He lowered his brush to the pan and looked down at her. "Tempting offer, but I need to finish this wall first."

She gave him a playful pout. "That's too bad. Berlin will be disappointed."

He had to laugh at that. "I doubt your girl will mind. She likes giving me a hard time."

"That's cause she likes you."

His brows rose. "Oh, really?"

"Yep, she just hasn't realized it yet." Then she turned on the heels of her leather boots and waved as she headed toward the side entrance.

As soon she was out of sight, Reginald thought about what she had said. Arianna might be right, but from what he had learned, Berlin would never admit it. She would continue to pretend he didn't exist. That's why he was determined to do something about it.

Even though he had known she would give him the cold shoulder, he had purposely bumped into her just to see her get all fired up. He couldn't help it. Her cheeky manner and sharp tongue intrigued him, not to mention the lush female curves he held briefly.

He found himself both irked and intrigued by the bourgeois woman who thought he wasn't good enough for her. With her manicured nails and expensive clothes, he knew she was high maintenance. She had an air about her that made a man's pockets go on alert. Yet, on some unknown level, her disinterested, high-siddity attitude made her appealing to him to the point that Berlin had become a challenge.

Hearing someone calling his name, he glanced over his shoulder at Dr. Bigsby, the clinical director, and waved. He decided he had better get back to work before someone thought he was goofing off. Reaching for the paint brush he shook his head. It was amazing how easily he was distracted by Berlin.

As he completed the last wall on the left side of the wing, he revisited those few minutes he'd had Berlin's breasts in his hand again. Perfect fit. He had always believed anything more than a mouthful was a waste and Berlin's were round and perky and too damn tempting. He couldn't resist touching her again, and no matter how much she tried to deny it, Berlin had enjoyed every second of it. Otherwise, she would have slapped his hand away. Instead, he had stroked her firm round breasts, and instantly her nipples had become hard and erect.

Without a doubt, there was more to Ms. Dupree than meets the eye. Last night she had been wild and passionate, and today she was back to trying to point her nose down at him. And he wasn't having it, which was why he had grabbed her in the first place. He now knew for a fact she would be a very passionate lover.

If it hadn't been for last night, he would have thought of her as a cold dead fish. He wouldn't have known how firm and ripe her breasts were or the way she moaned when he suckled her nipples. He wouldn't be feeling the lust he was experiencing now.

He knew he was crazy to feel even the slightest bit attracted to the stuck-up woman, let alone be aching to drag her to the nearest closet and strip off that conservative outfit and explore every inch of her body. Last night wasn't enough. He spent most of the evening hard and frustrated. The cold shower hadn't even helped.

He'd been imagining for weeks how she looked underneath her clothes, and his imagination had gone wild. And last night he'd had a chance to slip his hands beneath her clothes.

He shifted slightly, trying to ease some of the pain. She'd left him in a bad way. He could think of several women more than willing to alleviate the situation, but the woman who came to his mind was Berlin. More often than he wanted, he imagined laying her on her back, spreading her legs wide and burying his entire length inside her sweet core. And he was certain it was quite delicious. Those kisses in the coatroom had shown more passion and excitement, and now that he'd had a taste, he hungered for more. Last night he'd wanted to claim her fully, to possess her. The scent of her skin ignited his senses, his need to caress her curvaceous body with his hands.

Heat gripped his entire body.

She planned to make that task close to impossible to continue. She didn't have to worry; he wasn't interested in commitment. Burned by his ex, he had decided to leave serious relationships to other men. He wasn't dealing with that type of drama again.

While he added the final strokes, he thought about his high school sweetheart, who was now some NBA player's wife. An aspiring actress determined to have the finer things in life, Ayla Bennett had been given a better opportunity than any cereal commercial could have provided thanks to her millionaire husband.

Two years ago, Ayla had flown to California to audition for a part on a soap opera. She had come home three days later; tossing back his ring and any dreams he had of living happily ever after. Since then he swore off relationships. Women were for dates, casual conversation and mind-boggling sex. Emotions from the heart were not allowed. As soon as they became possessive, he extracted himself from the relationship.

Shaking off bad memories and regrets, he dipped his paintbrush in the paint one final time and moved over to the end of the wall.

But it had been three months since his last encounter. Sienna Hayes had tried to mess with his head, and he finally had to give her the boot. Three months was a long time for a man to go without sex, especially one with a high sex drive like himself. Yep, he was going to have to find a way, and fast, to get Berlin in his bed.

"I have to agree with Reggie, why do you dislike him?" Arianna asked the second their waitress sat their drinks down and left to check on their food.

A scowl touched Berlin's face. "Reggie? What, the two of you are now good friends?"

"No, but he's a nice guy. Very outgoing. And a helluva painter. You have to admit he is doing a fabulous job."

She reached for her glass. Arianna was right. Reginald was doing an awesome job. She was skeptical when he first started. As soon as she saw him walk in with his cornrows and pimp daddy walk, she knew there had to be some kind of mistake. Yet RDH Construction had a solid reputation in the community. After seeing the superb work they had done to the neonatal unit, she was quite pleased when they had outbid all the other contractors in the area to renovate the playroom in their clinic for children being treated for psychological issues. Construction on the new wing had begun in early spring and had been completed shortly after Thanksgiving. Color schemes had been decided on back in September, and two weeks ago, Reginald had begun. He had done such an excellent job, her medical director had extended his contract to paint the administrative office located on the left side of the building. Dr. Clarke highly recommended his work, and because of that, Berlin had decided not to call the company and asked for him to be replaced.

"Come on, I'm waiting. Why don't you like him?"

Berlin blew out a frustrated breath. For starters, Reginald Hodges reminded her a little too much of her ex-boyfriend. He was that sure of himself. Not that her ex had been anywhere near as fine as Reginald. Truly, Reginald dominated any room. Not even his paint-splattered clothes could hide a masculine physique.

Secondly, she didn't like the way those sepia-colored eyes of his made her go all shivery inside whenever he trained them on her. It was difficult to keep from squirming and wetting her panties beneath his burning look. The first time she had met him, it was like he had put a spell on her. However, last night, she'd been aware of an electrical jolt that hit her straight at her center and radiated through her whole body. Even now, her body was still tingling from his hand on her breasts less than thirty minutes ago. She assumed the heat that rushed through her veins was her body's way of warning her of danger. Painful experiences had taught her to trust her gut feeling.

And her gut warned her to stay away from him.

Berlin looked across the table and gave a nonchalant shrug. "He's all right. It's the flirting I could do without."

"He can't help it. He's naturally a flirt."

"I guess it takes one to know one, huh?"

Arianna gave her coworker a dismissive wave. "Just 'cause I'm married doesn't mean I'm dead. Besides, there's nothing wrong with looking as long as I don't touch."

"Ain't you something?"

Their waitress arrived with their food. Berlin glanced down at her plate piled high with southern fried catfish, coleslaw and hush puppies, and her mouth watered. Nothing beat Mabel's Fish House.

"Listen, it doesn't matter whether I like him or not. All I care about is that the renovations stay within the projected budget." *And that Reginald leaves me alone.* "Now, can we talk about something else?"

Arianna released a long breath, and Berlin knew she wasn't happy. *Tough.*

"I see you're still wearing your contacts."

She was relieved at the change of subject. "After you took my glasses, what choice did I have?" She couldn't resist laughing along with Arianna. "I figure since I spent all that money, I might as well get my money's worth. Besides, they were easier to put in than I thought."

"Well they look great," she replied and reached for a bottle of hot sauce. "Without those large bifocals you really draw attention to your face. Not to mention the new hairdo really helps."

"Thanks." She had spent almost four hours at the beauty shop getting her hair spiral curled. "The problem is Cameron never got a chance to see me."

"Yeah, that sucks. He is away at a conference until Monday."

"I know." Although Arianna was the staffing coordinator, Berlin had made it her business to ask the front desk when he was coming back. And when he did, she was going to be ready. The feel of Reginald's hand underneath her skirt raced through her mind, and she quickly shoved that thought away.

Cameron was more her type—a rich, resident physician. He was kind and less intimidating without the cockiness Reginald possessed. Her body didn't react in such traitorous ways either, which was a plus. Her heart was not part of the plan. Once burned…well, she planned not to experience that kind of pain again.

"That's alright. He'll see you when he gets back."

"By then my curls will be history." The thought of spending another afternoon at the salon, even for Cameron, was asking a lot of her.

"How about I come over on Sunday and fix it for you?" she asked between chews.

"I think if I learn to tie up my hair. It will last. Otherwise, I'll just pull it back in a bun again."

Arianna turned up her nose. "You do and I'll be knocking on your front door whether you like it or not. Girl, I'd give up my first-born for beautiful hair like yours."

Her friend hated when she wore her hair in a bun. Said it made her look like a librarian.

"Speaking of babies, when you and Lawrence gonna start a family?" she teased as she dug into her food.

Arianna gave her a long devilish look. "No rush, we're having a lot more fun practicing."

Chapter Four

Reginald spent most of his lunch hour in his Escalade, returning phone calls. A call to his assistant turned out to be exactly what he needed to hear.

"Reggie, don't worry. I got the bid in way ahead of schedule," she reassured him.

"Thanks, Kia."

He released a sigh of relief. He didn't know how his business had run without her. The woman could write a grant while blindfolded. She'd landed him numerous minority contracts over the last three years. After spending almost ten years working for someone else, he had quit and started RDH Construction with a beat-up old truck and a tool belt that had once belonged to his father. His business began with basic repairs, and then one contract led to another. He needed help in the office and hired Kia. Once a government employee, she was very familiar with minority grant programs.

He reached inside his lunch pail and removed a hoagie sandwich he had picked up at the grocery store on his way to work. Cooking had never been one of his strong points, but eating was. He tore open a bag of potato chips and stared off at the sky. Light flurries sailed through the air. Heavy snow was imminent. After weeks of freezing rain, they could use the break.

He bit into the sandwich and couldn't help thinking that the food at the restaurant across the street was better.

And it would have tasted even better in Berlin's presence.

He couldn't stop thinking about her golden eyes and passionate kisses. In his arms, she had been responsive and sensual and, most importantly, eager. He had learned a long time ago the danger of acting on impulse, but there was just something about her that made it impossible to control his actions.

Grabbing a soda from the pail, he glanced up in time to see Berlin and Arianna crossing the street together. He sat there soaking in her beauty and fiending for her. Never in his thirty-five years had he wanted someone so much.

Berlin was laughing. The smile softened her features. What he would do to have her look that way at him. Instead, all he got was lip and attitude.

Last night was something she'd rather he forget, but the memory of her taste wouldn't let him. Having her in his arms, moaning as he suckled hungrily at her breast, would not go away. He could still feel the smooth heat of her skin against his hand and the rapid pulse at her throat. He wanted more.

The muscle in his jaw twitched at the thought of the job ending and never seeing her again. Totally frustrated, he popped the tab on his drink and watched her enter the building. He would have to think of a plan—*fast*.

He had a good feeling all that would change sometime really soon.

When they returned from lunch, Berlin made it her business to walk through the clinic and take the long way back to her desk. The last thing she wanted was another encounter with Reginald.

The waiting room was filled with parents and children. Some were on their parent's laps crying, obviously not feeling well, while others were playing and laughing. She smiled down at a little girl with long hair and beautiful eyes who was reading a book to a little blonde girl. The little girl reminded her so much of her niece Gabrielle, whom she hadn't seen in over a year. As she moved past the treatment rooms, she made a mental note to call her sister. Maybe she would fly to Los Angeles in the spring for a visit.

Berlin stepped into her office and lowered into her seat, pleased that she had made it without any altercations. She reached for the financial reports from the previous month and spent the next hour going over the numbers and comparing them to another spreadsheet.

After double-checking the numbers once, and then a second time, she lowered her pencil and leaned back in her chair and frowned. She couldn't concentrate.

It's all Reginald's fault.

She exhaled a deep breath when she recalled how good he had looked staring down at her. It had taken sheer willpower to stay focused on his eyes and not look down at his lips. For a man, he had a fabulous mouth. It was full, supple and soft. And then there was that voice. She'd know that deep, rich tone anywhere. The sound made heat pool at her center. When he had pulled her in the corner and fondled her breasts, it took everything she had not to lean into him and beg him to make love to her. She was one hundred percent certain it would be amazing between them. She also knew one night would not be enough. If his kisses were addictive, she could imagine how potent making love would be.

Shaking her head, she swung around in the chair and gazed out the window. Light snow was starting to come down. The white flakes usually caused her to smile. Nothing was better than a white Christmas. However, with Reginald on her mind, it was impossible to appreciate it.

Scowling, Berlin swung her chair around and reached for her pencil. The reports needed to be verified and approved by her before the Christmas break. At the rate she was going, she wouldn't make the year-end deadline. Sitting up in her chair, she took a deep breath and started again. There was no way she would allow the hired help to stand in the way of her doing her job.

Still distracted by thoughts of Reginald, it was slightly after six when she finally decided to call it a night. She scowled. That man had a sensual presence about him that was driving her crazy. As far as she was concerned, completion of the project couldn't come soon enough. *Hang in there.* Eighteen more days until Christmas, and it will all be over.

A Delight Before Christmas

Walking across her small cramped office, she stopped and reached for her coat, then lowered a brown faux-fur hat on her head. She swung her leather purse strap over her shoulder, then turned off the light and closed the door softly behind her.

She moved down the hall toward the side entrance. Other than the sound of the janitor vacuuming, the clinic was relatively quiet and deserted. The support staff and medical personnel had left shortly after the clinic closed at five. She was used to being one of the last to leave. She wasn't worried. The clinic was located at a busy intersection in Dellwood, MO. There was a gas station, barbershop and a video store on the opposite side of the street. As she strolled out the building, the smell of barbecue wafted to her nose. Tempted to go and grab a plate, she glanced over at the rib joint next door. Noticing the drive-thru line was wrapped around the building, she declined. She wasn't that hungry.

Berlin moved around to the parking lot at the back of the building. It was already dark and snowing. She frowned. If she had known it was coming down so heavy and sticky, she would have left sooner. She pulled the hat down around her ears and moved quickly out to her car. As she reached her Lexus, she smiled. It always made her feel good to get off and see her hard work in the parking lot. She removed her keys from her pocket and hit the button, unlocking the door. It wasn't until she had moved around to the driver's side that she saw the flat tire.

"Damn!"

Just what she needed. The temperature had dropped down into the teens, and the snow fell heavily, topping the car hoods and the surface of the parking lot. Her hooded wool cape provided protection from the weather, but she shivered nonetheless. There was no way she was changing a tire. She pondered the possibility, trying to think of someone she could call and came up with no one. She couldn't afford triple A. She had no choice but to see if the janitor would help her; otherwise, she would have to call a tow truck. Opening her door, she tossed her briefcase onto the seat in the back, then shut it.

A light tap on the shoulder startled her.

"Looks like you need some help."

Swinging around, Berlin found Reginald standing behind her. He looked concerned, his straight brown eyebrows crinkling together. Her

46

skin prickled like the hair of a cat, sensing danger just as she had earlier today. The last person she wanted to come to her rescue was him. And as far as she was concerned, Reginald Hodges was dangerous with a capital D. The sooner she got away from him, the better. Checking her watch, she muttered, "I'm getting ready to call someone."

Reginald arched his right brow as if he didn't believe her. "You've got a spare?"

Oh yeah, she had a spare. A spare that she had known for over a month needed to be repaired. "Yes, but it's flat, too."

"Women," he muttered under his breath.

Berlin narrowed her eyes at him. "What did you say?"

Reginald shook his head. "Nothing." He moved around to the car. "Pop your trunk."

"For what?" she demanded.

He sighed. "So we can go and get your tire fixed."

We? No way, no how was she going anywhere with him. "I don't want your help."

Reginald gazed at her long and hard. When she didn't flinch, he shrugged his shoulders and said, "Fine. I'm out." He then turned on the heels of his Timberland boots, walked over to his Escalade, and climbed in.

Girl, are you crazy?

Berlin briefly shut her eyes. Why couldn't she just accept the man's help without thinking there was a hidden agenda? Reginald was trying to be nice, and she was acting like a stuck-up witch.

"Wait!" she screamed as he started to pull away.

Reginald put his foot on the brake and rolled down the driver's side window. "Yeah?"

She swallowed the lump in her throat. "I'm gonna take you up on your offer," she said in a soft voice.

He gave her a puzzled look. "I don't know what you're talking about? What offer?"

She pursed her lips. He was determined to make her grovel. She'd rather tell him where to stick it, but who's to say there was anyone else willing to help change her tire? "Your offer to help me fix my tire, *please*," she managed through gritted teeth.

With a smirk, Reginald put the SUV in park, then climbed out and moved around to her trunk. "Pop it." His voice was surprisingly calm and authoritative for someone who was standing out in the cold. As soon as it flew open, he reached inside and removed her spare. Just as she had said, it needed repairing. "What you do, drive over a switchblade?"

"Funny."

He chuckled and tossed the tire in the back of his SUV.

Berlin moved to the passenger's side. As soon as she opened the door, she heard loud rap music, booming from the CD player. Frowning, she climbed in and closed the door behind her.

Awareness cut through her the second Reginald climbed in the SUV. He carried the scent of a man, spicy and masculine. It disturbed her on a personal level that she didn't want to feel.

"Do we have to listen to rap?" she snapped as soon as he shut the door.

"No-o-o, we don't have to listen to rap." He glanced over at her with that irresistible smile that was all his own. She felt her breasts tingle against the material of her blouse. "I got something you'll like."

"How do you know what I like?"

"I got a pretty good idea, Ms. Dupree," he said, sending a rush of unwanted warmth across her face. He gazed at her for another long moment, and she gasped when she realized what particular *like* he was talking about.

Grinning, Reginald reached down and changed to another CD. Within seconds, the rap stopped and Jamie Foxx's "Unpredictable" filled the air.

She loved Jamie Foxx.

"So, was I right?"

She couldn't resist a grin. "Close enough."

Reginald chuckled, put the SUV in drive, and pulled out the parking lot.

Berlin leaned back and relaxed, hoping the music would lull her senses. But her traitorous body was keenly aware of Reginald. Her heart thumped a rapid pace, and her breathing increased. She caught herself staring at his profile. She absolutely, positively, didn't like what she felt when she was in his company. Shifting on the seat, she turned and stared out the window.

Once on the main road, even with the fresh show, Reginald drove like a fool. His cell phone rang, and he had no problem talking and driving at the same time. She took a deep breath. If they made it to the gas station in one piece it would be a miracle, she thought as she made sure her seatbelt was secure. She then briefly closed her eyes and said a silent prayer.

A horn blasted, sending her eyelids up and her scrambling on the seat with her heart in her throat. She glanced over in time to witness Reginald weaving out of the far left lane.

"Would you please slow down?" she snapped. It was bad enough he was leaning in the seat.

"Don't get your panties in a bunch. I got this."

She shook her head. "I don't think so. Where'd you get your license, in a Cracker Jack box?"

Reginald chuckled at her response. "Chill, we're almost there."

"Thank God," she mumbled while still clutching the armrest with white knuckled intensity. She decided to keep her eye on the road.

After several long minutes, Reginald was the first to speak. "You live around here?"

Unwilling to be drawn into a conversation, Berlin crossed her ankles and simply answered, "Nope."

There was a long silence, and she was glad he had gotten the hint.

As they rounded the next corner, Reginald put the windshield wipers on. "It's starting to come down. How 'bout I fix the tire for you later and go ahead and take you home?"

She didn't know how to react to his kindness. "I couldn't have you do that."

He took his eyes briefly off the road. "It's no problem. I can take it by my cousin's shop and have him fix it, then go back over to the clinic and change it."

After a few seconds of consideration, Berlin decided that the sooner she got away from him the better. "How will I get to work in the morning?"

"I can swing by and get you."

She should have known. The only reason why he had offered was so that he would have an excuse to come by her house. Maybe even try to finish what they started. The idea of him sticking something else between her legs turned her on, which pissed her off even more. "No thank you."

Reginald dismissed his suggestion with a shrug of the left shoulder. "Hey, that's on you."

She released a weary sigh. "Why don't we just fix the tire? I really don't like being without transportation."

Feeling her nose running, she reached inside her purse for a tissue and wiped her nose. Then, self-consciously, she reached for her compact and made sure she hadn't left anything behind. Her cheeks were pink from exposure to the damp, cold air, as well as her nose. Damn, she hated cold weather. Her nose would be raw and peeling before the end of the week.

"You still look good."

She looked to her left. "What?"

"I said, don't worry you still look good. Even with that crazy hat on your head."

She snapped her compact shut and rolled her eyes in his direction. "You just focus on the road and let me worry about how I look in my hat." She had to bite her tongue from saying anything further. If he weren't helping her, she would have told him about himself.

Reginald pulled into a small repair shop near the mall. He climbed out and moved to the rear for her tire.

Determined to pay for her own repairs, Berlin climbed out as well. She squinted as the chilly evening breeze tugged at her hat. The snow had begun to change to a mix of rain and sleet. She groaned. The roads would be messy in the morning.

Stepping inside, she was met by the smell of motor oil and the sounds of James Brown blaring from a speaker behind the register.

"Yo, Dashaun. Man, where you at?" Reginald yelled.

"Out here!"

She followed Reginald out to the garage where a dark, heavy-set man rolled out from under an old Chevy Impala.

"Hey, whassup, G-man?" Raising his fist, Reginald gave his cousin a pound.

"G-man?" she murmured. "What's the G stand for, gigolo?"

Reginald gave her another irresistible grin. "Aw, so now you got jokes."

She tried to mask her laughter by looking away.

"Hey cuz, Shorty, here needs her tire fixed."

Dashaun quickly looked the tire over, then shook his head. "Yo, baby girl, I can't fix this. But I can mount and balance another in a flash."

There goes my new comforter set. "I guess so," she said with a frustrated breath.

Reginald playfully nudged her in the shoulder. "Cheer up, boo. I got you."

She rolled her eyes at the endearment, then moved back into the waiting area and took a seat in a plastic white chair while she waited for him to prepare the new tire. Through the glass she watched Reginald and Dashaun shoot the bull. Reginald reminded her so much of her cousin with his friends. Relaxed. Laughing. Having fun. Watching his smiling face, heat flowed through her. He was too fine. She'd noticed practically everything about him from his jeans to the way they hugged his quads and glutes. Man, he had a body. If there were some way she could have one night with him and never have to see him again, she would jump at the opportunity to have that beautiful body lying on top of her. She already knew what he was working with because she had held it in her hand. Just thinking about its thickness caused her heart to jolt and her pulse to pound. She would like nothing more than to have all that buried deep inside her. She crossed her legs and tried to calm the heat throbbing between her thighs. Her sexual needs had definitely been neglected for far too long. Nothing would do but feeling his—

"Yo, Berlin. Your tire's ready."

"What?" she startled. She hadn't heard anyone enter the room. "Oh, okay."

Reginald gazed down at her with a look of concern. "Is somethin' wrong?"

"No, nothing," she replied in a sharper tone than intended. She didn't mean to snap at him, but she was pissed that she had been caught thinking about him.

Berlin swung her purse onto her shoulder, took a deep breath and moved out into the garage. She thanked his cousin who to her frustration "G-man" had already paid, and then followed him out to his Escalade.

On the ride back to her car, she didn't bother to comment on the rap music, although she was certain he had cranked the volume up just to annoy her. She was just glad for an excuse not to have to hold a conversation. Instead, she watched the wet mixture fall steadily onto the road.

Reginald pulled into the spot beside her car, then climbed out and opened the door for her.

"Thanks, Reginald," she replied as she slid off the seat and reached inside her coat pocket for her car keys.

He stepped around back and removed the tire and reached for a jack. She offered her assistance, but, to her relief, he declined. She hoped to never have to change a tire, but to be on the safe side, she then stood back and watched carefully as he jacked up her car and all of the proceeding steps just in case.

"All done." Reginald tossed her jack in and shut her trunk.

Berlin walked around to the driver's side. Before reaching for the door handle, she swung around. "Thanks Reginald. I owe you one." A snowflake landed on her eyelash that she wiped away.

He moved to stand beside her. "How about you pay up now?" He glanced down at her, his eyes darkening as he openly studied her, and it made her feel restless, excited, and a bit annoyed.

"What do you want?" she dared to ask.

His palm brushed her cheek lightly. "How about a kiss and we can call it even?"

For a long moment, she simply stared, hoping she hadn't heard him right. However, the look on his face told her otherwise. His gaze darkened, locking on her lips, tracing them. She couldn't breathe, feeling exposed with Reginald too close and too powerful. "I don't think so."

"Why? You scared?" he asked, eyes shining with determination.

She slipped her hands into her pocket and tilted her chin. "Being scared doesn't have anything to do with it,'" she said carefully. "I just think it is very inappropriate."

"It's not like we're strangers." His deep sensual voice curled around her. "I've already tasted you. I can still smell you on my fingers."

Berlin couldn't believe he had gone there, but he had. And thinking about his fingers buried between her legs was not a good thing when she was trying to decline his offer. "The answer is no."

"You know you want me to kiss you, so you might as well admit it."

She was about to deny it when her eyes betrayed her and traveled down to stare at his lips. Damn, she loved his mouth! His lips, thick and succulent. And when his tongue darted out to sweep his mustache, it took everything she had not to groan.

"What are you thinking about?"

She shivered when his warm breath fanned her cheek. "Nothing." He cupped her shoulders, drawing her closer. It was a simple gesture, but it seemed to have charged the very air around them with electricity.

"I think you're lying. I also think you want to kiss me again as badly as I want to kiss you."

He moved in slowly, and she knew he was giving her a chance to stop him if she dared. Despite how big a mistake she knew it was, she couldn't seem to find the words or the strength.

His lips feathered her mouth, before his tongue slowly stroked across her lips. His arms locking around her waist as if afraid she might run away. And that was exactly what she would have done if she'd had the strength. If she really and truly wanted to, and she was shocked to realize she did not. Her insides quivered with such a strong need; she didn't try to fight. Instead, she leaned in and enjoyed each and every stroke. Opening her mouth, she allowed him to slip his tongue inside. The kiss wasn't demanding like she would have expected after last night and this afternoon. It was soft and gentle, causing a burning desire between her legs, making her body yearn for release.

Reginald reached inside her coat and slipped a hand between the high splits in her skirt. "I want to finish what we started last night," he whispered against her earlobe.

She tried for logic and tried to convince herself that what she was experiencing now just wasn't reality. As soon as she opened her eyes, it would all be over. Only when she lifted her eyelids, their gazes collided.

A car hood slammed close by and she jumped.

She shivered as Reginald's mouth curved into a sensuous smile. "Relax. You're safe with me."

Berlin doubted that. Being around him was getting to be dangerous business. She glanced over his shoulder at the snow that had changed to sleet. "It's starting to get bad out. I guess I better go."

"Can I go with you?" he asked, studying her with that close, burning intensity that seemed to make the floor vibrate beneath her feet.

He leaned into her, allowing her to feel the evidence of his arousal. She felt every inch of it. As he rotated his hips and pressed against her, she was so tempted to say yes. She sensed that this man would know a lot about passion. His vehement study of her caused a wave of something she didn't want to define to slam against her. Again, his gaze slowly moved down her body. She would love to have him share her bed tonight. Only she couldn't. She'd never be able to face him the next morning at work.

"I don't think so." Flustered, she quickly turned around and slid behind the driver's seat, and turned the key in the ignition. The entire time she was speechless. Her body was still humming from the effect of his sizzling mouth.

Reginald reached down and snapped her seat belt in place. "Drive safely," he murmured. His mouth was so close to her ear that his lips actually brushed it. Something unfamiliar rippled through her body. She was unable to figure out what he had said.

"What did you…" Her body stiffened with surprise as his lips closed on the rim of her ear. She tilted her head back against the headrest and closed her eyes. She wasn't quite sure what he was doing. All she knew was that he had found her spot, and she had no choice but to go with the flow. He did something dark and dangerous to her lobe that had her turning to putty in his hand. Without the presence of mind to care, she lost herself in his gentle caress and the scent of his body. She had a strong suspicion if he pulled her into his arms and finish where they had left off, she would be too weak to resist. And then her car door closed, snapping her out of a trance. Glancing out the window, she watched Reginald walk back to his SUV.

Humiliated beyond reason, she put her car in reverse and pulled away from the parking lot.

Reginald watched her leave, and shook his head. The woman was too stuck-up for her own good. After she had turned down his offer of help, he could have left her standing in the parking lot, but his mama had raised her sons better than that.

He had no business kissing her earlobe. He had no idea what had come over him. Just having her standing in front of him smelling so good made it hard to resist. Now she had him so rock hard that he wasn't sure if he'd make it home.

Reginald stepped into his SUV. Once inside, he loosened his pants allowing a little relief. However, the only thing that was going to satisfy him was Berlin. Reaching inside his boxers, he stroked the head of his dick as he thought about Berlin spread across his bed with her legs spread wide open, inviting him to come inside. He wouldn't be happy until he was pumping red hot into her body, filling her with his seed. He planned to make her entire body quiver as he held her steadily by the hips. Just as she was about to come, he would flip her over and have her riding him until she begged for release. No matter how hard, he would hold back until she was ready to collapse from exhaustion. Realizing he was getting carried away, he removed his hand and started the Escalade. He was more determined than ever to have her.

Only living a short distance away, within minutes he pulled into his subdivision. Even in the four-wheel drive, he could tell the roads were getting bad. Visibility wasn't the best and the sleet had made the streets slippery. As he pulled onto his street, he couldn't help but to wonder if Berlin had made it home safely. He tried to push the thought and her to the side. The last thing in the world he wanted to start doing was worrying about Ms. High & Mighty. Nevertheless, by the time he had pulled into his garage the feeling resurfaced.

Quit thinking about her!

Reginald climbed out and stepped through the side door. He never locked it. The only way anyone could break into his house was if they had the combination to his garage opener. He hung his coat on a hook in the garage, removed his wet boots and moved through the side door into the kitchen.

He padded across the linoleum over to a large stainless steel refrigerator. After removing a beer, he turned on a small portable television in the corner and had a seat at the small oak kitchen table. Popping the tab, he took a thirsty slurp and listened to the news. Three minutes later, his brow bunched with worry. The newscaster reported numerous accidents in the area tonight. Lowering the beer to the table, Reginald stood abruptly and went to the window, considering the mix with his hands thrust into his pockets.

I wonder if she made it home safely.

He moved over to the far right hand drawers and removed the phone book, then returned to his seat. The only way he'd be able to relax and enjoy a quiet and peaceful evening was to contact her. As he flipped to the D's, he was certain someone like her would have her phone number unlisted. If not, then he would feel relieved, knowing that he had at least tried.

Dupree Berlin.

His pulse raced. He couldn't believe she was listed. What were the chances of another person by the same name living in St. Louis? Convincing himself that it was the right thing to do, he reached for the phone on the wall and dialed her number.

The phone rang, once, twice, while he worried his bottom lip dropped and tried to think what he would actually say once she answered the phone. By the fifth ring, he sighed with relief when her answer machine picked up. He trembled as the sultry sound of her voice vibrated through every nerve in his body. It took him several seconds before he realized the silence was his signal to leave a message.

Quickly, he ended the call, and sat their breathing heavily. Calling her hadn't made things any better. It had made things worse. Why wasn't she at home? Glancing over at the clock, it had been at least thirty minutes since he had watched her drive away from the lot. Where could she be? Thoughts of her being in one of the accidents that was reported on the news, started to worry him again. Reginald picked up the phone and hit redial. Pacing across the floor, he was seconds away from hopping back into his SUV and driving over to the address in the phone book, when he finally heard her pick up the phone. The heavy breathing, told him she had rushed to get it.

"Hello."

"Berlin?"

"Yes?"

"What took you so long to answer the phone?" he snapped.

"Excuse me? Who is this?"

"I asked you a question."

She sucked her teeth and replied with attitude, "And I asked you one. Now either you answer or I'm hanging up."

Reginald realized they were both yelling, which wouldn't get him anywhere. He paused and took a deep breath. "This is Reggie."

He heard her quick intake of breath, "*Reginald Hodges?* Why…why are you calling me?"

As much as he was tempted to hang up and pretend she had the wrong person, he couldn't. "I called because I was concerned. There are a lot of accidents this evening, and I wanted to make sure you had made it home safely."

There was a slight pause. When she finally spoke again, her voice had softened considerably. "Yes, I made it home a few minutes ago. I was outside tossing salt in my driveway. With all that sleet coming down, I didn't want to take a chance at it being icy in the morning."

He closed his eyes and grinned. "That's a good idea. I probably need to go out and do the same."

"Well at least you have a four-wheel drive. I could just see the wheels on my Lexus spinning in the morning." He chuckled along side of her, which was followed by an awkward silence.

"Well, now that I know you're safe, I'll let you get back to your work."

"All right." There was another pause. "Uh, Reginald?"

"Yeah, whassup?"

"Thanks for helping me with my tire. There is no telling how long I would have had to wait for help if you hadn't come along."

"No problem. Although a beautiful woman like yourself, I'm sure you would have had the brothas lined up ready to help."

"Yeah, right."

He chuckled. "I'll see you tomorrow."

Berlin walked over to the window and stared out at the icicle-laden trees and blankets of white snow. She loved fresh snow. It was the ice she could do without. Luckily tomorrow's forecast promised temperatures ten degrees warmer than today, which wasn't saying much, although it was better than the years she spent growing up in the Windy City. A shiver snaked up her arm. Her house was cold as usual. Anyone else would have moved to the thermostat and cranked up the heat, but not Berlin.

After talking to Reginald, she had changed into a red sweat suit and fluffy house shoes and moved down to the kitchen to make herself a chef's salad. She then spent the last hour curled in the corner trying to read a book and had found the effort useless. Moving to the family room, she flopped down onto a burgundy couch and tossed a throw cover across her legs. She decided to read until bedtime and reached for the book again. However, five minutes later she realized she had read the same page twice. She couldn't stop thinking about Reginald.

Berlin released a long sigh and lowered the book to the beige Berber carpet. As long as Reginald acted cocky, like he was man's gift to women, it was easy for her not to like him. However, after his behavior this evening she wasn't so sure anymore. Reginald had shown a compassionate side that was hard for her to ignore. Not only had he helped her with a flat in the middle of a snowstorm, but he had taken the time to look up her number in the book and make sure she had made it home safely. No one had ever done anything like that for her.

Leaning back against the deep cushions, she lowered her eyelids as her lips tingled, reminding her of the heated kiss they shared. She wanted so badly to stay angry with him for taking advantage of her. She took a deep breath, knowing what she was thinking was nowhere near the truth. He hadn't taken advantage of her. She'd had every opportunity to say no. She could have hopped into her car and left. Instead, she had stood there willingly, and as soon as his lips had touched hers, she had met each stroke with an urgency of her own.

This isn't supposed to be happening.

The last thing she needed was to be attracted to Reginald. There was no point in denying it, but that didn't mean she had to like it. Yeah, he was gorgeous, and yes, she appreciated his help this evening, but she was under no obligation to him. Not now or otherwise. She had a mission, and the sooner she stuck to it the better off she would be.

Cupping her legs to her chest, she pushed Reginald aside and tried to focus on Cameron. He would be back in the clinic on Monday. What she needed was a plan to get his attention. She had three days to think about it and have a plan ready to execute. Cameron was everything she needed to complete her carefully laid out life. All she had to do was get him to realize it.

The phone rang. Reluctantly, she rose from the couch and moved down the foyer into a spacious kitchen. She reached for the phone and glanced at the caller ID. She blew out a frustrated breath, then put the phone to her ear.

"Hi, Mom."

"Well, hello, dear. How's the weather there?"

"Nasty. I'm just getting in from salting the driveway," she said while leaning against the counter.

She sighed heavily into the mouthpiece. "I wish you'd find a man to help you. Your father and I hate knowing you're all alone down there."

"I'm fine, Mom, really."

"Where have you been? I tried reaching you several times yesterday."

A Delight Before Christmas

"I was at the company Christmas party last night." She closed her eyes. What would her mother think if she knew she had spent it in the closet making out with a man? Knowing her mom, she'd probably shout, "About time!"

"I spoke to Eileen yesterday. She and Darryl are going to Paris for Christmas."

"How wonderful," she mumbled under her breath. She half listened as her mother went on about how wonderful a time the two of them were going to have. Berlin envied her older sister. She hated she felt that way, but she did. It wasn't fair. Eileen had the life she wanted.

Shortly after graduating from high school, Eileen had fallen in love with a second year law student who asked her to marry him the day after he passed the bar exam. He was now a partner at one of the largest firms in Los Angeles. The couple had a six year old, Gabrielle. At Thanksgiving the happy couple announced that they would be having their second child in May.

Paris at Christmas was something she had dreamed about and hoped to experience. The hard part was finding a man of similar status.

"Did you hear what I said?" her mother said, breaking into her reverie.

"I'm sorry, I was listening to the weather report. What did you say?"

"I said, since their leaving the country and you're going to be all alone for the holiday, your father and I decided to come and spend Christmas with you in Missouri."

"What?"

"Won't it be wonderful? This way we can spend Christmas together."

"Actually, I was planning to clean my house and catch up on some reading."

"Nonsense. I'm sure your house is spotless. We've been dying to see your house, so this is going to be perfect."

Her mother was bubbling over with excitement. Berlin didn't know what to say, or rather she did. She just didn't know how to say no in a way her mother would understand without her feelings being hurt. Unfortunately, by the time they said their goodbyes, she still hadn't come up with a reason. Hanging up the phone, she knew she was in trouble. Her parents were coming to St. Louis for Christmas.

"Stupid," she muttered after she had strolled back into the family room and noticed the horrible walls. The wallpaper had been stripped months ago, but still needed scraping and priming. She should have told her mother no. Now what would she do? There was no way she could finish painting the entire house before they arrived Christmas Eve unless she took off from her job and worked nonstop. Even then, she had to be in the mood to paint. Otherwise, she'd do a sloppy job. She would have to find a painter. She didn't know of anyone. Then just as that thought left another entered and a sexy painter in a silly red Santa suit came to mind. *Reginald.* She shook her head and moved back into the kitchen. There was no way she would ask him to paint the interior of her house. That would mean being around him alone, and that just wasn't a good idea. Dr. Clarke was due back on Monday, and she already had enough damage to repair, she didn't need to offer any other reason for the office to gossip about the two.

Moving over to the microwave cart, she reached inside the bottom shelf and removed the phone book. She took a seat then quickly flipped through the yellow pages to Paint. There were several companies listed that had reasonable rates. A smile tipped her lips. She didn't need Reginald's help at all. Closing the book, her shoulders sagged with relief. First thing tomorrow she would start calling every number listed until she found the best deal. Everything would be just fine because there was no way in the world she would ask Reginald for help.

Chapter Five

Berlin hung up her phone and groaned. She was in trouble. After spending the latter part of the morning contacting every painter in the phone book, she discovered she had hit a dead end. Most of them were off for the holiday season, and the others' prices were way out of her league.

"You look like you lost your best friend."

Berlin glanced up at Arianna's concerned expression, and then dropped her face into the palm of her hand. "Worse, my parents are coming to spend the holiday with me."

"That's wonderful!" her friend cried as she lowered in the seat across from her. "Does this mean I'll get to finally meet them?"

"I guess," she mumbled.

"So what exactly is the problem?"

"The problem is my house is still under construction," she explained as she raised her head and slumped back against the chair. "If my father sees the paint peeling from my walls, he's gonna insist on completing the project for me."

Arianna looked confused. "What's wrong with that?"

"He has a bad back." She gave her a grim look. "The worse part is that I've been bragging to my family for months how nice my house is. Once they see it, they'll know I've been lying."

"I saw your house. It isn't that bad."

Berlin gave her a hard look. "Arianna, puhleeze."

"Well, then again, I barely had my foot in the door when you kicked me out."

Last June she was home with a stomach virus when Arianna had offered to stop by the pharmacy and pick up some medicine for her. She had barely stepped into foyer when Berlin insisted she wasn't up for company and booted her back out the door. "That's because I wasn't ready for guests."

Her coworker crossed her legs. "Well, you better get ready because your parents are coming."

She groaned. "I know and they will take over. I cannot deal with my parents trying to make my home theirs. Besides, their taste and mine are not on the same level. They shop at thrift stores and Wal-Mart."

Arianna frowned, then replied defensively, "Hey, I shop at Wal-Mart, too. They have some fabulous deals."

Frowning, Berlin didn't feel like getting into a long discussion of how she liked to shop not only for price, but for quality as well. She'd rather pay extra in order to have the luxury of sleeping in a set of six hundred thread sateen sheets. Berlin loved Arianna like she was a sister, but decorating was not one of her strong points. She and her husband Carlton, a police officer who painted as a hobby, had decorated their new home with IKEA furniture and his abstract paintings. She wasn't knocking it. If the shoes fit wear them; however, for her, quality was a key element to finding that perfect pair.

Folding her hands on the desk, she tried to clarify, "I wasn't implying that Wal-Mart doesn't have deals. Lord knows I live at the Super Center. I just want to do things my way."

Arianna gave her a look that said she didn't understand her way of thinking. "Okay, so what's the plan?"

Berlin blew out a long breath. "I need a painter. I've called every one in town, and either they are not available or I can't afford their prices."

The other woman waved off her words. "Is that all? The way you were looking I was thinking it was something impossible."

Her eyes grew wide with excitement. "You know someone I can call?"

"You don't have to call," she began with a chuckle, and then pointed toward the door. "All you gotta do is walk down the hall and ask him yourself."

Berlin frowned. "Who? Reginald?" She shook her head. "No way."

"Why not?"

Damn, what could she say without Arianna reading something else into it. "Because, I…uh…don't want him to know where I live."

Her friend lifted an arched brow. "That's crazy. Why not?"

Berlin broke eye contact to glance down at her keyboard. "I just don't like him," she lied.

"Why not?"

Despite herself, Berlin laughed. "You're beginning to sound like a parrot."

"I'm waiting," Arianna said with her lips pursed impatiently.

Berlin quickly sobered and looked across the desk at Arianna. "Reginald rubs me the wrong way."

Arianna's face softened with a smile. "Girl, I would give anything to have that brotha rub on me."

That figures. She grinned. "You're too much, you know that?"

"Yeah, so I've been told," she said with laughter in her voice. "Well, what other choice do you have besides Reggie?"

Berlin gave an exasperated sigh. "None."

"Then you better go ask him."

"I don't know," she returned with skepticism.

In one quick motion, Arianna rose from the chair. "Well, person-ally, I think you need to get past your hang-ups and ask Reggie to help you. Otherwise, get ready for your parents to decorate your crib."

Berlin shuddered at the possibility.

Long after Arianna had gone back to her office, Berlin sat behind her desk, pondering what she would do. She could drop by the paint store on her way home and get started tonight. However, as slow as she was it would take her all night to complete one wall, and even then it would look like she had done it herself.

Armed with nothing but determination, Berlin assessed her options. Though female intuition warned her to run for cover, she desperately needed Reginald's help. No matter how much working with the man might stir her sexual needs that were best left sleeping; she had to have her house completed in sixteen days. The latter was not even an option. Now was not the time to let her emotions interfere with her good sense.

By noon, she moved from behind her desk and went out in the hall, following the smell of paint. Near the end of the hall, she spotted Reginald painting a wall outside the nurse's triage station. He glanced over his shoulder and gave her an irresistible smile.

"How's your tire?"

Just two feet from him, she'd stopped and slowly looked him up and down. Three inches shorter than his six-foot height, her high heels brought his sepia-colored eyes to her own.

Berlin nodded. "Just fine. Thanks again for your help."

"No problem," he replied, then stared with intensity as if he already knew the thank you wasn't the reason why she had stopped to talk to him. She could bet free lunch for the next two weeks that Arianna had already blabbed her mouth. She groaned inward. They were going to have to have a long talk. *Too late to chicken out now.*

"Can I speak to you?" she asked, and then noticed a nurse glancing over the half wall, taking it all in. "In *private.*"

"Sure."

As he lowered the brush to a pan of paint, Berlin moved in the direction of her office for privacy. The last thing she needed was for the staff to know she was inviting him to her house to paint. She stepped inside the room with Reginald only seconds after.

"Whassup?" he asked.

Berlin swung around to find his massive body blocking the doorway. She swallowed tightly. His relaxed stance in those loose fitting jeans was sexy as all get out. With Reginald invading her space, again she felt the strong need to get as far away from him as possible. Unfortunately, she needed her walls scraped, primed and painted.

Okay, so what if she was attracted to him? She thought, trying to convince her hormones to snap out of it. Having her house completed before Christmas was the most important thing, and she wouldn't allow an attraction to jeopardize that. She felt this was a phase that would eventually go away. She was certain of that. All she had to do was not allow Reginald to kiss her again.

Standing in the center of her office, she shifted her weight to her left leg and cleared her throat. "I need your help."

The corner of his mouth lifted. "What kind of help, beautiful?"

A Delight Before Christmas

Such a charmer, isn't he? She smiled sweetly at Reginald, reminding herself that she was a big girl who needed to separate past experiences from the present. She needed his help. As long as she didn't get involved with him, there was nothing to worry about. "I need a couple of rooms at my home painted before the holidays."

Amusement and something she couldn't put her finger on flickered in his eyes. His voice was soft and almost sensual when he spoke. "And you want me to do it?"

"Yes, depending on how much you charge." She hesitated. "I really don't have a lot of money to spend."

His voice was soft and husky. "Cost."

There was no way she heard him right. "Cost?"

He nodded. "That's right. Paint and materials."

Uh-oh, ol' boy was up to something. She folded her arms defiantly across her chest. "Okay, what's the catch?"

He gave her a look that was far from innocent. It was downright sexy. "There is a catch. You just hafta be willin' to pay the price."

She swallowed. "The price?"

He smiled sheepishly. "There's always a price. You know it and I know it. I'll be more than happy to paint your house for you before Christmas, but on one condition."

The way he stared at her as if he were ready to sop her up with a biscuit, she was almost afraid to ask. "And what's that?"

He moved forward. "Three dates. I set the rules."

Berlin gave him a long puzzled look. "Three dates? Why?"

"Because I want you."

His price sent a flurry of goose bumps over her. She had to take a few deep breaths before she responded. "You can't make me sleep with you."

His eyes slid down to her breasts where she was certain he could see her nipples were hard and erect. "Believe me, boo. By the time I get done with you, you'll be begging me to make love to you."

She resented the sexual challenge. "I doubt that," she countered, although her voice lacked the conviction she had expected to hear.

"Fine. The choice is yours." He shrugged slightly. "But either you play by my rules or find yourself another painter."

Damn him. She clenched her jaw against the retort that sprang instantly to mind. The last thing she wanted was to be his sex slave, but it was either that or her father doing the job with his bad back. And that was not even an option. She hesitated, thinking about her father. But the only other choice she had was being at his mercy. There was no telling what he'd insist that she do. And despite her protest, the idea of making love to him made her clit tingle.

"I guess so," she finally said.

Reginald lifted a single black eyebrow, challenging her. "Don't do me any favors. It's either yes or no."

Oooh! She knew there was something about him she didn't like. If she didn't need him, she would have told him where to shove it. "Yes."

He took another step forward. "Yes, what?" he demanded in a low husky voice that sent a shiver over her skin.

She swallowed hard and moved back slightly away from where she was leaning against her desk. He was too close and too masculine for her own good. "Yes, I agree to all of your terms, Reginald."

"From this moment on I want you to call me Reggie," he replied as he eased himself closer to her.

She swallowed again. This was not going to be easy. Not easy at all. Before she could fathom his intentions, Reginald had backed her against the wall near the window and braced his arms on either side of her. He was so close, his breath brushed across her nose. Her heart leaped then dropped into her stomach and quivered there. She feared the intimacy circling the room. While watching him lick his luscious lips, she unconsciously tilted her chin with anticipation. Anticipating what? Another kiss?

Berlin quickly reminded herself of her ten-step plan. She couldn't afford to make a mistake. She couldn't possibly be stupid enough to fall for the same kind of man again. The kind who cut a woman's heart in two. Or could she?

Reginald trailed a path up her arm, toward the soft flesh of her neck. When his hand lightly touched her cheek, her eyelids fluttered. He then grazed along her delicate jaw, and traced the outline of her lips. "Say my name, Berlin," he whispered.

Her breath caught in her throat, cutting off any ability to form words.

"Say it, Berlin," he demanded, his voice controlled. She felt the warmth of his breath on her forehead.

"Reggie," she said, then bit her lip.

"Tell me who'll be making all of the rules." His hand dropped and caressed the side of her breast. Desire pushed to the surface, and even though she should have shoved his hand away, she could not.

He fixed her with a determined gaze. "I'm waiting, Berlin."

"You get to make all the rules," she managed to breathe out the words as she stared up at the wicked gleam in his eyes.

"Good, girl," he murmured, rubbing the rough pad of his thumb across her covered nipple in a slow motion that drove her mad. Even through the blouse, her breasts tingled and sent an ache down to her clit. She shifted slightly, trying to ease some of the pain.

"Why are you doing this?" she asked.

His mouth was a millimeter away from hers. "I already told you. Because I want you."

His words brought on shock and thrill. She couldn't think straight when he was standing this close, surrounding her with his heat and his touch. Reginald made her just want to close her eyes and go with the flow, allowing her body to control the moment. Staring up at him, she swallowed. The look in his eyes told her he wanted her as much as she wanted him. It also warned her, she was in for a ride.

And what a ride it will be.

There was nothing shy about him. Reginald was going to pursue her for his own pleasure, and she had better decide quickly if she could handle him or not. She knew in her heart she wouldn't be able to resist for long. Eventually, she would weaken. Deep down, she was curious at what he had to offer. So she'd have to make a decision. Soon. Now. Was she really willing to let him set all the rules? If she did, then she was going to have to be ready to play his game.

And what a game it would be.

His hand moved to her other breast where he kneaded and plucked her nipple until it puckered, sending a burst of pleasure through her body. "How do I know you're not going to change your mind?" he whispered.

"Because my word is all I got." Wetness slid down her inner thigh, and the ache became unbearable.

Bending his head, he kissed her.

The brush of his lips over hers was soft and gentler than she had thought him capable of. A sigh escaped her, then she raced to meet each skillful stroke of his tongue. The sensation of his mouth was powerful, and she felt powerless to fight. Heat raced up her. Fire ignited. Wrapping her arms around his neck, she pulled him closer against her body as he took complete possession of her mouth. Any thought of stopping what was happening was swept away by a tidal wave of desire. Instead she strained against him, wanting so much more. She whimpered his name as he nibbled at her lower lip, catching it gently between his teeth, and then thrusting his tongue into her mouth again. She could feel him hard against her stomach.

Reginald gave her buttocks a gentle squeeze, and for a second she thought he would swoop her up into his arms and carry her over and lay her across her desk. Instead, he gave her one final kiss, then released her. She opened her eyes.

Her shoulders sagged with relief when Reginald strolled over to the door. She thought he was leaving. Part of her was angry that he started something he had no intention of finishing, while the rest of her was pleased that he had walked away. However, instead of leaving, he reached up, turned the lock, then swung around and faced her again.

"Open your blouse."

Momentarily speechless, she watched Reginald's expression. The look in his eyes told her he was as serious as a heart attack. His commanding words changed the rhythm of her heart. It wasn't what he said but how he said it while staring over at her with deep penetrating eyes. It was a test. Reginald wanted to see if she would allow him to truly be in control.

Well, are you? If so, it's now or never, girlfriend.

Reaching up, she pushed one button through the hole followed by another. Berlin couldn't believe she was doing what he asked. Especially

69

at work, right inside her office. It was crazy, but something about his aggressive personality excited her. Made her want to live on the edge.

When her blue blouse finally hung open, Reginald held out a hand to her. "Come here."

Berlin swallowed hard, then moved toward him. As soon as she was close enough, he grabbed onto her waist and drew her closer. In one attempt, he unfastened the front clasp to her bra, freeing her breasts and watching with appreciation as they bounced freely. He then released her and reached up and stroked the side of her breasts, molding them gently in his hands. Heat generating from his fingertips traveled though her skin, overwhelming her with pleasure. A moan escaped her lips. Reginald brought her against him and pressed his lips to her throat and moved lower. Her breath caught when Reginald dipped his head to catch one of her rock-hard nipples between his teeth. He licked. Nibbled. Sucked. Her eyes drifted shut while she arched against him with soft whimpers. Pressed against him she felt his dick jerk.

Reginald teased each nipple with his tongue, moving from one to the next. Her breasts ached. Her nipples throbbed.

"You like that?" he whispered.

"Oh yes," she moaned as her sex clenched. It gave her a rush of pleasure that he could make her feel so good with minimal effort.

Reginald suckled a little longer, then released her. "Good. I just wanted to make sure you're going to be obedient."

Yes, master, was right on the tip of her tongue. She was willing to say or do whatever he had to do to get him to continue doing what he was doing. She gazed up at him and saw amusement burning in his eyes. She pursed her lips together. "What is this, some kind of game?"

"Not at all." His gaze slid down to her exposed chest, lingered for a long satisfying moment. "Now that we understand who's in charge, give me the directions to your house, and I'll drop by tonight and check out the work."

She panicked. "Tonight? Why tonight?"

"If you want me to start this weekend, then I need to drop by and see how much paint. We also need to discuss colors. I'll bring by some samples to choose from."

"Fine," she said as she reached up to button her blouse. Somehow, she would have to keep reminding herself why she had desperately agreed to this arrangement in the first place. She was suddenly anxious for him to leave her office. "I'll make sure to give you directions before we leave today."

He chuckled and headed toward the door. "I look forward to it."

Outside her door, Reginald leaned back against the wall with his legs crossed at the ankle. Berlin's eyes and expression called to mind the word stubborn, yet he had a feeling she was nowhere near as stuck-up as she pretended to be. Behind that hard exterior he believed was a woman who was fragile and compassionate. And he planned to find out.

As he returned to his work area, he decided his reasons for agreeing to help her weren't purely sexual. It was apparent she had asked for his help out of desperation. Considering that the holiday was two weeks away, it was obvious everyone else either turned her down or wanted way too much money. Reading between the lines, it was easy to conclude she had no other choice but to agree to his terms, which told him she was short on cash. Now he couldn't swear to the last, but what he had discovered that Berlin wasn't afraid to ask for help. She was so sexy that he made his decision to help her, but it would cost her. He hadn't lied when he said he wouldn't make her do anything she didn't want to do. But he was getting ready to turn up the heat. He intended to take advantage of those three dates and uncover the passionate woman underneath that still exterior. And that was where it would end.

He would sleep with her, and when the work was done, they would go their separate ways.

A Delight Before Christmas

Berlin rushed home and allowed herself ten minutes, start to finish, to change out of her work clothes and slip into a pair of sweatpants and an oversized T-shirt. She paused long enough to gaze into the mirror. With the new look, she hardly recognized herself. When Rolesta had first suggested the wild new look, she had cringed at the idea. But when she combed through the hundreds of curls using her fingers, she found she loved the new hairdo. Despite the hours it had taken to accomplish the look, she was already planning her next beauty appointment.

Taking one final glance, she went downstairs to straighten up before Reginald arrived. Her house was not a mess, but she wanted to impress him as well as show Reginald how different they really were. As she slipped her feet into a pair of fluffy pink house shoes, she moved downstairs to straighten up.

Berlin sprinkled carpet fresh over the plush blue carpet, and then moved to dust the dark oak furniture. He was arriving at seven, which barely gave her enough time to clean. She didn't know why she was going to so much trouble. He would be her first houseguest, and she wanted to impress. She tried to brush it off, thinking that he wouldn't show up at all. And even if he did, he probably wouldn't be able to get all the work she needed done in less than two weeks. Then there was always the possibility that after looking at all the work she needed, he might decide he would rather get paid, and then she probably couldn't afford him. Her biggest problem was her deadline. If he couldn't meet her deadline, then there was no reason for him to start. Although, she told herself, something was better than nothing at all. She was getting a headache from worrying about it. *Where there's a will, there's a way.* At this late stage in the game, the best thing for her to do was to let everything fall into place on its own.

As soon as the downstairs was spotless, she moved into her bathroom and washed the makeup from her face. She wanted to make sure Reginald saw her at her worst so that he wouldn't get any notions in his head of taking things from a business level, yet there was a fine line between worst and horrible, and in those beat up sweats and bleach stained T-shirt, she looked horrible. Moving into her room, she

72

changed into a pair of worn jeans and a clean pink T-shirt. She planned to keep things strictly business, not run the poor man away.

Berlin was afraid of her overreaction to being alone with a man she was sexually attracted to. She wished she could rationalize away her thoughts as easily. Maybe his intentions were legitimate—cost in exchanged for three dates. Maybe it really was no big deal. And maybe she was imagining that predatory interest in his eyes. Although after this afternoon in her office, she wasn't taking any chances.

She had just stepped into her bedroom when she heard the phone ring. She scowled and as much as she hated to admit it, she hoped it wasn't Reginald calling to tell her he wouldn't be able to make it. The thought of being his sex slave for three dates was bad enough, but the thought of her parents seeing her house less than perfect was even more than she could bear.

She quickly said a silent prayer, and reached for the receiver.

"Is Reggie there yet?"

Her shoulders sagged as she blew into the phone. If anyone was to call at the most inconvenient time, it would be her good friend and matchmaker. "No, Arianna, he isn't here yet."

"You did give him directions to your house?"

Berlin rolled her eyes. "Yes, I even drew him a map."

"Did you give him your number?"

She took a deep breath. Arianna wasn't going to let up. "Yes, I wrote it on the bottom of the map. Besides, I'm listed in the phone book." She hadn't bothered to tell her friend about Reginald's help the night before.

"Well something must have happened," Arianna said as if it was all her fault. "What time is he supposed to be there?"

Hearing a sound outside, Berlin moved toward the window. "Any minute—listen, I got to go. I think I hear his SUV pulling in the driveway right now."

"Wait a minute, don't hang up!" her friend cried.

"What?" she asked impatiently.

"If he tries to kiss you, you better go for it. I think—"

A Delight Before Christmas

Berlin didn't want to hear what Arianna had to say. The trouble with her friend—she was a hopeless romantic. She was in love and believed everyone else should be.

Fat chance.

Without giving it a second thought, Berlin slammed down the receiver. She would ask for her friend's forgiveness later.

Peering through the glass, she spotted an old pickup truck in her driveway, different from the one she'd seen him drive before. She wasn't sure it was even Reginald until she spotted him climbing out of the cab and moving toward the door.

Berlin drew in a deep breath and exhaled. Scraping up what little strength she had, she turned away from the window and walked downstairs. It was not the time to think about the way he made her feel. She could not think about what had happened in her office or that she had given him complete control over her body for three dates. She just had to find a way to concentrate, or else she would be in big trouble.

Her doorbell rang. After shutting the curtain, she glanced up at the clock and frowned. Just like a man to be late. As she moved toward the door, she glanced at herself in the mirror. Plain and boring. Good. She swung the door open, and finding him standing there, she almost fainted.

Rocawear jeans and Timberland boots on his feet. *Oh my goodness.* She was definitely in trouble.

"Hey, whassup?"

His spicy scent filled her empty lungs and a thrill of awareness sent goose bumps prickling her skin. Unable to speak, she simply smiled and moved aside so he could enter.

Reginald couldn't stop looking at her. Her full lush lips were pursed perfectly. Her reddish curls framed her face and shoulders. Looking down at her shirt, he could see her nipples and couldn't help wondering if she was wearing a bra. He remembered how her nipples had tasted. How soft her chin had felt beneath his fingers. He wanted her…wanted her naked beneath him.

She shut the door, breaking into his daydream.

"Let me show you around."

Berlin gave him a tour, and he watched the swing of her hips as she led him through the house. He had to force his eyes away to pay attention. But his body wasn't listening to his brain. He didn't know why he was getting himself all worked up; yet he was. For a stuck-up woman she was quite fine.

"What are you looking at?"

He stood over six feet, yet she still seemed to have a way to look down her nose at him.

"I don't think you want me to answer that question."

She stared at him and must have realized he was probably right. She swung on her heels and moved through a fairly large kitchen.

Reginald followed her into a sunken great room and studied the area. From any vantage point in the room, there was a spectacular view to the wooded backyard and soaring cathedral ceiling. Unlike the front of the house, the walls were either covered in outdated paisley wallpaper or had already been scraped and were ready to be primed and painted.

"I'd like to have the rest of this wallpaper removed, then painted to match my furniture. I hope it won't be too hard."

He thought about what she had suggested, then as a visual came to life. He nodded his head in agreement. He knew of the perfect color to bring out the gold couch and rustic chair.

They stepped back into the two-story foyer where an elegant chandelier hung decoratively over an oak hardwood floor. Off the foyer was an oversized formal dining room with crown molding and plenty of natural light. The room had been painted in a baby blue. There was a large dark wood table for eight with a matching china cabinet and buffet table.

"Let me show you the rest." She waved a hand toward upstairs.

Reginald followed her up a turned oak staircase. She moved past the first room, which he assumed was the master suite. At the end of the hall were two roomy bedrooms boasting large closets and windows, separated by an adjoining bathroom. Each room was simply furnished with a bed and matching dresser and nightstand with a thirty-six inch television on a corner shelf. He sized up the rooms and made a mental list of what needed to be done with an eye trained by over ten years in the contracting business. The paint was peeling and the wallpaper faded and worn.

"You said the house was this way when you bought it? You get a good deal on this house?"

"Government foreclosure. Back taxes." She quoted a price way below market price that made him whistle.

"The woman who owned it had been in a nursing home for several years, and none of her children wanted to live here."

"How long have you lived here?" he asked, looking around, touching the walls. There was still paste.

"Almost a year now."

After one final sweep of the room, he turned to her and nodded impressively. "You've got a nice crib. Just a little work, and you'll have quite an investment."

She gave him a soft smile. "That's what I'm hoping."

He stepped aside to allow her some room. When she tried to move past, she brushed one hip against his thigh. A flash of heat passed between them. Without another word, she turned and headed back downstairs.

When she reached the foyer, she allowed her arms to fall to her side. "Well that's everything. You think you can have everything ready by Christmas Eve?"

"No problem," he replied confidently.

He then moved into the living room and reached into the bag on his shoulder and pulled out a portfolio full of paint samples, then took a seat on the couch.

"Why don't we move to the table?" she suggested.

He fixed her with a puzzled look. "Why?"

"Because this room is for guests only."

Reginald shook his head at the ridiculous idea. "I never understood why people spend thousands of dollars on furniture they never use."

She gave him a stubborn look. "That's how it lasts."

He chuckled. "Yo, I promise not to mess up your furniture. Now sit."

Reluctantly, she moved and sat beside him, and together they looked at the samples he had. She realized their shoulders were touching; she was leaning against him.

"Who decorated this room?"

"I did with the help of a painter I hired last summer," she answered defensively, then wiggled her butt away from his.

He leaned back against the cushions. "You did a good job."

Obviously stunned by his compliment, she lowered her gaze to the floor.

"So let's have it," he asked briskly. "Why'd you ask me for help, especially since it's obvious you don't like me?"

"I…" Her lids were lowered. She ran her manicured nails across her thigh, and lifted her face to him. "Because I didn't know who else to ask."

"At least you're honest," he replied, eyes dancing with laughter.

There was a long pause before she spoke again. "I don't dislike you."

"No?" he said playfully.

Her golden eyes caught fire, and then slid downward, shielding her expression. "I don't want to mislead you, so don't take this the wrong way."

He reached out and captured her chin and lifted it. "And what is that?"

He could tell she took the time to choose her words carefully before her eyes slowly rose to meet his. "I need your help around the house, not in my bed."

Reginald nodded and simply said, "Uh huh, I'm listening."

Her golden eyes studied him coolly. "I'm serious. This is business. And if I have to write you a check to remind you of that, I will."

Reaching out, he caressed her cheek. Beneath his palm, her skin was smooth. He felt the heat beneath the surface. Silence surrounded them, and he knew she was waiting for his response. He had a different agenda. Without realizing it, his thumb moved to stroke her neck, then drifted down to the limited amount of cleavage spilling out from her shirt.

"You don't have to pay as long as you stand by our agreement. I want three dates. I get to decide when, where and how."

"How?" she asked huskily as his fingers glided across the tops of her breasts.

"How we spend the evening."

She pushed his hand away as if she disliked him touching her, and leaned back on the couch. Seeing the look of discomfort on her face, for a second he thought maybe he might have gone too far and decided it was time to quit while he was ahead. "So what do you have in mind for your bedrooms?" he asked, changing the subject.

Her smile returned as if the intimate moment had never happened just seconds ago. "Peaches and cream."

"Okay."

She leaned across the couch for his samples and flipped to the orange family. "Here, let me show you what I'm talking about."

His breath caught as her soft breast lightly brushed across his arm. He held it savoring the sweet shudder that slid down the length of his spine. There was plenty of room. It was only his imagination that made it feel the walls were shrinking, pushing them closer together. He didn't dare move as she showed him the exact shades she wanted to dominate the guest rooms, her office, and the master bedroom, which he had yet to see. When he suggested a more subtle effect, she countered with a shade that was a little more daring, just like the way he was feeling right now. Not daring enough unfortunately. Otherwise, he would swing her onto his lap and slip a hand beneath her T-shirt. Instead, he sat still, her breast continuing to brush his arm while his body ached for a repeat of the incident earlier in her office.

Berlin finally said, "I can't look at anymore," then slid over slightly. "The colors are all starting to look the same."

"I understand." He closed the notebook and rose from the couch while he still had the strength to do so. "I'll swing by the paint store in the morning and will be by shortly after."

Suddenly, she chuckled softly. "I'm sorry, it's so rude of me. Regin...I mean, Reggie, would you like something to eat?"

Reginald grinned. "No, but thanks. I had a burger and fries on the way over here."

Berlin nodded and folded her arms across her breasts.

"But I wouldn't mind something to drink."

She returned his smile with one of her own. "Okay. I've got tea, soda or wine."

"A soda would be great."

Turning on her heels, she moved down the hall and disappeared inside the kitchen.

Berlin reached inside the refrigerator and retrieved two orange sodas. For the life of her, she didn't know why she had offered him something to drink when he was seconds away from walking out the door. For some reason she wasn't ready for the evening to end. Somehow, some way, she would have to find a way to get her hormones under control. She felt exposed. Not bothering to put on a bra, she knew her nipples were hard and erect and the evidence visual through the thin, pink cotton material. Hopefully, Reginald hadn't noticed.

"You have a nice fireplace," she heard him say. The only one she had was in the family room. Following the direction of his voice, she moved into the room and found Reginald standing in front of her fireplace.

Goodness, he looked handsome with the lights bouncing off his reflection. It should be a crime for a man to look that good in clothes, she thought as she watched him lean against the marble mantel. The shirt strained against his firm back muscles.

Her nipples tingled as she pictured rubbing her breasts against his solid back. Good God, he was handsome; tall and broad shoulders. His face rugged and inviting. She was tempted to walk over and remove his clothes. He turned around and she shivered.

"Is something wrong?"

Berlin snapped her gaze upward to his face. Wrong? Hell yeah, something was definitely wrong. She wanted those muscular arms holding her. His skillful hands touching her in every aching place. "No, nothing's wrong. Just a little cold."

"I started a fire."

Yes you have, and it's racing through my body.

Walking over, he took one of the sodas from her hand and popped the tab.

Berlin moved and took a seat on the floor in front of the fire.

"You ever ride on a motorcycle?" he asked as he took a seat beside her.

"You have a motorcycle?"

Reginald nodded, then moved to sit on the floor beside her. "Yep. I take it out from time to time. Riding motorcycles has always been a means of escape for me. I can hop on one and drive for hours with the wind blowing on my face. I get this rush that feels almost as satisfying as sex."

She snorted rudely. "Then I must be missing something, because sex has never been quite that good. I guess I need to buy myself a bike."

"Dang, girl," he paused to chuckle. "Sounds like you've been with the wrong brotha."

"Maybe so." Which was why she was marrying for social status and financial security. Sex and love where overrated. "But sex has never been a big deal to me. I can do with or without it."

"Are you kidding?" When she shook her head, he continued. "That's because you haven't met the right one."

She popped the tab on her soda and frowned. "Nah. I don't think that's it. Sex just isn't that important to me."

"What could possibly be more important than sex?"

She glanced over at him. "Shoes."

He tossed his head back with laughter. She smiled as she took a sip. Maybe he knew something she didn't.

Reginald reached out to stroke a finger down the side of her check. "I bet I could change your mind."

"I doubt that," she said, although something told her he could.

"Wanna bet?"

His hand cupped her chin, tilting her face toward his in a way that sent her pulse in overdrive. His challenge caused her blood to race through her veins.

"I don't think that would be a good idea," she stuttered nervously. "We're getting along quite well, why complicate things?"

"Who said anything about complications?" His thumb moved slowly along her bottom lip. "It's only if we allow things to be. I'm not looking for a commitment, and I assume neither are you. So what's wrong with two people who are attracted to one another spending time together?" He released her and took another sip. "I promise you won't be disappointed." Reginald leaned back, resting his weight against his arms and sipped from his can, giving her a few seconds to think about what he had just said.

Man is it tempting.

Damn, she believed if there was any man capable of changing her mind, that person was Reginald Hodges. The thought of him making love to her in front of the fireplace had her body hammering. But common sense kicked in. "Over the years, I've met people I've liked or disliked. I like you. If we sleep together, that might change."

Reginald stared into the fireplace for so long she thought maybe he was lost in his own thoughts and hadn't heard him. But as she got ready to speak, he turned to look at her. The heated impact of his gaze was unnerving. "I guarantee if I make love to you, you'll never look at sex the same again. If you choose to dislike me after that, then that's your choice." He paused to lick his lips. "However, I doubt you will."

She was intrigued beyond words. Her whole being sparked with anticipation, longing for more hot kisses, dying to feel his hands on certain parts of her body. She didn't think she wanted anything as much as she wanted Reginald to make love to her.

But she also had an agenda that was far more important.

"I don't think so," she said regrettably.

He finished the last of his soda, then moved into the kitchen and tossed the can in the trash. With a sigh, she followed and lowered her can on the counter. She was relieved when Reginald headed toward the door. He stopped suddenly and startled her when he swung around and met her gaze.

"What do you have planned tomorrow night?" he inquired and took a couple of steps forward.

"What's tomorrow? Saturday?" She frowned thoughtfully while pretending to give it some serious thought. The last thing in the world she wanted him to know was that she didn't have plans on a Saturday night. "Uh…nothing, I was planning to spend the evening catching up on my reading." She arched an eyebrow. "Why?"

"I want date number one," he said without taking his eyes off her.

Berlin swallowed. She hadn't expected the dating to start so soon. "I…okay." There was no time like the present. The sooner they got the dates out of the way, the sooner she could get on with her life. She forced her lips to curl upward in agreement. "Yes, that would be fine."

His gaze ran provocatively down her full-length before coming back to meet hers. "You know you're beautiful when you smile. I wish I had a camera to capture this rare occasion."

She hadn't heard a word he said. As she looked at him, she couldn't help thinking about that evening in the coat closet. Goodness, this was not the time.

He took another step closer, and she felt his breath on her nose. "You need to smile more often."

Her breath caught. The room snapped, crackled and popped with sexual tension. If he reached out and tried to kiss her, she wouldn't be able to stop him. The shocking part was that she wouldn't want to. While he stood there and watched her, her knees wobbled.

Reginald gazed at her for a long strained moment before he blew out a breath and replied, "I'll see you in the morning." He turned and had barely taken two steps when he swung around and gave her a serious look.

Berlin inhaled deeply. "Did you forget something?"

One corner of his lips turned upward. "Yeah, I have."

Caught by her shoulders, Reginald pressed her back against the door, his knee sliding between her legs. She turned her head and found his mouth, her tongue unconsciously seeking his. With skillful strokes, he caused a series of shudders to ripple through her.

His hands moved to her waist. Moaning, mindlessly, she let her head drop limply back. She wasn't quite sure what she was doing, and, for now, she didn't really care one way or another. It felt so damn good that she didn't even notice his hand slipping beneath her T-shirt. When he reached the mounds of her breasts, a hungry groan slipped from her. She arched closer to his hand, pushing her breasts forward. His lips then left her mouth and traveled down to the area now exposed. Wheezing, Berlin pressed her back against the cool metal door, arching her breasts out as he teased her nipple.

"They're beautiful and taste delicious. I've been thinking about them all evening."

This is insane, she thought, yet she did nothing to stop it. Her body wouldn't allow her to. Reginald wasn't what she wanted or needed in her life. The timing was all wrong. Yet right now she wanted and needed him with a violence that would have scared her if she had foreseen it coming.

And then he stopped.

She was left blinking in amazement, her chest heaving as she watched Reginald move toward the door.

"Like I said before. I'll never force you to do something you're not ready to do." He winked. "When you're ready, just let me know. See you tomorrow."

Gasping, she stood for the longest time in the doorway. Her chest heaved with each deep breath as she watched him drive away.

Goodness gracious, she had never been kissed like that before. Even the kiss at the Christmas party was tame in comparison. She wiggled her toes to uncurl them. How in the world would she be able to work with him? Every time she looked down at his lips, she knew it would become close to impossible.

Somehow, she would have to find a way.

As soon as he climbed into the truck, Reginald breathed deeply, shaken by an awakening desire too harsh to ignore. He was stunned by the strong need to make love to Berlin. If he had stayed in her presence a minute longer, he would have done something stupid like begged to share her bed tonight. It was one thing to lust after her, but what he felt ran deeper, and he didn't like it.

He could almost taste her smooth honey skin beneath his tongue. Her curvaceous body was any man's dream. But he didn't want her with any man. He wanted to be the only man touching her.

He recognized her need; it surrounded her, radiated from her eyes. The man in him recognized her resistance. She didn't want to get involved. He understood. He felt the same way. Where would getting involved get them? Nowhere. But, the attraction was too strong to ignore. He realized that the night of the Christmas party. He realized it again last night while fixing her tire. Even with Dashaun in the garage, he hadn't been able to miss the heat, the desire. Typically, he kept his business and personal life separate, but with her he was willing to make an exception. He wanted her every night in his bed.

What if she already has a lover?

Unknown jealousy brewed in his head and taunted him as he headed toward home. He hadn't felt this strongly about a woman in years, and that bothered him. Of all the women in the world, why did he have to fall for Berlin?

Chapter Six

Berlin woke up the next morning tangled in her sheets. Shifting on the bed, she glanced out the window and watched fresh balls of snow fall from the sky. The weather was definitely getting persistent. The chance of having a white Christmas this year was more than likely. She smiled, finally warming up to the idea of her and her parents gathered around her tree opening presents. She would have to make a trip up into the attic to retrieve a six-foot artificial she had bought last year, after the holidays, during a fifty percent off sale. She would do whatever it took to make this a holiday to remember. As long as the rooms were painted, everything else would fall into place.

After propping another pillow behind her head, she allowed her mind to wander to forbidden territory, Reginald. Thinking about him was inevitable, especially the next several days while he prepared her house for her parents.

Last night, after he had left her house, she had been too tired to do anything but shower, slip on a flannel gown and climb under the covers.

She closed her eyes, and memories of his hands on her breasts, between her legs, replayed in her mind, the heat of his touch anchored her.

Reginald was handsome, good with his hands and one hell of a kisser. Heat flowed freely through her chest as she remembered how good he had made her feel. Of course, she tried to convince herself she hadn't kissed many men in her lifetime, so who was she to gauge how good a kisser he really was. He was better than anyone she had experienced before. She shivered at the memories of how good his arms had felt around her, how good his lips had felt against her. And goodness, her lips were still tingling, not to mention her nipples where he had suckled just long enough to make her body yearn for more. Man, she had gone to bed last night wishing he had carried her off to bed and spent the night making love to her. Instead, she had to settle for her vibrator. After slipping on a condom, she had plunged the plastic device in and moved it in and out. She had imagined it was Reginald's long, fat dick bringing her pleasure. It wasn't long before she reached an orgasm, and her legs collapsed. Just thinking about him caused warmth to flood the area between her legs.

Remember the ten-step plan.

Berlin squeezed her thighs tightly together. The last thing she needed was to be fantasizing about him. They had a business arrangement, nothing more. She couldn't afford to jeopardize everything she had been working on by getting involved with him. During the next several days, it would take everything she had to fight him. She would have to find a way to constantly remind herself that he was just a man, and she had made a vow to herself to never lose her head to another man again. She had an agenda to marry a doctor who she wasn't in jeopardy of losing her heart to, and doggone it, that was exactly what she was going to do.

Groaning, she rolled over and glanced at the clock. It was barely eight o'clock. She could afford to lie in the bed just a little longer this morning. It was warm and felt so good in the bed she didn't even want to get up.

She closed her eyes as forbidden thoughts of Reginald returned. A smile curled her lips, and she squeezed her pillow close to her aching breasts and was prepared to go back to sleep when she heard a truck pull into her driveway. She dashed out of the bed and glanced out the window. Reginald was already here. Good lord, didn't he believe in sleeping late on Saturdays.

Quickly, she moved into the bathroom and splashed water over her face and gargled. She removed the scarf from her head and fingered her curls with womanly vengeance, then reached for her pink terrycloth robe on a chair in the corner of her room. She slipped it on, and then hurried downstairs just as the doorbell chimed.

"I'm coming. I'm coming," she muttered impatiently before swinging the door open.

Reginald smiled down at her. "Whassup, sleepy head?"

"What are you doing here so early?" she didn't mean to snap, but she was pissed that he managed to see her at her worst, while he managed to look as sexy as ever in paint splattered jeans and a T-shirt.

He stepped inside, carrying a large can of primer. "I figured the sooner I get started, the earlier we can hit the town," he said as he wiped his boots on the mat in front of the door.

Berlin had almost forgotten they were going out tonight. "Where are we going?"

"It's a surprise. Just be ready by seven."

"But what if I had plans this evening?"

"Cancel them." He moved toward the stairs.

"I told you before I'm not letting you tell me what to do."

"We have a deal, remember?" At her silence, he winked and continued. "Now go get dress so we can get started."

It took a few seconds for his words to register. "You didn't say anything about me helping."

"Why not? It's your house. This way you can make sure things get done the way you want them."

She couldn't argue. He did have a point. Although the reason why she had hired him was so she would haven't to do it herself. "How about I make a pot of coffee and some breakfast, and then we can talk about it?"

Reginald chuckled. "You're on."

As he walked upstairs, Berlin found herself thinking she liked it when he laughed. It was nice, deep and robust. His eyes sparkled and his teeth flashed. *Snap out of it!*

Shaking her head, she moved toward the kitchen and started a pot of coffee. She turned on the coffeemaker, and then dashed up to her room to change into something more appropriate.

Reginald carried the rest of his equipment inside the house and tried to take his mind off seeing Berlin. Dressed in a robe, she looked sexy with curls tousled all over her head. Soft, sexy and a little wild. For just a brief moment he saw her beneath him, her moans of pleasure, her long legs wrapped around his waist.

He sighed as he removed his coat and tossed it in the corner, then moved to his supplies and removed a scraper from the box. He was seriously overqualified for this job, he thought as he began removing old wallpaper from the wall. But she would never know that, at least not until it was time for her to know.

"Breakfast is ready."

Reginald glanced down at his watch. He had been so absorbed in his work as well as his thoughts that it had been well over a half hour since she suggested making coffee. He looked at her thoughtfully as she shifted in the doorway. She had changed into blue jeans and a yellow cotton blouse that hugged his two new friends perfectly.

"I hope you like pancakes," she taunted.

Common sense told him to decline her offer. After all, he'd had toast and sausage before arriving. But the idea of sitting down at a table eating breakfast with her was too good an opportunity to pass up. He glanced down at the can of primer, then back at her again. "Pancakes, huh?"

She smiled. "Yep, with sugar cured bacon, scrambled eggs with cheese and grits."

"Dang, girl. You doing it like that?"

Berlin shrugged. "Mama always said to start your day off with a hearty meal."

He nodded and lowered the scraper. His impression of her was changing by the minute. He followed her down to the kitchen, admiring the sway of her hips and scolded himself for having such a weak resistance to her.

He stepped inside the kitchen where the aroma of fresh brewed coffee wafted by his nose. The food was already on the table. He paused. The scene reminded him of many Saturday mornings at his grandmother's house. Eleanora always made it her business to have a large breakfast on the table by the time her grandchildren rolled out of the bed.

Berlin was looking at him strangely. "Is something wrong?"

He gave her a warm smile. "No. Everything is right." *That's the problem.* He turned and met her gaze. She was looking at him with vulnerability shimmering in her eyes. "Nothing's wrong. Everything smells great."

Her shoulders softened. "Good then what are you waiting on? Let's eat."

He smiled down at her. "I can't wait. Let me go wash my hands."

"You know what?" Reginald asked quite awhile later.

"What?"

"You've got skills," he replied as he popped the last piece of bacon into his mouth. "Who taught you how to burn like this?"

She beamed with pride at the compliment. "Grandmother, that's what everyone called her. I spent a lot of weekends in her kitchen watching her whip up pancakes from scratch, bacon, fluffy eggs with cheese. She had everything timed so well that it all came off the stove at the same time, piping hot. My sister and I used to rush to the table."

"I don't blame you. I would have knocked someone over for that food."

She laughed, and then her gaze shifted to his mouth as she watched him lick away a drop of syrup. It took everything she had not to lean across the table and press her mouth against his. Instead, she reached for her glass, and drank the last of her orange juice knowing it was time for the meal to end. She was feeling more than she cared to be feeling. Sitting at the table felt too comfortable for words. It was almost as if they were a couple sharing breakfast after a night of making love. The notion sparked a throb of warmth in Berlin. It was shocking, appalling. She ought to be repulsed yet a thrill enveloped her body. She quickly subdued the feeling by thinking about every reason why he was wrong for her. Reginald was cocky. Arrogant. And most important, a blue collar worker. He probably hadn't gone to college. He was not what she wanted or needed in her life and the sooner she remembered that the better. The only problem was that the more she got to know Reginald, the more she liked him. He wasn't any of those things and she knew it.

Berlin stood. "I guess I better let you get back to your work while I clean up the kitchen."

Reginald wiped his mouth then rose as well. "I appreciate it. You need some help? I can't cook a lick, but I can bust some suds."

Her eyes crinkled with laughter. "No, I got it." The sooner she got away from him the better.

He nodded. "All right. Ima go and get to work."

Berlin watched him leave the room, loving the way he looked in loose-fitting jeans. When she heard his foot hit the top step, she turned and moved to the sink then sighed. Her mind was working in overdrive. She thought as she began loading the dishwasher. Reginald's presence had her thinking about things she'd rather not be thinking. But he was handsome and so appealing what woman wouldn't be attracted?

You're not other women.

This woman had an agenda she'd better stick to; otherwise, her carefully planned future would be destroyed.

She loaded the last glass, then reached for the box of soap and filled the dispenser. *Why can't I stop thinking about our kiss?* She locked and started the dishwasher.

During breakfast all she did was watch his lips as he spoke and couldn't help remembering the way they felt against hers. She didn't want to notice. She didn't want to be attracted, but it seemed her efforts were useless. Now he expected her to work side by side with him for the rest of the afternoon and feel absolutely nothing. *Yeah, right.* The very thought of going upstairs was giving her a heated rush.

While reaching for the dishrag, she tried to shake off the feeling and immediately came to the conclusion that she was simply horny. Reginald aroused her in the worst way and it was only natural that her body reacted.

Frustrated, she flopped down in the chair and rested her elbows on the table. She cursed herself for having offered to make breakfast. The last thing she wanted was for him to start thinking she was interested in him. He was used to women falling all over him, and she had no intention of being one of them.

She wanted so badly to convince herself it was just her hormones working overtime, but now she wasn't so sure. Her brow bunched. What was it about Reginald that made her want to forget about her ten-step plan? The fact that he was a blue-collar worker should have been enough reason for her to stay clear of him. Despite her agenda, one look at Reginald and she forgot everything, but what she felt when he was around.

"Good grief!" she mumbled in annoyance. "You've got better things to do with your life than to fantasize over him." Starting now. Instead of helping Reginald paint; she would spend the rest of the morning hiding in her room.

Reginald fixed his gaze on the door across the hall. He was tempted to walk over to her room and find out what was keeping her, but he talked himself out of it. If she didn't want to paint, that was fine with him. Keeping distance between them was probably a good thing. Last night he had gotten next to no sleep. Memories of full, lush breasts had kept him aroused and wide-awake.

He removed the last of the wallpaper and focused on scraping the remnants from the wall. In another hour, he'd be ready to apply a coat of primer.

Hearing footsteps, he moved and stuck his head out the door just as she stepped away from her room.

"Did you forget you're supposed to be helping me?"

She froze, and then turned around. "I am?" she asked with a look of surprise.

He knew she was faking ignorance. "Yes, remember I said we're going to do this together?" He studied her features closely. "You feeling okay?"

She gave a nervous laugh. "No, I'm fine. I was on the phone with my mother discussing Christmas and once she starts talking, it is hard to get her off the phone."

"Sound like my mom."

She nodded, then tried to escape down the hallway toward the stairs.

"Berlin?"

Holding the banister, she spun on her heels.

"You haven't forgotten about dinner tonight?"

"Nope."

"You better not," he said, then turned and went back to work.

I can do this.

Berlin repeated her silent mantra as she put the finishing touches on her makeup.

She could do this. She could work with Reginald regardless of how attracted she was to him and keep everything strictly professional between them. She could get through the three dates without sleeping with him. She was no longer a teenager controlled by hormones.

The doorbell rang, and she took one final look in the mirror.

"I can do this," she chanted again as she moved down the steps and swung open the door.

There Reginald stood in a black Dickies outfit. Charcoal gray turtleneck. Black Timberland boots and a black leather jacket. He looked sexy as hell. Despite her resolve, she experienced another rush of involuntary heat. It made her skin tingle and her cheeks flush.

I can do this.

She wasn't a teenager by a long shot. She felt grownup feelings and hormones that were screaming at her to grab that man around his neck and beg him to skip dinner and carry her up to her room instead.

Snap out of it!

She'd always been goal-driven. Competitive. She would just look at their time together as a big challenge. Lust vs. common sense.

"Did you hear what I said?"

Berlin shook her head, clearing her thoughts and focused on Reginald's puzzled face. "I'm sorry, what did you say?"

"I said, damn, you look good."

She didn't realize how much his compliment meant to her until his words warmed her to her toes, heating a couple of other things along the way.

"Thank you. You don't look half bad yourself."

His eyes sparkled with excitement. "Ready to have some fun?"

Ready as I'll ever be. Berlin slipped into a long winter white coat and reached for her gold purse. "I'm all set."

"Good. I'm getting ready to show you how to really have a good time."

"Where are we going?"

A grin tugged at his mouth. "Somewhere you've never been before."

When Reginald came to a complete stop in front of *Lula's Southern Fried Kitchen*, he had to do everything in his power not to laugh at the look on Berlin's face. He wished he had a camera. Her mouth dropped. Her eyes were wide and round.

"Ready?"

Slowly, she turned to look at him. "We're eating here?"

"Yep. Is there a problem?" He had a strong suspicion she was expecting dinner at some five star restaurant.

She quickly shook her head and mumbled, "No, there's no problem."

He slipped out the SUV and went around to her side and helped her out. "You won't be disappointed. The food here is off the hook."

Nodding, she released her seatbelt and took his hand as he helped her off the seat. God, she was beautiful. He just stared. He couldn't look away. Not with that soft smile on her lips. The way her eyes sparkled beneath the moonlight, she looked good enough to be on the cover of any magazine. Although he'd rather see the red of her beautiful auburn-colored hair spread out on his pillow.

Berlin's face was unreadable. He knew Lula's was totally out of her element, and that's why he took her. He had purposely gone out of his way to test the waters tonight.

He strolled inside, welcoming the familiar setting. Large exotic plants. Tables covered with fine linen. Dim intimate lighting was supported by lanterns at the center of each table.

He helped her out of her coat, admiring her shapely body in the chocolate-brown suede skirt and matching jacket before she lowered into a seat. He moved to the seat across from her.

"It sure smells good in here. What do you recommend?" she asked as she reached for a plastic menu. He was amazed to see a hint of interest softened her expression.

"Everything," he declared. "Fried chicken is finger lickin' good." He glanced at her studying the menu intently. He figured she was looking for the prime rib or lobster, and hid a silly grin behind his menu.

When their waitress came to their table, Berlin lowered her menu to the table.

"Good evening, y'all ready to order?"

Berlin glanced up and smiled. "Yes, ma'am. I'm gonna have fried chicken, macaroni and cheese, greens with hamhocks and banana pudding for dessert."

Startled, Reginald dropped the menu to the table. "You're kiddin, right?"

She gave him a silly grin. "Why would I do that?" She turned to her waitress again. "I'll also have an ice tea, sweetened."

Nodding, she scribbled down her order, then looked over at Reginald. "And what about you?"

Still looking at Berlin with surprise, he finally shook his head and gazed up at the waitress. "I'll have ribs, macaroni and cheese and collard greens. I'll also have tea and a slice of sweet potato pie."

"Ooh! Change my dessert to sweet potato pie, too."

Their waitress nodded, then left to get their drinks.

Reginald stared across the table.

"What?"

Grinning, he shook his head. "Nothing."

She leaned across the table and whispered, "You act like I've never been to a place like this before?"

"Well have you?"

Berlin lifted a brow as if the answer should have been obvious to him. "I'll have you know my grandmother is from Mississippi. I grew up watching her cook everything with pork," she paused long enough to release a tinkle of laughter. "My parents used to send us to our grandparents for the summer. Grandmother believed in you earning your meal. So I used to spend a lot of time in the kitchen. I told you I could throw down."

He nodded his head, clearly impressed and took a few seconds to stare at her. Seeing some friends of his across the room, he waved then focused on Berlin again. She was definitely worth getting to know.

The waitress placed their drinks on the table, then moved to help another couple.

Soft holiday music filled the air from an old jukebox in the corner. It took him a few minutes to identify Nat King Cole's voice as he sang "The Christmas Song."

"So is this a regular spot for you?" she asked as she raised the glass to her lips.

Reginald nodded and reached for his own tea and took a sip. "I grew up three blocks from here."

"Really? Is your family still there?"

He lowered his glass and shook his head. "My mom moved to Memphis to be near her sister. My sister and younger brotha live around here. Yvonne's a child support enforcement officer and Jay, well, Jay is Jay. You never know what he's doing from one day to the next."

"Sounds like my cousin. Kwane is a sophomore at Morehouse, and he changes his major every semester. He drives my aunt crazy." She giggled.

"Do you have any sisters or brothers?"

Her expression stilled. "I have an older sister."

Reginald noticed the prim line of her lips conveyed displeasure.

"Eileen has always been the princess. Cheerleader. Popular. Pretty. Never been much of a student, however, she met and started dating a college student her senior year. Now Darryl's a big-time criminal defense attorney in Los Angeles. The reason my parents are coming down for Christmas is because 'lifestyles of the rich and famous' decided to go to Paris instead."

His brow arched. "You sound envious."

Berlin released a heavy sigh. "Yeah, I guess I am. I worked my butt off to have a better life, and my sister married the rich guy and got her future on a silver platter."

Things were starting to become clearer. She wasn't some rich girl. She was a girl who grew up poor, striving for something better. Isn't that what he had done?

"So because your sister married a lawyer, any rich man will do?"

She tilted her chin defiantly. "You don't have to put it like that."

Reginald shrugged. "If the shoe fits…" He purposely let his voice trail off, reached for his drink and took a sip. "So, in other words, a hard-working brotha like me doesn't have a chance?"

She took a while to answer. "Nothing personal. It just would never work. After the sexual attraction wore off, what would we have left?"

Love. He scowled and wondered where that thought came from. That is if he was stupid enough to allow such a thing to happen again.

"Money doesn't buy happiness," he reminded.

"But it's better than being broke. I grew up watching my parents argue over bills and money. When my dad hurt his back and was unable to work, my family had to go on food stamps. That was the most humiliating time in my life."

Food stamps had been a part of his lifestyle until he was fifteen. He and his family would have starved without them. "But your parents are still together. That must count for something."

"Don't get me wrong, my parents have been married thirty-five years, but for me love isn't going to be enough."

"And my boy Cameron is your knight in shining armor." Reginald tossed his drink down and laughed. When she flinched, he realized he must have hit a nerve. He didn't mean to, but he found her idea of living happily ever after, funny.

96

Cameron wasn't the slightest bit interested in settling down with anybody. He was having way too much fun. She'd be better off with him. That is if he were interested in a commitment, which he was not.

It was different for him. He'd spent the last several years protecting his heart from women who had ulterior motives. He hadn't even been conscious of his behavior until an airline stewardess he'd once dated got tired of his "take it or leave it" attitude and no desire to commit.

"Where's your father?" he heard her ask.

Reginald stroked his chin. "Dead."

Her eyes grew big and round with alarm. "Oh, I'm so sorry for asking."

"Nah, my pops bounced when I was barely two years old."

"How sad." Her expression softened. The last thing he needed was sympathy for growing up in a broken home.

"He left my mom with three kids and never bothered once to send her a dime to help support us." He took a sip of his tea. Henry Hodges and the way he had treated them was something he rarely talked about to anyone. "My mom busted her butt working two jobs to support us and never once complained."

She looked at him, steadily meeting his gaze. "She sounds like a wonderful woman."

He smiled. "Yes, she is."

Their waitress arrived with their food. And Reginald was glad for the interruption. The last thing he wanted was to ruin the evening discussing his deadbeat dad. She put their plates in front of them, and asked if they needed anything else before departing.

"Wow! Everything looks fabulous," Berlin replied.

"They have the best food in town." He watched with intrigue as she reached for the hot sauce and sprinkled it generously over everything but her dessert. She was obviously no stranger to soul food.

Berlin caught him staring. "What?"

He scratched his bearded chin and didn't try to hide the smirk from his lips. "I see you like hot sauce."

"Oooh yes! Soul food ain't the same without it."

"Ain't?" He chuckled. Tonight was turning out to be one intriguing evening.

She brought a forkful of greens to her mouth. "I use bad English every now and then, when the sentence requires it."

His brow rose with amusement. "Oh, yeah?"

"Yeah," she challenged, eyes dancing with excitement.

Reginald relaxed against the chair and watched her dig into her macaroni and cheese. "Berlin Dupree you are really something else."

"Thank you...I think."

He reached for a rib, and the two ate in silence while listening to Destiny's Child's "Eight Days of Christmas." Glancing to his right he spotted someone he knew from high school. He waved and returned his attention to his plate. He'd recognized quite a few people at Lula's. He wasn't the only one who returned to the old neighborhood for a good meal.

"Do you have any children?"

He almost choked on his food. "Where in the world did that question come from?"

Berlin reached for her glass and shrugged. "Just curious."

Immediately, Reginald shook his head. "No way."

She paused as if surprised by his answer. "You say that like you don't like children."

"I love children, but I don't want to have any unless I am settled down and married. I want my kids to grow up with two parents," Reggie replied as he finished the last of his macaroni and cheese. His gaze collided with hers, establishing an understanding that surpassed logical explanation. Years ago he had made a vow. No children until he was ready to start a family. He would never do his children the way his father had done them.

While eating dessert he found himself watching Berlin as she talked about the roses she had planted all over her yard.

"Why are you staring at me?" he heard her say, breaking into his thoughts.

He gave her a wide irresistible smile. "Because you are beautiful."

Berlin dropped her eyes and blushed. "You make me feel sexy when you look at me that way. And I'm not used to it."

"Then get used to it. During our time together I plan to look and touch you every chance I get."

Reginald knew the last thing he needed to do was touch her. His need battled his want and lost. He reached under the linen covered table and stroked her bare knee. He was so glad she wasn't wearing tights with her knee-high suede boots. Her skin was softer than anything he'd touched in a long time. Very feminine. His hand glided over to the inside of her thigh where he stroked and slowly moved his hand up. He locked his eyes with hers, watching her expression as he slid over to the chair beside her. Her breathing became labored, and Berlin bit down on her bottom lip as he moved closer to her sex. He stroked against the satin crotch, feeling the heat against his fingers. He pushed her thighs apart, and then searched for access beneath the material to her most sensitive area.

Berlin pushed her thighs together. "Don't," she whispered.

"Don't what?" he challenged as he continued to stroke her. "You want me to stop?"

He heard the pleasure murmur rise up from her throat, and he managed to push her thighs apart again with ease.

"Tell me you want me to stop, and I'll stop." Reginald teased her inner thigh, caressing first one leg, then the other. All the time he watched her face for some kind of sign that she didn't like what he was doing. He found none. Instead, Berlin bit down on her bottom lip as if trying to stifle a moan.

With his other hand, he reached for her fork and cut into the sweet potato pie. "Open your mouth." She obeyed, and he put the food in her mouth. "Now you have an excuse to moan. That's right. Let me know how good my hand feels."

Berlin closed her lips around the fork, and he slowly removed it from her mouth. He pressed against her heat more forcefully. This time her eyes fluttered shut. "Mmmm, that is so good," she moaned.

He continued to rub against the crotch. "Me or the pie?"

She opened her eyes and gazed over at him. "Both," she said barely above a whisper. He slipped his thumb under the edge of the silk she wore and moved across cropped hair toward her lips where he found her. He eased his thumb inside, and she startled, and then spread her thighs wider.

He glanced to his right and left, then leaned over toward her and whispered near her lips. "You like that?"

"You know I do."

He pressed his mouth against hers and pushed his tongue between her lips at the same time he moved his finger in and out of her creamy wet heat. The thought of making her come in a public place had him hard and erect.

"Have some more pie."

Obediently, she took another bite. As soon as she put the pie in her mouth, she moaned again.

"That's it, baby," he whispered huskily against her lips. "Let it out." He inserted another finger and drove deeper. "Baby, you got me hard as a rock." Her head lolled against his forehead. He could tell she was only seconds away from coming, when their waitress returned to see if they needed anything and filled their glasses with more tea. Slowly, he removed his fingers. Berlin slowly opened her eyes again. He could tell she was disappointed about the interruption. That's okay. He had every intention of making it up to her later.

As soon as the waitress left, he brought his fingers to his lips and slipped them inside his mouth. "Mmmm, you taste good," he whispered with a smirk.

Berlin playfully slugged him in the arm. "You're wrong for that."

Her face sobered, and he stared at her with heated intensity. "No, I'm not. Admit it. You liked every minute of it."

She blushed. "Okay, I'll admit that."

They shared a laugh. Reginald was discovering how real the sistah truly was.

"He-e-e-y Reggie."

He glanced up to see his ex, Jasmine James, standing beside their table. Skin-tight jeans. Turtleneck that showed off her large round breasts. Cornrows hanging down her back. "Hey Jaz, whassup?"

"Obviously nothing between us." She pursed her thick lips together. "I guess I need to stop waiting for that call."

He noticed Berlin arch her eyebrows. Uh-uh, he wasn't even about to go there. "Jasmine, you should have stopped waiting a long time ago."

She rolled her eyes, spun on her heels and headed toward the bathroom, where she was going in the first place, before she had the audacity to stop and try to ruin his date. Reginald glanced in the direction of the restrooms and scowled. He was glad to get rid of her. Not that he didn't like her. They just never had anything in common. She wanted a commitment. He did not. Noticing another chick he used to date coming through the door, Reggie was beginning to think coming to Lula's was not a good idea. He knew too many people, and right now was not the time. Tonight he wanted Berlin all to himself. He wanted to finish where they had left off, and if he was lucky, replace his fingers with something ten inches, pulsating and ready to do business.

Damn, why'd you even have to go there? He shifted slightly on the chair, trying to fight a damn hard on. Reaching for his glass, he took a long thirsty drink, then met Berlin's amused smile.

"Ex-girlfriend?"

"Something like that," he said with a sheepish grin.

"She's pretty."

He leaned forward. "And you're prettier." He nibbled playfully at her neck, and Berlin giggled like she was ticklish and pushed him softly away. Reginald watched her, liking the way she dropped her eyes and cupped her mouth when she blushed. She reached for her drink and took another sip, her lashes long and thick resting on her high cheekbones. She barely wore any makeup, and he liked that. She didn't have to. Her features were already perfect.

During the rest of their meal, they talked and laughed about growing up. Reginald was glad there were no more interruptions. Jasmine had stayed over at her table with her girl, Tamika, mean mugging him for the first few minutes or so before she finally got the hint—he wasn't paying her the slightest bit of attention.

After dinner he took Berlin to a small—hole in the wall—nightclub, a couple of blocks away. There was always a live R&B band on the weekend.

"I hope you can dance," he said only seconds after they had settled in their seats.

"Probably better than you." Berlin shrugged out of her coat, then pushed back her chair and shuffled out onto the floor with Reginald right behind, guiding her to the center.

The first was a fast number. He wasn't much of a dancer, but he enjoyed watching her bounce her J-Lo booty around the dance floor. Nevertheless, he was happy when the music finally slowed down. He smiled and brought her close so that she pressed her cheek against his throat. This was where he liked to be, close enough to smell and taste her. He slid both arms around her, resting right above her butt. He'd been waiting for this moment. He wanted to feel her breasts against his chest. Feel her thighs moving with his.

"I've been waiting all night for an excuse to hold you in my arms."

Berlin tilted her head back to look at him. "You should have asked. After all, you make all of the rules tonight."

Since he was making all the rules, he wished that he could demand she share his bed tonight, but he had made a promise not to make love to her until she asked.

The dance floor had gotten more crowded. Good. It gave him an excuse to pull her even closer so that she could feel the evidence of his growing erection.

"You feel that?" he asked.

"Yes," she replied, then blushed and looked down again.

"That's what you do to me," he whispered against her forehead.

There was no denying they were attracted to each other sexually. She leaned in close, inhaling his cologne and wrapped her arms tightly around his waist.

Reginald lowered his lips to the side of her neck and blew softly on her exposed skin. As shivers raced down her spine, Berlin moved closer in the circle of his arms.

"Berlin, look at me."

Pulling back slightly, she met his penetrating stare.

"Thanks for a lovely evening."

She swallowed the lump in her throat. "I should be thanking you."

"You can properly thank me later."

Lowering her head, she rested it at his shoulder. Berlin couldn't believe it, but she was having such a wonderful time with Reginald. Dinner, conversation and his hand beneath her dress. She swallowed, thinking about how naughty he made her feel. And to end the evening dancing in his arms. If this was their first date, she could only imagine what would happen between them by date three. Which was why the sooner she ended their date, the better. Otherwise, she might end up doing something she'd regret later.

They danced two more slow songs before she decided she was ready to call it a night. Reginald escorted her off the floor. He helped her into her coat, and then draped an arm around her waist as they moved out to his Escalade.

He assisted her onto the bench, then went around to the other side and climbed in the SUV.

Reginald started the SUV and pulled away from the parking lot. The sounds of Jaheim filled the silence.

Berlin settled on the bench beside him. Reginald reached over and stroked her knees. She loved the way her skin tingle on contact. For someone who was skilled in using his hands, he was gentle as a kitten.

His hand crept higher.

"Berlin?"

She glanced over at him. "Yes?"

"Take your panties off," he demanded.

"What?"

"I want you to slip your panties off and open your legs."

For some strange reason, his demand had her throbbing. She hesitated.

"Either you take them off or our deal is over," he challenged in a low voice.

She was pissed by his demand. What he didn't know was that she had every intention of granting him his request before his demand. Angrily, she reached up and pulled her silky red panties down her hips and past her ankles. "There, satisfied?"

"I will be when you slide over to me and open your legs."

Berlin slid over and leaned back against his shoulder. She then raised her feet onto the seat and parted her thighs. Her knees shook because she knew what was going to happen next.

"Good, girl." He planted a kiss to the top of her head, then reached over and placed his hand on her knee. She trembled as his fingers moved slowly up, drawing erotic paths on her legs. As he neared her core, she trembled, aching to feel his hands there. She closed her eyes and bit on her lower lip to stifle a groan. There was no way she would let him know how good he made her feel. She couldn't. Not again. But the only way to do that was to stop him before he even got started. And there was no way she would do that.

He tickled her pubic hairs, then barely grazed her fold before moving over to caress the inside of her right thigh. His hands traveled up again, and this time to her delight, he tickled her clit. Uncontrollably, she squirmed.

"Recline your seat."

Obediently, she reached down and pulled a lever that lowered the seat back. Closing her eyes, she allowed her knees to fall further apart. His palms traveled down her hip, and then under her skirt where his fingers moved higher. Her knees trembled with each inch. Reginald stroked her clit, and she felt on fire. His fingers moved slowly, circling, teasing. She tried to catch her breath and couldn't. The heat and the friction were causing a rush of sensation. His fingers then moved down and parted her dripping slit. Her juices freed and he plunged one finger in followed by another. She arched with unexpected pleasure and shifted her hips, allowing him better access. He pushed all the way in, then removed his fingers halfway before dipping into her honey again. Unconsciously, her hips bucked against his finger, meeting each thrust with one of her own.

"Does that feel good?"

"Yes, Reggie. Yes, it feels so good." All she wanted was to feel his hard thrust inside her body.

"You want me to stop?"

"No, no, please don't stop!" She was practically begging him to keep making love to her with his fingers.

"You're so wet you've got my dick hard." His voice sounded a little strained.

She was so close to coming, so close to losing control. "Yes, oh please that feels so good."

A truck drove passed them. She didn't care if anyone saw what was going on. All that mattered was the magic he created with his fingers. What in the world was she doing allowing a guy she had no future with to make love to her with his finger on the front seat of his Escalade? But when his finger found her spot, she couldn't have ended it even if she had wanted to. Her walls gripped him, unwilling to let him go. Reginald pushed inside of her again, then retreated, then plunged some more, again and again. It was growing hard to think with him stroking her just right. The man was no stranger to a woman's body. That much was obvious. Each time he thrust harder and deeper, she enjoyed the ride. She needed this. To hell with her conscious and resisting. The rhythm was so good. Her nipples yearned for attention. Her toes curled as he pushed her toward the edge. She rode his fingers until finally an orgasm hit her hard and fast. Her body shook, and she gripped the bench, and within seconds she let out a husky cry.

She was left weak and heaving. Reginald removed his wet fingers from her body and continued to caress her inner thighs while her breathing slowed. She couldn't believe how good he always managed to make her feel.

The Escalade came to a complete stop. She opened her eyes and glanced up at Reginald staring down at her. He had made her come with only two fingers, and she could tell by the sparkle in his eyes, he was damn proud of it.

"We're here," he announced.

She immediately sat up on the seat and peered through the glass. He was right. She was home. Embarrassed beyond reason, she reached down for her panties and stuffed them in her purse and climbed out of his SUV. Walking, she could feel the sticky wetness of what he had done. Her lips were moist, swollen and ready for something stiff, long and hard to finish the job.

He took the key from her hand and unlocked her door and pushed it open. She paused in the doorway, the glow from a lamp backlighting her.

He framed her face, his palm upon her jaw, allowing his thumb to trace her bottom lip. "I want to thank you for a wonderful evening."

Unable to find the right words, she simply nodded, the aftershocks of the orgasm still vibrating through her body.

Reginald swooped down and kissed her on the lips. A simple goodnight, but once his lips touched hers, he couldn't stop; he wanted more. She parted her lips and he enjoyed the taste as his tongue touched hers.

Slowly, he lifted his head and stared down into her eyes. His breathing grew heavy. Her eyes sparkled with desire. Her face flushed. If he asked, if he just pushed a little bit, he was certain that he could have what he wanted tonight. He wanted to hold her tits in the palm of her hand. To replace his fingers with his tongue, and then after making her come, replace it with his dick for the ride of her life. However, the sparkle had vanished for her eyes. Watching her nibble nervously on her bottom lip, he groaned inward. She wasn't ready for what he had to offer. He was too good a guy to take advantage of his power over her. He had promised to allow her to make the choice, and he was a man of his word.

"See you tomorrow." Reginald turned and walked away.

Reginald hopped into his Escalade, and it took everything he had not to turn around, carry her off to her room and bury all ten inches deep inside of her.

He couldn't remember the last time a woman fired him up in minutes. He wanted to take her to his bed. He wanted to finish what they had begun tonight. He wanted to taste, tease and possess her.

He wished he could have replaced those fingers with another part of his body. He wanted to mold her body to his, without clothes, so he could run his hands over her curves while he tasted her. But he couldn't do any of those things because he had given her his word. He wouldn't make love to her unless she asked.

Okay, so make her beg.

Yep, that was what he would have to do if he wanted to hit it. And he definitely planned to have her before the holiday season was over. If he had his way, he would have her down on all four bringing in the new year.

Now why'd you even go there?

A hard-on strained against his pants. Berlin had him so turned on that for a moment he couldn't even remember his way home.

He pulled off the highway and turned onto the Forest Parkway. Halfway down, he made a left and pulled onto his street.

He forced his mind away from the last half hour of their date and back to their dinner conversation. He couldn't remember the last time he had shared his personal life with anyone. Yet tonight, it had felt like the most natural thing. He felt so comfortable talking about his childhood with Berlin.

As he pulled into his driveway, he thought about his father. He couldn't remember the last time he'd thought of the man who fathered him. Staring up at his two-story brick home, he was reminded that the man's death had benefited them quite well.

Henry Hodges was worth more to his children dead than alive. Shortly after his untimely death to alcoholism, an attorney appeared on Reginald's doorstep with a check for a quarter of a million dollars payable to him, each of his siblings, and his mother. At first he hadn't wanted anything to do with the money, but at his mother insisted that her estranged husband owed it to them. Reginald had deposited the check and decided to start his own company, painting and remodeling homes. RDH Construction started as a small room in his studio apartment and had grown to a large office located in downtown St. Louis. He had stopped working in the field years ago. Reginald's main focus was checking out sites for bids. The only reason he was working at the pediatric clinic was because the fall was a busy time for interior work before the winter months rolled around, and he was short-staffed. By the holidays, business slowed down considerably and didn't pick up again until mid-spring.

Reginald climbed out and moved into his house. He paused in the foyer, feeling a since of pride. The row house had been a project of love. He had gutted out half the building and remodeled it from top to bottom.

He reached for a beer in the refrigerator, then moved into his living room and took a seat on a black leather couch. Taking a deep breath, he was hit by a lingering scent of Berlin. He brought those fingers to his nose and took another sniff. Yep, her cum was still on his hand. Flooded again by memories of their evening caused his dick to thicken. The taste had been sweet on his tongue.

Tonight he saw a side to her that told him he had been so wrong about her. The beautiful woman was vulnerable. He felt slightly guilty for demanding that she go out with him. His intentions had been to teach her how to let her hair down and truly live. Instead, he had found a woman who deserved love and that was one thing he could never give her, no matter how badly he wanted her.

He twisted the cap off the bottle and took a long drink. One thing for sure, no matter what, he was putting out no stops to make her his.

Chapter Seven

Berlin woke early the next morning with a queasy feeling in her stomach. She had gone to bed last night tossing and turning with her body on fire and believing that this morning everything would be all right. After hitting the snooze button on her alarm clock for the fourth time, she decided there was no point in hiding under the covers any longer. Nothing had changed. Her traitorous body was still playing tricks on her.

Rolling onto her side, she tightly squeezed her thighs together as the strong urge for sexual relief flowed through her body. She wanted Reginald so bad, she'd even dreamed about the two of them making love.

Why now? She groaned. Why when she was so close to creating the perfect life would she start lusting after the brotha? For the last year she had had little to no desire to be with a man, yet after one evening in the coatroom, she had been horny as all get out. Every encounter with him only seemed to add more fuel to the fire. Last night was no exception.

Pulling the covers tightly around her shoulders, she allowed herself a few minutes to relive the events of the previous night.

Reggie made her feel naughty and wicked, and instead of being appalled by the behavior, she welcomed it. What had happened at Lula's Kitchen under the tablecloth she would have never imagined in a million years, but the idea of doing something so bold in public with the risk of getting caught had turned her on.

What she'd discovered about Reggie was that no matter how much she tried to deny it, she liked him. He was a wonderful conversationalist with a wonderful sense of humor. She liked the way his irresistible dimple deepened when he laughed. But what turned her on the most to her amazement was his confident and aggressive attitude and his ability to arouse her with a single grin. She shivered as she remembered him ordering her to take her panties off with one simple command that she followed without hesitation. His words caused an uncontrollable heat to radiate through her body and settle down below. His touch had refueled a fire. The mere thought of the pleasure his fingers had caused brought a flush to her skin, an ache to her breasts. Reggie. She had become Reggie's with the magical touch of his hand.

She released a sigh, then lowered her eyelids and tried to block out the memories. She tried to calm her arousal but could not. Reaching inside her cotton nightgown, she ran her palm over her nipples. Her nipples responded and encouraged her hand to trail down her hip to touch the same spot Reggie had played with. Her heart rate increased as she allowed her mind to replay the drive away from the restaurant. His long fingers traveling between her folds and plunging deeply.

On a shivered sigh, Berlin withdrew her finger and rolled onto her back. This was not the time for self-gratification. She needed a man. However, the last person she needed to be fantasizing about was Reggie.

The fine brotha from the projects made her feel things she didn't want to feel. Last night he had reached inside and touched her soul. And she was terrified. That was why she needed to stay as far away from him today as possible.

Dragging herself from the bed to the bathroom, Berlin surveyed her disheveled image in the mirror. She then hurried through her shower and dressed in record time.

While sipping her coffee, her thoughts wandered once again to Reginald. It wasn't regret she was feeling this morning. It was more like confusion. That brotha managed to make her feel things she hadn't felt in…well, never. She wondered what it would be like being truly in love with someone like him.

Burning her tongue, she scowled, and blamed it on having such foolish thoughts. Falling in love was a matter of choice. Only romantics and budding teenagers could believe anything else. Who else but the most naïve individual could believe there was really a man named Cupid who zapped you with his bow and arrow? And next thing you know you have fallen helplessly and hopelessly in love with a man.

After her last painful lesson she had finally come to the conclusion that finding the right man was no different than shopping for clothes. It was up to you to pick out the shade and style that was right for you. That's what she had done. She had decided marrying a doctor was the right choice for her, and she refused to settle for less no matter how tempting he might be.

No matter how fine he was. Regardless of how horny she felt. Nothing could ever come of their relationship. She was a fool for ever allowing anything to happen. Allowing a man to finger her in a car; wasn't what she was about. It wasn't her style. It was against her morals, yet she had been so caught up in the moment she hadn't been thinking straight. In the next half hour, she sipped her coffee and came up with a decision. She would pretend last night never happened.

At ten o'clock she heard the doorbell ring. Her heart thundered wildly in her chest. She took a deep breath, then smoothed down the front of her sweater and moved to the front door. Suddenly thrilled to see him again, she deliberately hesitated. She didn't want him to know how anxious she was to see him. As he rang the door a third time, she turned the locked and opened the door.

Reginald stood on the other side dressed the way she saw him every day at work. Looking super fine.

"Hey whassup, boo?"

"Good morning." She stepped aside and gestured for him to come inside.

Reginald brushed past her, smelling too damn good this early in the morning.

"I hope you're planning to help me today," he said.

She shrugged, then shut the door, trying her hardest not to look at him for too long. "I was hoping to spend the morning filling out my Christmas cards."

He nodded. "Well as soon as you're done, come in and give me a hand."

She watched his nice round ass as he ascended her stairs and entered the second bedroom. It would have been nice if he had made a left instead and moved into hers. There was nothing better than to find a naked man lying across her bed.

A Delight Before Christmas

Shut up girl. You don't know what you want.

She sighed. Yep, that was the gist of it. Feeling more confused than ever, she moved into the kitchen where a box of cards had been sitting for the last month. Berlin lowered in the chair and reached for the first African-American greeting card. She gazed down at the artist drawing of a family standing in front of a Christmas tree. Her imagination took over, and she thought about the family she hoped to have some day. Somehow, the man became Reginald, and he was holding in his arms a little girl with his eyes and dimples and Berlin's skin complexion.

Grabbing a pen, she shook the ridiculous thoughts away and began filling out the first card. She had made it halfway through the stack when she heard footsteps. Glancing up, she watched Reggie move into the kitchen.

"You think maybe a brotha could have some water."

"Sure." Nervously, she moved over to the refrigerator and removed a bottle of water from the bottom shelf.

"I had a great time last night," she heard from behind.

Sweat beaded her forehead at the heat of Reggie close behind her. She hadn't even heard him move. Feeling his breath against the back of her neck, her nipples hardened.

Dang, she wanted him again.

"So did I," she replied, hoping he hadn't heard her voice crack at the end.

"I'm glad to hear that." He brought his hands to her waist and leaned her back against his chest. Surprised to discover his stiff dick pressed against her back, her body stiffened.

She tried to fight the memory of holding its thickness in her hand, but could not. Closing her eyes, she nibbled on her lower lip and tried to think of a response, but could not. In the meantime, an arm snaked around her waist and tugged her back against his chest. His breath feathered her neck and his arm only inches below her breasts caused her nipples to yearn for attention.

"Last night I dreamed you went home with me. I slowly undressed you, then carried you over to my bed where I kissed your lips, your neck, then suckled your nipples. When you begged for more, I draped your legs over my shoulders so I could taste your juices on my lips," he whispered near her ear. "After I made you come with my tongue, I spread your legs wide and grabbed your firm juicy ass and held you firmly in place while I buried my dick inside of you." He shifted his hips making sure she felt exactly much he was working with. She moaned. "Then I stroked you until you begged me to stop."

Her tongue slipped from her lips. Thank goodness the refrigerator door was open cooling her off because suddenly it had gotten seriously hot in there. As he explained every detail of their erotic escapade, she felt wetness slide down her inner thighs. She wanted so badly to feel all he was working with buried deep inside of her. But she couldn't. Not if she planned to seduce his friend Dr. Clarke.

It took everything Berlin had to step away from him. Shutting the refrigerator, she swung around and faced him. Why did she do that? His eyes were dark and filled with lust. Glancing down, she stared at the evidence of his arousal. The brotha was blessed. She should feel lucky he wanted to share all of *that* with her. And she definitely wanted everything he had to offer. If only he were Cameron, she would have jumped at the opportunity.

Shaking her head, Berlin tore her eyes away from his package and took another painful step back. "Last night shouldn't have ever happened." When he prepared to speak, she held up her hand. "Look, Reggie I like you, but nothing can ever come of us. I've got an agenda, and frankly, you're not part of it."

He gave her one of those irresistible smiles that made her toes curl. "I'm not talking about a commitment. I'm talking about making each other feel good for the time being."

She had to stifle a moan at the suggestion of making each other feel good. That was definitely one thing he knew how to do, which was why she had to end things now or deal with the consequences later.

"I don't need a sexual fling. I want a lifetime commitment with the right man."

Reggie stepped forward until they were standing toe to toe, and then pressed his lips against her forehead several times as he spoke. "That's what your mouth says, but your body is telling me a totally different story."

"Why are you doing this?" she asked in a husky whisper.

Reginald put his finger beneath her chin and tilted her head so that she had no other choice but to look at him. "Because I want you, and I know that you want me. I guarantee you sex between us will be like nothing you've ever experienced before."

Berlin went all warm inside at the images his words conjured. Her breathing came in shallow gasps, and her pulse raced. Being appalled by her reaction did absolutely nothing to lesson the feelings she was experiencing. Staring up at his mouth, she longed to feel Reginald's lips on hers. She was dying to discover if there were more than empty promises smoldering behind his dark eyes. She longed for one brief encounter with him to indulge in what she was feeling headfirst and worry about the consequences later.

She suddenly remembered the last time she had jumped headfirst into a relationship and the heartache that had followed. Berlin tried to tear her gaze away from his full sexy lips. Yet it was impossible. It was as if her brain had gone on strike and had given her body complete authority.

"It wouldn't be a good idea," Berlin said, trying hard to regain control of the situation.

"Why not?"

"Because nothing will ever come of it."

"Then let's concentrate on the here and now." Reginald scooped her into his arms and carried her over and lowered her onto the kitchen table. He then took a seat in the chair and sat between her legs.

Reginald stared up at her puzzled face as he spoke. "I think you misunderstand my intentions. I'm not trying to insult or take advantage of you," he said softly. Draping his arms across her thighs, he gripped her butt and slid her closer to him and held her firmly in place despite her resistance. "I'm not gonna lie to you," he began as she continued to struggle free of his grasp. "I want you, but I don't want you to feel pressured to do anything that you'll regret later." Pausing he released a heavy sigh. "I want to be with you, but that is totally your decision. As I said before, if you want me to make love to you, you're gonna have to ask."

Berlin stopped tugging to be released.

Berlin felt a fire build behind her eyes. That was not at all what she had expected to come out of Reginald's mouth. He was a wannabe mack daddy, or so she thought before he had responded with so much tenderness; she wanted to mold her body against his. For him to say something like that then his words had to be honest as the evidence of his desire that brushed against her back. It was quite flattering and oh so very tempting. She would have liked nothing better than to tell him yes, and then have him carry her up to her room and make love to her until their dinner. Only that was the world of make believe. She had learned a long time ago there is no such thing as happily ever after. As much as she longed to give in to her emotions, she could not. It was time for her to make wise decisions, and sleeping with Reginald, no matter how good he made her feel, reacting on impulse was not the right thing to do.

Swallowing the lump in her throat, she replied, "I'm sorry, but I can't."

As if he hadn't heard a word she had said, Reginald reached inside her shirt and fondled her breasts. Her breath caught as he captured one pebble-hard nipple between his fingers. "Like I told you before, that's what your mouth says." Raising her shirt, he leaned forward and kissed a trail along her stomach, his breath hot against her skin. "But your body says something else."

His tongue moved down to her belly at the same time he reached for her sweat pants and lowered them over her hips. He dropped to his knees, breathing in her womanly scent, then kissed a path to the cropped black patch of hair.

"Reggie," Berlin moaned as her hands came up to rest on his head, pushing his head lower.

"I got you baby." Her legs trembled as he pushed her thighs apart and licked a path along her inner thighs.

Berlin leaned back across the table and closed her eyes as his tongue drew closer to where she needed to feel him most.

"Berlin?"

"Yes," she whispered.

"Look at me." When her eyelids fluttered open he added, "I want you to watch me taste you."

Their eyes locked before he lowered, and she watched as he kissed the inside of her other leg. He was torturing her. Wanting her to plead for release. She could feel his warm breath, and her sex yearned for his touch. Finally, while she was watching, Reggie lowered his head, and the tip of his tongue parted her private folds, causing her to shudder. Her legs trembled as he licked one long stroke across her heated sex. Her body relaxed as he teased and suckled lightly on her clit.

"Yes!" Berlin cried out and arched against him, drawing him closer. "Right there." He had her hot and bucking against him. He started with a slow rhythm that slowly increased and as his tongue move in and out, she rocked back and forth. She focused on the heat of his mouth, the gentle caress of his tongue and the need to have him inside of her. Every so often he looked up from between her legs to see if she was still watching. Each time turned her on even more. Reaching under her shirt, she found her own nipples and fondled one and then the other, squeezing and releasing. Returning to his seat, Reggie pulled her thighs forward until she was almost hanging off the table and draped her knees over his shoulders. With her ass in his hand, he buried his tongue inside of her while he held her steady. Berlin heard labored breathing and realized that it was her. She didn't care. All that mattered was the masterpiece he was painting with his tongue. He was torturing her, making her beg for release. She closed her eyes while he focused on her clit. He suckled, then stopped and suckled again, bringing her close to the edge but refusing to let her have it.

"Please," she murmured.

Reginald raised his head and met the strained look on her flushed face. "Please what?" he asked.

Berlin wanted to scream. He knew exactly what he was doing. Teasing her to the point that she had to beg for release. Opening her eyes, she looked down at him. "Make me come, please."

After a long intense moment with their eyes locked, he plunged two fingers inside her heat. She gasped, then stared down in his dark eyes. He watched her as she moaned with pleasure and bucked wildly against his fingers. She was so wet she could hear the sounds as he stroked in and out of her heat. Her head fell back and her eyes rolled close. Reginald lowered his head and suckled her clit while his fingers drove deeper. Within seconds her muscles tightened, then she cried out and trembled around him as her body found pleasure.

She went limp across the table. Reginald rose. The evidence of his hard-on grazed her sensitized clit, and she flinched. She slowly opened her eyes and found him staring down between her legs. He reached for his belt buckle and she watched as he removed his dick from his pants.

"See what you did."

Her breath caught in her throat. All she could do was stare.

"I want to give all this to you. Just like I did in my dream."

Berlin gulped when he pressed against her and rocked his hips from side to side. The head of his dick only inches away from her warm wet passage.

With her legs wide open, he continued to grind against her. Her knees began to tremble as desire brewed through her body again. He stared down at her long and hard, and she knew that he was waiting for her to ask him to finish what he had started, for him to making love to her. She couldn't, she thought as she dropped her eyes. Make love to him would be a mistake.

She shook her head, took a deep breath and lifted her eyes to his. "Reggie, Please, I—"

"Oh, yeah, I forgot. I'm not good enough," he answered. He gave her a grim smile, then stepped back and put his erection back inside his pants. "The front guest room is done. I'll be back tomorrow to start on the second," she heard him say only seconds before strolling out of the kitchen. By the time she had gotten herself together, she heard the front door close.

"Hey, Reggie, dawg, you playing or not?"

Markeith's question captured his attention, and judging by the weird looks on everyone's faces around the table, they found his lack of concentration on the game quite amusing.

"Man, quit sweating me. Yeah I'm playing," he replied, annoyed that he had gotten caught a third time thinking about Berlin.

"Yo, then step up your game. We're fin to lose," Markeith complained as he fingered his mustache nervously.

"I got this," Reginald said with confidence.

"Then do the damn thang."

Reginald glanced down at the last card played, then looked at the last two cards in his hand and slammed down a card that won him the book. He removed the cards and placed them in a stack beside him, then slapped down an ace of spades on the table.

Looking over to his right, he watched Tyrone glance at Byron out the corners of his glasses, trying to give signals. Reginald relaxed in his chair. He didn't have anything to worry about. He'd had the majority of the aces in his hand.

Tyrone dropped a ten of hearts, which meant he didn't have any more spades. He chuckled inwardly. The hand was in the bag. He glanced across the table at his partner and tipped his head as if to say "We got this."

Markeith dropped a five of spades. Reginald was all set to take the book when Byron slammed down a two. He groaned. He had forgotten the deuce was wild, beating out his ace.

Markeith sprung from his chair. "Dang, dude, that's the fourth hand we lost to these cats!" Turning, he stepped into the kitchen.

"Hey if we're good, we're good." Byron chuckled as he dropped his last card on the table.

"Nah, Reggie needs to step up his game. Dude, whassup?" Markeith asked as he returned to his seat with a fresh beer.

Reginald waited until he threw down the joker before answering. "Ain't nothing up."

Markeith shook his head as he dropped a jack on top. "Yeah, whatever, dude. Your mind is somewhere other than this game."

"Probably between some chick's legs," Byron joked, causing the others to roar with laughter.

Reginald simply glared across the table at the light-skinned brotha and reached for the last book. He should have known hanging out with his boys was a bad idea. After his afternoon with Berlin, he desperately needed a distraction from her or he was going to lose his mind.

Of all the years he had been engaged in sex, he never had a woman tell him no until now. And it bruised his ego to say the least, not to mention he was also challenged by her. It was time he stepped up his game. Having her legs draped over his shoulders while he ate an afternoon snack had him so worked up that he needed some and soon. Only no other woman would do but Berlin. But she was playing games.

"Yo, earth to Reggie."

Reginald refocused on the group. "Let's just finish the game." He reached for the cards and shuffled the stack.

For the next two hands he tried again to focus and could not, and was glad when the game was over, even though they lost.

"Dawg, thanks for the fifty bucks." Byron chuckled as he slid the money off the table and gave Tyrone half.

He frowned at the two clowns. "Consider it a loan, cause I'll get it back plus interest next week."

Tyrone chuckled boisterously. "As long as that honey is on your mind, I doubt that."

The others joined in with jokes about him being sprung over some woman.

With a glare, Reginald rose from the chair, tossed the empty bottle in the trash and went into Byron's small apartment sized kitchen to retrieve another.

"So, Reggie, man, all jokes aside, who's this that's got you all bent out of shape?"

He gazed over at Markeith and saw the sincerity in his question.

Reginald brought the bottle to his lips. "You wouldn't know her," he mumbled. He wasn't ready to put his business out there in front of the others. He, Tyrone and Bryon went way back, but the two bubble heads were years away from thinking about being with one woman.

And what about you?

As he took another sip, he pondered that question. Last week he would have been quick to answer, "Absolutely not." However, after the last few days, he wasn't sure. Hell, he wasn't sure about anything lately except that he wanted Berlin and he wanted her bad.

"She wouldn't happen to be that fine sista I saw lay it on you thick at the Christmas party?"

His head sprung up in surprise. He had forgotten Markeith and his wife had been there. Knowing her, she had blabbed how he had come out the closet with his pants open.

"What sista?" Tyrone asked, his ear hustling on the conversation.

To his annoyance, Markeith told them about the beautiful woman in the short leather skirt.

Tyrone tossed his hands in the air. "Dang, dawg, can we get some details?"

"Hell, I want to know if she has a sister," Byron cried with his long dreads swinging across his shoulders.

Reginald's keen dark eyes held his boys; they were all watching him, waiting for his response. "None of y'all damn business."

"Aw, come on dawg! I told you about Deanna," Byron whined.

"That's cause you like putting your business out on the street." Reginald took one final sip from the bottle then tossed it in the trash. "Yo, I'm out."

Markeith simply nodded as he watched him move toward the door.

Chapter Eight

On Monday Berlin stepped into the building dressed to impress in a navy blue pants suit. Dr. Clarke was due back into the clinic, and today she planned to get his attention and take her mind off her weekend with Reginald. Which wouldn't be easy to do, considering he had been occupying her every thought since…well, since that night in the coatroom.

She turned her computer on, and then took a seat. While she waited for the modem to warm up, she thought about the little afternoon snack Reggie had in her kitchen. That was the first time anyone had eaten her out and had done it right. Even when she pleasured herself, not once had it come close to what he had made her feel.

Dropping her head, she briefly closed her eyes. The look on Reginald's face when he left her house still haunted her. He had misconstrued her behavior in the kitchen and was under the impression he wasn't good enough for her. Quite the contrary, Reginald was damn good. The problem was regardless of how good he made her feel or even how much she enjoyed being around him, she had an agenda she needed to stick to. Berlin sighed. Even still, it bothered her that she had hurt his pride.

"How was your weekend with cutie pie?"

Berlin looked up from her desk and scowled as Arianna waltzed into her office in dark green slacks and a cream blouse and dropped in the chair across from her desk.

She shrugged. "Okay I guess."

Her brow rose. "What do you mean, you guess?"

"I mean, the weekend was just fine," Berlin said, trying to choose her words carefully.

"Uh-huh." Arianna pushed a strand of hair from in front of her eye and leaned across the desk. The scent of her expensive perfume tickled her nose. "And what else?"

Her girl was determined to work her nerve. "Nothing. He worked on the guest rooms."

"Are you sure that's all he worked on. Did you give him some?"

"Of course not." At least not the way she'd suggested. Just thinking about his fingers buried inside her, caused Berlin to shift uncomfortably on the seat. Thinking about his magic tongue, she flinched and pretended to be reaching for something from her inbox.

"What about kissing?" she pressed on.

"Arianna," Berlin warned.

She clapped her hands with glee. "You did kiss him! Was it as good as the last time?"

No, it was ten times better.

Berlin leaned back in her chair, knowing her girl wouldn't give up until she gave her something. "Okay, he's a good kisser, so what?"

Crossing her legs, she leaned back in the chair and fanned herself. "Girl, good kissers are hard to find. For some unknown reason, a brotha doesn't think about chewing a piece of gum or grabbing a breath mint before kissing. So if he had fresh breath and didn't slob in your mouth, then Reggie is definitely a winner."

Slobber? Goodness, Arianna could be so graphic at times. One thing she could say about Reggie, fresh breath was one of his strong points. Kissing was definitely one of his greatest strengths and making a woman come—

Swiveling around in her chair, Berlin immediately ended the thought and reminded herself the weekend had been one big mistake. Today was a new day, and Cameron was at the top of her agenda.

Arianna glanced down at the cell phone at her hip and frowned. "Look, I gotta go take this call, but we're not done with this conversation." She rose and reached down to her phone as she strolled through the door.

Shaking her head, Berlin swiveled in front of her keyboard and logged onto her computer. Before Arianna returned, she would have to think of something to tell her friend, because she wouldn't let up until she did.

"Good morning."

Her pulse skipped a beat as soon as she heard the deep soothing voice. She looked over at the door to find Reggie standing there.

"Hey."

"We need to talk," he said, then stepped into her office and shut the door behind him. "I have a little bit of a problem." Reading the serious expression on his face, Berlin moved from around her desk and came to stand in front of him.

"What happened? What's wrong?"

Reginald's expression softened as he stepped forward and wrapped his arms around her waist, resting on her butt. "I was hoping to have some time alone before the others arrive," he murmured, pressing a kiss to her neck that made her jump despite her best attempt not to.

"You can't be doing that. Someone might walk in and see us," she snapped, pushing his shoulders away with her hands, squashing the shivers his touch sent through her.

"So, let them see," he said with a wicked smile. He circled his arms around her waist and pulled her close again. "I want you. I said I wouldn't pressure you, but I've changed my mind." Again Reggie's hands slid down to her behind where he pressed his erection firmly against her. "See what you do to me?"

Berlin took a deep breath. She couldn't see but could definitely feel what she had done to him. Gazing up into his eyes, she watched as he leaned forward, his lips growing closer. She felt herself tilting her chin, anticipating his mouth against hers. When their lips finally met, she found herself meeting each stroke with one just as bold.

"What's going on in here?"

When Berlin jumped out of his arms, Reginald slowly turned around to see Arianna peeking around the door, smiling.

"Nothing is going on!" Berlin snapped as she tried to step around him.

Reginald caught her around the waist and despite her objections, he held on. Laughing, Arianna stepped into the office, pushing the door behind her.

"I kissed her and now she's mad," he stated boldly. "I don't know why your friend can't just admit how much she likes me."

"I agree." Arianna's smile widened and actually sparkled with laughter as she moved to rest her hip on the corner of the desk.

Berlin wiggled out of Reggie's arms, then glared at him, trying to hold her temper in check. "I'm going to get you for that," she warned.

He chuckled, obviously finding her threat amusing.

Arianna's eyes traveled from one to the other before she finally said as she pushed off the desk, "Why don't I come back later?"

"No!" Berlin cried. "Don't go. Reginald was just leaving."

"I was?" He still had that irresistible grin on his face.

She folded her arms beneath her breasts. "Yes, you are."

Arianna gave Reggie an apologetic smile. "You have to excuse my girl. She can be extremely rude at times."

"I know," he said chuckling. "Although the last couple of days I also learned that beneath that hard exterior is a warm and giving individual."

Arianna's eyes sparkled with interest. "Ooh! It sounds like the two of you spent quite a bit of time getting to know one another."

Berlin inhaled roughly and shot back, "Probably more time than needed." She then gave a dismissive wave, and moved around her desk. "Now if you two would excuse me, I have work to do."

Reginald nodded still seemingly amused. It appeared he enjoyed embarrassing her. "I'll talk to you later."

As soon as he departed, Arianna shut the door behind him and rushed over and leaned across Berlin's desk. "Ooh! You better give me every juicy detail and don't leave anything out."

Berlin pretended to be working. "I thought I asked you to leave. Don't you have work to do?"

"Nothing that can't wait. So quit stalling and tell me what I want to hear."

Berlin lowered the pen and folded her arms on the desk. "Reginald agreed to paint my house as long as I agreed to three dates. We went out Saturday night."

Her friend clapped her hands with glee. "You don't say? And how was it?"

Berlin couldn't resist smiling as she thought about him thinking she thought she was too good for soul food. Man, he had her pegged wrong. But there wasn't anything she could do about that without giving him the impression he had a chance at being with her. Regardless of how much they had in common, she wanted more than a painter could ever offer her. "He took me to his old neighborhood in Wellston, and we had dinner. Then went dancing at some nice little club."

Arianna lowered into the chair. Obviously, she didn't plan to leave until she had gotten every little juicy detail. "From the look on your face, I can tell you had a fabulous evening."

Berlin glanced over her head with thoughts of Reggie dancing in her head. Even with him barging in her office, she couldn't help smiling at his boldness. "I did."

"So, I'm going to ask you again, did you give him some?"

Berlin blinked twice and turned her attention to her nosy friend and frowned. "None of your business." There was no way she was telling her the things Reginald had done to her. It was still hard for her to believe it herself. Without even making love, he had made her feel more things than she had ever felt with anyone before.

"Fine. Keep your secrets," Arianna pouted. "However, from the look on your face, I can tell it was definitely a weekend to remember."

That was an understatement.

Arianna rose from the chair and started toward the door. "If you haven't noticed yet, Dr. Clarke is here."

Long after her friend had left, Berlin sat back in her chair, staring out at the clear sky. She shook her head, then dropped it to the palm of her hand. What was wrong with her? Here she was trying to get Cameron's attention, and all she could think about was making love with Reginald.

Reginald agreed to meet his boy Ron for lunch.

A Delight Before Christmas

He dropped in the restroom long enough to clean up his hands, then strolled to the coffee shop across the street. The Grind had been around for almost a decade and was a regular evening hangout spot for college students in the area. Not only did they serve every type of coffee imagined, but they also offered sandwiches with fresh oven-baked bread and homemade soups. The food was both good and affordable. Last year the owner had decided to station two computers at the back with free online services. The idea was an instant success.

Reginald entered the building and glanced around. The Grind had a casual atmosphere with booths and tables covered with red-and-white-checkered tablecloths. A jukebox in the corner was playing a classic Isley Brothers' tune. He couldn't recall the title, but knew it had been one of his mother's favorites that she often played in their home.

Finding a seat in the corner of the shop, he lowered onto the bench. Within seconds, a waitress came to take his order. Cameron had asked him to go ahead and order him roast beef and Swiss cheese on rye, and he also ordered one for himself. After she left with their order, Reginald leaned back in the chair and gazed out the window.

He still couldn't believe how stupid he had been. He had honestly thought that after spending the weekend together, Berlin would have forgotten her ridiculous quest to marry a doctor. Only nothing had changed. He was only a substitute for what she really wanted, and nothing or no one for that matter would stand in her way. He scowled. The woman would drive him insane if he wasn't careful. The best thing for him to do was step back, but unfortunately, he had never been one to accept defeat so easily. Which was why he had dropped by her office with the hope of putting something on her mind to think about.

He glanced up in time to spot Cameron coming through the door in nothing more than a lab coat. Breathing heavily, it was obvious he ran across the street.

"Man, it's cold out there," he said as he slipped onto the bench across from him.

"I guess so, if you come out the door without a coat on," Reginald replied sarcastically.

"I was distracted."

"So what's up? What you want to talk about?"

Angie Daniels

The waitress arrived and hung around long enough to put two lemonades on the table.

Cameron took a long drink before he spoke. "Look, Reggie man. I need some advice."

"Sure, shoot."

"There's a particular woman I'm interested in, and I need to know how to approach her. Nice body, auburn curls, light golden eyes."

He knew immediately the woman he was talking about was Berlin. He groaned inwardly. He didn't want to discuss Berlin with his best friend or anyone for that matter. As far as he was concerned, if he couldn't have her, then no one could.

Cameron gave a nervous laugh. "I'm talking about Ms. Dupree."

"I figured as much."

"How'd you know?"

Reginald reached for his drink and gave the only obvious answer. "She's a beautiful woman."

Cameron gave a nervous laugh. "Yes, she is definitely fine. I wonder why I haven't noticed her before."

"Because before she was wearing thick eye glasses and her hair pulled back in one of those old-school librarian hairdos."

He nodded. "Yeah, that's probably right. But now, damn, she looks good."

Reggie had to grit his teeth. Ron was his good friend, and since he didn't have any dibs on Berlin, it meant she was free game.

"So when are you planning to ask her out?"

"Well I was kind of hoping you could put in a good word for me."

He immediately declined. "I'm not getting involved in that."

"So what's she like to work for?"

Sexy. Vulnerable. Has the power to turn him on at the drop of a hat. Pushing the thoughts away, he simply shrugged. "Stubborn, difficult, but when she cracks a smile, it's like she changes into another person."

Cameron's brow arched. "Sounds like you feel some type a way about her."

"Me?" He frowned. "Nah."

127

Raising his hands in the air, Cameron replied, "Hey, man I'm not trying to step on anyone's toes."

Nothing would have pleased him more than to tell his boy to step off, but Berlin wasn't his to claim. Besides, at the Christmas party, it was Cameron she had wanted, not him.

"Our relationship is strictly business." He shrugged. "Go to her office and ask her out." He liked Cameron, but the thought of him being with her didn't set to well with him.

"You think I should?"

"Since when is mack daddy unsure about a woman?"

"I usually don't have workplace relationships."

Typically, his boy was out for one thing and one thing only—sex. And as soon as he succeeded, he would move on to his next victim. The thought of him using her irritated him more than he was prepared to admit. "I'm no matchmaker. If you want her, go for it. Just don't treat her like an old pair of shoes."

Their food arrived, although suddenly he had lost his appetite. He didn't want Cameron dating Berlin, but it wasn't his place to stand in the way. She would have to find out for herself what type of man Cameron was. Although he planned to also make sure she also knew what she was giving up in the process.

All during lunch Berlin tried to clear her thoughts. She was reeling from the sensual assault. His skillful lips. All she could do was think about them down between her legs. She couldn't get him off her mind. She had spent practically the entire afternoon trying to budget one of their grant-funded accounts, and instead found herself thinking about Reginald. His talk. His walk. His dick.

She scowled. The last thing she needed was to be sidetracked so close to Christmas. She had to stay focused. Next Monday was her last day until the New Year, although she had to come in the Wednesday after Christmas long enough to submit payroll. The clinic itself was scheduled to close at noon on Christmas Eve until the Monday after

New Year's Eve. As soon as she had everything done, the sooner she could enjoy her holiday vacation. She had to do whatever to keep him off her mind.

Hearing a light rap on the door, she glanced up and was startled to find Cameron.

Swiveling around in her chair, she faced him. "Dr. Clarke? What a pleasant surprise! Please come on in."

"I won't take up too much of your time," he began as he moved into her office. "I'm getting ready to begin seeing patients, but I wanted to stop by and ask you something."

She smiled up at his gentle face. "Sure, anything."

"I would like to know if you'd be interested in dinner Friday night?"

She couldn't believe her ears. After weeks of drooling over the man, he was finally asking her out on a date. So why wasn't she excited about it? She knew why. She just wasn't ready to admit that she had allowed Reginald to get in her head. Which was exactly why she needed to accept the date. Goal number eight was to marry a rich man, not a union worker.

Berlin swallowed hard. Was she falling in love? Flinching at the ludicrous idea, she looked Cameron directly in his brown eyes and replied, "Dinner? I would love too."

His grin broadened. "Great. I look forward to it."

As soon as he moved out of her office, she slumped down in the chair and forced a smile. She was finally getting what she wanted. A date with the gorgeous and single Dr. Cameron Clarke. A feat she thought a long shot was miraculously falling into place, which was why she needed to stay clear of Reginald.

Her door opened, and Arianna barged in, interrupting any further thoughts.

"I just saw Dr. Clarke leaving your office."

She rolled her eyes. "Don't you have better things to do than to be watching who's coming in and out of my door?"

Arianna shook her head. "Who can work with all the action popping off over here? So spill it, what did the good doctor want?"

She couldn't resist a grin. "He asked me out on a date."

The glint in her eyes faded. "I can't believe he finally asked you out on a date."

"Well, believe it. We're having dinner on Friday."

Looking up from her desk, she noticed Arianna giving her a curious look. "What?"

She frowned. "What about Reginald?"

Berlin gave a nonchalant shrug. "What about him?"

"Well, I thought maybe the two of you were…"

"Together? No way. He is doing me a favor, and in exchange I have agreed to go out with him." She couldn't make any more of it than it really was. A business arrangement, nothing more. "Besides, he knew when I kissed him that I was interested in Dr. Clarke."

"Dr. Clarke is like all the other brothas with good hair—playas."

She laughed at the ridiculous statement. "What does the texture of your hair have to do with it? For all we know, Reggie is also a playa. After all, they are homeboys."

"Yeah and they are both interested in you," Arianna pointed out.

Could what she say be true? Was her relationship with Reginald more than a business arrangement? She shook her head at the nonsense. The last thing she needed was for Reginald to think she was interested in him beyond the physical. She had made it perfectly clear from jump, he fit nowhere in her perfectly planned life.

"So where is he taking you to eat?"

She shrugged. "I don't know."

"I'm sure it's somewhere bougie."

Berlin simply nodded. She was certain it would be nothing like Lula's Kitchen.

"You still owe Reginald two more dates," Arianna reminded. "What if he wants to go out on Friday?"

She practically choked on her own spit. "I forgot about that. I'll just have to tell him I'm going out with you."

"Oh yeah, just use me why don't you?" Arianna was quiet for a long moment. "I hope you know what you're doing." Her voice was low and concerned.

"Sure I do. The only person I'm interested in dating is Cameron."

"I hope you're right."

Berlin watched as Arianna returned to her office. Her words were still ringing in her ear. She hoped she was making the right choice, even though her body was saying one thing and her mind was saying another.

She didn't know what to do. Reginald made her feel like no other, yet Cameron was everything she had dreamed of in a man or so she hoped. And that hope was enough reason to push aside any feelings she might have for Reginald Hodges.

Chapter Nine

On Tuesday Berlin worked on a grant proposal all morning and was so absorbed in it that she startled when the phone rang. She took a deep breath, lowered her pen and glanced over at the phone. Her private line was blinking. She picked up the phone before the fourth ring.

"Berlin speaking."

"Hey, boo."

"Reginald?" She glanced around as if someone was in her office listening. "How did you get my private line?"

"I have my ways." She didn't miss the hint of laughter in his voice.

"Uh-huh, I can just guess Arianna has something to do with this," she retorted with an angry breath. She and her dear friend were going to have to have a long talk real soon. "Aren't you supposed to be working?"

He chuckled. "I am working. Why don't you come out of your office and have lunch with me?"

Berlin glanced over at the clock and noticed it was already after twelve. Where had the morning gone? She groaned inward. She knew where the time had gone. She had spent it hiding in her office all morning, trying to avoid him. Yesterday she had conveniently disappeared, Christmas shopping most of the evening and was relieved when she had returned home to find him gone. She had to avoid him as much as possible, which was why there was no way she was going anywhere with him for lunch no matter how tempting. "I've got to get this proposal done."

"Lula's Kitchen is having a fabulous special; sweet potatoes, corn bread dressing and smoked ox tails."

Now *that* was definitely tempting. "No. I better pass."

"I think you're avoiding me."

"No I'm not." With that she abruptly hung up the phone. Hearing a knock at her door, she moved around her chair and swung the door open. She found Reginald standing on the other side.

"Yes you are."

Her breath caught in her throat as she studied his features. They were the same strongly prominent features that had invaded her dreams for the last couple of days. Staring up at him, she inhaled, breathing in a scent that was warm and inviting, causing her pulse to beat rapidly.

Reginald cleared his throat, and she realized that she hadn't breathed a word since she'd open the door.

"Invite me in, Berlin."

She let out a breath in an audible sigh and tried to ignore the dimples he flashed. "I got work to do."

"You can't work all day." He pushed past her, and as soon as the smell of food hit her nose, she noticed he was carrying two Styrofoam containers. "You can spend thirty minutes eating lunch with me."

Without saying a word, she moved around her desk and lowered back in her seat. Reginald took the seat across from her and pushed one of the containers in front of her. She pretended to hesitate, but her stomach growled and gave her away. With a sigh, she reached for her fork and dug in. She couldn't resist a moan.

"Ooooh, that is so good!"

He made a grumble sound in his chest as he resumed eating, although his eyes never left her face.

Berlin brought her food to her lips and caught him staring. "What are you looking at?"

"You. Wondering when you're gonna stop playing games and let me make love to you."

Lowering her eyes to her floor, she said, "This isn't a game, Reggie. This is my life."

"If you say so," he said between chews.

"What do you mean by that?" she asked with attitude.

Reginald pointed his fork at her. "I think you're scared."

"I'm not scared."

"Then prove it. Come here."

She hesitated, then lowered her fork in the container and came around from behind her desk.

"Okay, I'm here, now what?" she said as if suddenly bored with him.

"Have a seat."

"Where?" she dared to ask.

"On my lap."

She shook her head. "What if someone walks in?"

"What? Now you're scared?" he taunted. "Come, have a seat."

Slowly, she moved over and lowered onto his lap. He draped an arm around her waist and turned her around so her back was facing him. He pressed a kiss to the skin at the back of her neck. Turning, she was about to say something when she saw him grin.

"Relax and finish eating your food." He reached across the desk and put her food in front her.

While they ate, Reginald stared up at her profile, taking in her full lips he envisioned sometime real soon wrapped around his dick. He had asked her to sit on his lap as a test to see if she would really do it. His dick pulsed in his pants making it hard for him to think straight. While they ate he moved his hand to her knee. The forked paused halfway to her mouth.

"Relax, Berlin. I asked for thirty minutes of your time, and I plan to utilize every second of it."

While she resumed eating her cornbread dressing, he smoothed his hand up her thigh underneath her skirt.

"Open your legs."

Obediently, she draped her legs over his knees and leaned her back against his chest.

"Good girl," he murmured against her hair. He dropped his fork and brought his other hand to her leg. He was going to show her how good it could be between them. That his boy was no match to him.

His hand slid up high beneath her skirt. Damn those pantyhose. He wanted to dip his fingers in her heat, but this afternoon it wouldn't be possible.

"I want to make you feel good," he murmured against her ear as he took the lobe into his mouth and suckled. As soon as she turned her head to the side, he dipped his tongue inside and moved in and out of her ear, mimicking sex.

Berlin released a grumble from her chest.

"You like that don't you?"

She responded with a shrug as she continued to eat her food as if to pretend he didn't affect her.

Reginald chuckled. Well, he'd show her.

His hands slid higher beneath her skirt. When he reached the heated apex between her thighs, he stroked and stroked some more until her breathing changed.

"You like when I stroke your clit?"

Nodding, Berlin dropped the fork and leaned back against his chest. Her legs fell further apart, and Reginald used his palm to rub the entire crotch.

"I want to be all up in that. Stroking. Tasting. Sucking every drop of cum." There was something about teasing her that turned him on. His dick pulsed, making it hard for him to concentrate on simple foreplay. He wanted more.

"You feel that against your ass. You got me hard as a brick."

She released another moan.

"You want me to make you come?"

She nodded, her heavy breathing escaping between her lips.

His hand moved between her inner thighs some more and could feel the heat dampening her panties. He could feel her engorged folds as he traveled higher. This time when he reached her crotch, he used his thumb to tease her clit.

Berlin practically came off his lap. "Yesss!" she cried. "Don't stop."

"Don't stop touching you? You like when I do this." He rubbed along the seam of her folds. Over her clit. At the same time he nibbled and sucked along her neck and ears. He felt her body shudder.

"Oh, yesss."

Reginald moved his other hand to her breast, cupping it, then sought out her hard nipple and rolled it between his thumb and finger. "You like?"

"Yes," she moaned.

Through her pantyhose, he managed to slide his finger underneath her panties and find her swollen clit. She was wet, and he was enjoying every minute of it. "Tell me what you like."

Berlin bucked her hips against his hand. He rubbed harder, pressing into her, soaking his fingers.

"Tell me Berlin," he said, his breathing became jagged. His erection demanding relief.

"I like it…when you play with my nipples," she panted. "I like the way you stroke my…my clit." Her body arched against his hands. She rocked back and forth.

He didn't know how much more he could take. He reached inside her blouse, slipped his fingers into her bra, found her swollen chocolate nipple and captured it between his fingers.

Her body tensed, and he pressed firmly against her clit and rubbed harder. She was so wet, his dick jerked in his pants. That's where he wanted to be. Down there. Inside of her.

"Ooooh!" her body tensed, then trembled against him. "Yesss!" she cried out.

Reginald removed his hand from her blouse and cupped his palm over her mouth as she climaxed. "That's it baby, let it go," he whispered against her cheek. She clung to him. Her breathing was ragged and a series of tremors continued to travel through her body. He about came himself from the thrill of giving her an orgasm for lunch.

He looked over at her. Her eyes were closed and her mouth hanging half open. He wanted her. Right now. Bent over the edge of her desk. Only it wasn't the time. She needed to figure out for herself that he was the right man for her.

"Reggie?"

"Yeah?"

"Thank you. I needed that," she whispered.

His dick throbbed in response. What about him? He needed some, too. He kissed the side of her neck. "Anytime, baby."

"I'm glad you understand that even though I'm sexually attracted to you, I have an agenda."

He did understand. He didn't want to. Didn't want to accept this world she was trying to create with his boy Cameron. But he respected it. He had no other choice.

Chapter Ten

Berlin gazed across the table, trying to stay focused on what Cameron was saying no matter how hard it was getting.

Oh my goodness. Dr. Clarke was a complete bore. For the entire evening, all he had done was talk about himself. First, they went to see the Broadway musical *Wicked.* She had been waiting anxiously for months to see the production when it toured through St. Louis. She was even more thrilled that Cameron managed to get floor seats, two rows from the orchestra. However, only minutes after the show started his mouth began to run nonstop throughout the entire play, analyzing each and every one of the characters. She wanted so badly to tell him to "shut the hell up," but was much too polite for that so she grit her teeth and said nothing.

Afterward, he had taken her to dinner at Shana's, an upscale restaurant in the Central West End, where he took the liberty of ordering dinner for the two of them. Not once had he considered the fact that maybe she didn't like salmon. She did, but that was beside the point. Berlin brought her cup to her lips. It had been an hour since they had first been escorted to a quiet table near a window, and she had barely managed to get in more than two words at a time.

"So," Cameron began, after finally coming up for air. "How do you like living in St. Louis?"

She stopped sipping her espresso, stunned that he had finally asked her a question. Berlin thought she had imagined it, but the still expression on his face told her she hadn't imagined a thing.

"Uuh, I like it. I'm from Chicago and—"

"Chicago? Really. I've been there several times myself. The weather there is just like it is here."

Again, he started rattling on and on about how familiar he was with the Windy City. With a sigh, Berlin reached for her fork and took a bite of white raspberry cheesecake. *Mmmm.* At least she was getting something out of the evening.

While she ate and finished her espresso, she tuned Cameron out of her thoughts. As she gazed down at her plate, she found her thoughts drifting to Reginald. She couldn't help wondering who he was spending the evening with. Not that she cared, but she knew good and well someone as fine as him wasn't alone on a Friday night.

Reginald had been ignoring her since Tuesday. He'd come to her house and work for a couple of hours, then leave. At work, she barely saw him since that afternoon in her office when he had given her an orgasm for lunch. Heat seeped between her thighs just thinking about him. *Oh, my!* Squeezing her thighs together, she pushed the thought aside and reached for her fork.

The waiter arrived with their bill, drawing her attention. Cameron smiled over at her as he reached in his breasts pocket for his wallet.

After removing a platinum credit card and sliding it in with the receipt, Cameron leaned back in his chair wearing a cocky smile. "Well, Berlin, I must say this evening was a success. Don't you agree?"

All she could do was smile with relief that the night was finally over.

Half an hour later he took her hand as he led Berlin up the sidewalk to her front door.

She turned the key in the lock. "Thank you for a wonderful evening."

"The pleasure was all mine."

He leaned forward and pressed his lips against hers. This was what she had dreamed about for weeks; yet the kiss was wet and sloppy and she felt absolutely nothing. She tried to turn her head, but he pushed his tongue between her lips and met hers with clumsy strokes. With a push of her hand, she managed to pull apart.

"I better get in."

"Don't you want to invite me in for a drink?" he asked suggestively.

She faked a yawn. If he thought he was getting some booty tonight, he thought wrong. The sooner she got away from him the better. "I'm really tired, but maybe next time."

He tried to hide his disappointment. A man like him was obviously not use to being turned down by women. *Tough.*

Before he could try and change her mind, she hurried into the house and shut the door. She took a deep breath. She couldn't believe how disappointing the evening had been. Moving up to her room, she quickly shrugged out of her clothes and climbed under the covers. Reginald was due in the morning, and she couldn't wait to see him.

Berlin was up early the next morning making breakfast when she heard Reginald's truck pull into the driveway. Quickly, she raced into the bathroom in the hall and checked her face and hair. She was smoothing down the front of her red blouse when the doorbell rang.

She had to make herself slow down as she moved to the door.

Her breath caught in her lungs. He had a fresh cut and the earring in his lobe glittered against the sun.

"Hey."

"Whassup. Let's get this morning started."

Without even cracking a smile, he brushed past her and moved toward the family room.

"Would you like some breakfast?" she called after him.

"Nope. Ate on the way over."

Frustrated she returned to the kitchen to eat alone.

Reginald moved into the guest room. He planned to have the first coat completed before lunchtime. He carried his boom box over to one of the huge windows, taking up the majority of wall space that flooded the room with light. The radiant sun filled the room, highlighting the greenery surrounding the opposite end of the room. Hanging plants had been removed and carefully placed on newspaper on a long dresser to the far right. Plastic had already been draped across the chaise to protect the ecru printed fabric.

He stuck a Kanye West CD in his boom box and got to work. He was secretly upset with her for her going out with his boy. He couldn't understand it, especially since he didn't care that much for her. As he dipped his brush in paint, he asked himself why he was even trying to fool himself. Despite her siddity ways, he liked her and couldn't stop thinking about her. Last night his mind burned with memories. Her cries of delight raced through his brain and her scent, even though he had bathed several times, still lingered on his hands. Feeling a strong need to be with her, he had to resist the urge to drive by her house early this morning to see if Cameron's Jaguar was parked in her driveway.

Reggie man, you need your head examined. Yeah, that was probably true, but right now he'd rather ignore his opinions of Ms. Dupree and her ten-step plan, and follow his instincts.

The smell of amber flooded the room. He glanced over his shoulder to find Berlin standing in the doorway.

"Berlin Dupree, reporting to duty."

His breath stalled. She was wearing a pair of green spandex shorts and a T-shirt that had "Got Milk?" across the breasts.

Milk definitely does a body good, he thought as his eyes traveled from her ponytail down to her pink painted toes. How in the world was he supposed to work with her looking that good? There was only so much spandex a brotha could take, and her outfit hugged every curve including her breasts.

"Don't worry about it. I can get this room done myself."

"Too bad. Like you said before, the more I help the sooner we'll get done."

She reached for a brush while he filled a tray with paint. He taped off a wall for her since she didn't have a steady hand like he did. All the while, he watched her breasts jiggle.

Reginald swallowed. "Don't you have something…uh, old to wear?" he asked, hoping like hell she did.

Berlin glanced down at her clothes, then back up at him again. "This is old." She swayed toward him. "What's wrong with what I'm wearing?" she pushed her chest forward and her breasts rose.

"Nothing."

"You're lying," she challenged.

"You're right. I am lying, but you don't want to know what I'm thinking 'cause if you did, you'd race back to your room and change into something else."

For a long moment neither of them said anything. She stared up at him with surprise, lips parted invitingly. From her expression he could tell she had no idea how tempting she looked.

"I'll be right back."

Watching her leave, Reginald sighed with relief.

Berlin returned in less than five minutes in a pair of faded loose-fitting jeans and an oversized T-shirt. "Is this better?"

His lips curved upward. "Much."

Berlin reached for the brush and moved to the wall facing the window.

She was thankful for the music. Although the rap wasn't her taste, she decided to leave her comment to herself rather than risk working side by side in silence.

They had been working for about fifteen minutes before Reginald finally asked, "How was your date?"

She wondered how long it would take before he asked. Without looking in his direction, she answered, "Okay."

"Just okay?"

There was no way she would let him know her date had been a flop. "I had a good time."

Reginald snorted rudely. "Yeah, knowing Cameron, I'm sure you did."

Berlin stopped painting and turned toward him with her hand on her hip. "What does that mean?"

He continued painting. "It means I know my boy. And he definitely knows how to have a good time."

"Well he may know how to have a good time, but he definitely didn't with me," she answered defensively. "We went and saw a play and had dinner. End of story." Berlin didn't know why she felt obligated to explain to him, but it burned her up when someone assumed something about her that wasn't true.

"Uh-huh," he mumbled under his breath as if he didn't believe a word she had said.

Irritated, Berlin tossed her paintbrush at him and got him square on the back of his arm. It wasn't until she saw the look of retaliation on his face that she regretted her move. "Don't do something stupid," she warned as she slowly backed away.

"Now why would I do that," Reginald said as he moved forward.

She held her hands up in surrender. "Okay, I'm sorry, really."

"Sure you are."

Before she could take off, he caught her by the arm and wrestled her kicking and screaming to the plastic covered floor. No matter how hard she tried to guard her face, soft bristles brushed across her cheeks and forehead. She couldn't help laughing as she fought to no success with him chuckling along with her. She wasn't sure when the laughter had stopped and she gazed up at him and realized he was straddling her hips. The look in his eyes told her he was well aware. She swallowed, then racked her brain for something catchy to say.

"I guess I now look a sight."

He shook his head. "No, you're still as beautiful as ever," he whispered, then he felt her squirm beneath him.

"Babe, I respect my boy, but if you don't stop moving, I'm going to do something that you might regret later."

She tilted her chin." What's that?" she challenged.

His lips felt firm and hot against hers, demanding her to react. Desire flowed through her, building slow then bursting in every direction. He lowered on top of her, and instinctively she wound her arms around his neck, pulling him closer. Unconsciously, her lips parted and Reginald swept his tongue inside. She kissed him back, meeting his mouth with matching passion. She heard a long, uneven sigh of pleasure, and recognized it as her own. Heat exploded inside her mouth as his tongue moved skillfully inside her mouth. Against her stomach his arousal was impossible to hide. She could feel his dick buck in his pants. She wanted it. It had come from an emotion so deep; she didn't even know it existed. All she knew was that if he tried to make love to her, she wouldn't give him any resistance. A jolt sent the blood rushing down between her legs. Startled, Berlin sucked in a quick breath, the kiss halted momentarily.

"We're going to have to stop this," he murmured heavily, his warm, thick breath fanning her burning cheek. He then rolled off her and rose.

"I guess we got a little carried away," he said, reaching for her hand to help her up.

Berlin nodded, then reached out her hand and allowed him to help her off the floor. She wanted him and all that was straining against his pants. She lowered her eyes to his crotch and was pleased to see he was still hard. If she could just hold it, taste it, feel it just one time, she—

"You might want to go get that paint off your face before it dries," he said interrupting her thoughts.

Eager to escape, she nodded and practically ran down the hall to the bathroom. As soon as she was alone, she leaned against the sink and closed her eyes. Taking several deep breaths, she tried to slow her heart, which rattled her whole chest. What was she thinking, kissing him like that, she scolded. There was no telling what he now thought of her. She was dating Cameron, and here she was spending the afternoon rolling on the floor with his best friend. She should be ashamed of herself.

So why aren't you?

While splashing cold water on her face, she took a few seconds to think about it. Kissing Cameron was absolutely nothing like the kiss she had just shared with Reginald. Instantly, her fingers went to her still sizzling lips. She straightened and looked at her face in the mirror with paint streaks still on both cheeks. Reaching for a bar of moisturizing soap on a ceramic holder, she rubbed it across her hands, then lathered her face and neck.

Reginald wiped the paint from his tingling lips and face, and then reached for the paintbrush. He hadn't meant for things to get out of control, but he just couldn't help himself. Something about Berlin made him temporarily lose his sanity. And the way she had melted against him, responding to his kisses with passion made the task of leaving her alone almost impossible. She made him crazy with desire.

Shifting, he tried like hell to calm the raging hard-on Berlin had left him with. If he hadn't gotten her out of the room when he had, he would have made an even bigger fool of himself. He was throbbing. In pain with no relief.

He scowled. Here he was hard as a rock over a woman who was dating his homeboy. It just wasn't fair. Unfortunately, that's just the way life was.

Regardless of how bad he wanted her, he had no right disrespecting his boy the way he was. If the shoe had been on the other foot, he definitely wouldn't want his homeboy disrespecting him like this. Somehow he would have to keep reminding himself that Berlin was off limits. As far as he was concerned, Berlin already belonged to Cameron.

Hearing footsteps, he glanced over his shoulder to find Berlin standing in the doorway.

"Looks like you didn't have a hard time getting the paint off," he said with a smirk.

"Nothing a little soap and water can't fix. Um," she began, and then dropped her gaze briefly to the floor. "I think I'm going to spend the rest of the afternoon Christmas shopping, that's if you think you can handle the work without me."

He stopped painting long enough to glance at her waiting expression. "I think I can handle it."

She lowered her eyes again. "Good, then I'll see you later." With that said, she turned and headed down the hall to her room.

Arianna waited until they had finally gotten a seat at the Cheesecake Factory before she asked the question Berlin had been avoiding all afternoon.

"Okay, Berlin, I want to know how your date went last night."

Berlin carefully placed her packages on the seat beside her, then looked up at her good friend and rolled her eyes. "Boring."

"Boring?" Arianna's eyes grew large with disbelief. "Oh my goodness, you're saying Mack Daddy Wannabe, Dr. Cameron Clarke is a drag?"

"Dang, Arianna, why do you have to be so loud," she scowled as she glanced around to see if anyone had heard. "You putting that man's business all out in the street."

She chuckled. "My bad." Resting her elbows on the table, she leaned forward and spoke in a lower voice. "So what was boring? The dinner or the sex?"

"Sex? Who said anything about sex?" Berlin gave her friend a disappointed look. "We saw a play and had dinner and that's it."

"That's it? Well no wonder your evening was boring. You should have suggested going somewhere where y'all could have slow danced and held each other and really got know what y'all are about."

Berlin reached for her menu. She doubted dancing and drinks would have made that much of a difference. "I don't know. He's just not at all what I had expected."

"That's because you want him to be like his boy Reggie."

"I do not!" she cried defensively.

"Look at you, getting all upset. You like Reginald and just don't want to admit it."

Dropping her eyes to the menu, she released a sigh. The last thing she needed was for Arianna to see it in her eyes. If she knew she had spent most of the evening wishing Cameron were more like Reginald, she would never hear the end of it. Just thinking about Reginald made her panties wet.

"Maybe you're right," she said after a long thoughtful minute. "I think next time Cameron and I need to go dancing."

Arianna gave her a long stare. "You think you're slick don't you?"

"Yep."

They started laughing. Their waitress arrived and took their orders. She wasn't really hungry but ordered a large slice of New York-Style Cheesecake and a large cup of black coffee. Arianna included a sandwich with her order.

"So how's the painting coming along?" her friend asked after their waitress left.

The mention of Reginald caused her heart to flutter. "Actually, quite well. I think he'll be done in plenty of time."

"Good. I'm dying to see your place," she replied, eyes sparkling with interest. "You better invite me over to your house. Otherwise, don't be surprised if I just show up at your door."

Berlin smiled over at her friend. "You're welcome to come and join me and my parents for Christmas dinner."

"Sounds wonderful. Just let me know. Carlton has to work, so I was planning to spend Christmas alone."

From the look on Arianna's face, she could tell she wasn't too happy about the idea, but as a St. Louis County police officer, he didn't have much of a choice. It was his turn to work a holiday. "What are you getting him for Christmas?"

She batted her eyelashes. "He doesn't need anything. He already has me."

Berlin pretended to choke on her water. "Yeah, right."

"I was thinking about getting him a new leather jacket."

She nodded, then found herself remembering how good Reginald looked in his. She was a strong believer that clothes can completely transform a man. However, Reginald had the ability to look good in just about anything he wore.

"What are you thinking about?"

She swallowed. "Nothing."

"Girl, listen. If you don't hop on Reginald while you have the chance, someone else will." Arianna leaned back in her chair. "Shoot, if I wasn't married, I'd be all over his fine behind."

Berlin was shocked at the jealousy she felt at her good friend's statement.

Oh boy, I'm in a world of trouble.

Hours later, Berlin returned home with a trunk filled with gifts and totally exhausted. She pulled into her driveway expecting to see that Reginald had gone home, and a part of her was pleased to see he was still there. As soon as she climbed out the car, he came down the walk to help her with her bags. "Looks like you had fun."

She returned his smile. "I did. I really did."

He took the bags from her hands, moved into the house and set them n the kitchen table while she removed her coat and hung it on the back f one of the kitchen chairs.

"I finished the first coat. Tomorrow I'll put on the second coat."

"Sounds good."

He took her hand and led her into the family room. She stared, speechless. There was a fire roaring and a bottle of champagne in a bucket of ice, chilling on the coffee table with two flute glasses beside it. But what got her attention most was the black table he had set up in the center of the room.

"What's that?" she finally said.

"A massage table." His gaze traveled from the table to her, and she thought her skin might sizzle from the weight of his stare. "I'm a certified massage therapist."

The word sent quivers through her stomach.

"Tonight I want date number two."

She started shaking her head. "I really don't feel like going out—"

He placed his fingertips to her lips. "Nobody asked you to go out. What I want you to do is go up to your room, put on something comfortable and come back down so I can help you relax."

She was speechless.

"Go," he ordered. He then leaned forward and pressed his lips gently against hers. As soon as she moaned, he pulled back, swung around, and swatted her on the butt. "Now get."

She moved up to her room and lowered onto the bed. She was definitely in trouble. The last thing she needed was for Reginald to be feeling all over her body. Because if he touched her in the right spot, she doubted she would be able to say no. She was surprised he even wanted to touch her after the way he had reacted earlier when she had put paint on his arm.

Reluctantly, she slipped into a pair of sweat pants and a T-shirt and came back down the stairs.

Reginald was standing in the family room. The big stone fireplace was ablaze and gleaming on the wood paneling and hardwood floors, broken by thick woven rugs.

"Come have a seat," he said, slipping over to the two slender flutes beside the bucket. "We'll have a drink, then I'll have you climb up on the table."

Popping the cork on the bottle, he poured bubbling froth into the chilled glasses. She took a seat on the opposite end of the couch and curled her legs beneath her.

He held out a glass of champagne to her and raised his own with the other hand. "Here's to you and Cameron. May he be everything you want in a man."

She tapped her glass lightly against his, then brought the flute to her lips. The room was silent except for the sound of Floetry vibrating through the room.

"So tell me a little about yourself," she said. The flames crackled, fire-light flickering on his face, catching his hair.

Reginald found her question amusing. "What would you like to know that I haven't already told you?"

She knew the question was dumb, but she needed to do something to take her mind off the romantic mood he set. "You are very talented. Are you any good at art? Like watercolors and acrylics?" she asked, thinking about the abstracts Arianna's husband called art.

He frowned. "Neither."

Okay, let's try this again. "What made you decide to become a painter?"

Leaning forward, he rested his forearms on his knees. "I like seeing something better. With a quick trip to the nearest home improvement store, a person can transform their home into something they'll be forever proud of," he said between sips.

"Do you own or rent?"

"I own. I bought a rundown house a couple of years ago, gutted it out and have slowly been renovating it."

"You have a great eye. I can imagine your home could be displayed in a magazine."

He grinned. "Something like that."

"I would like to see it."

"I plan for you to see it soon." He put his glass down. "Now quit stalling."

"Stalling?"

He nodded then rose. "Yeah stalling. Go climb onto the table."

Taking a deep calming breath, she moved over to the table and climbed onto it. As soon as she was comfortable, Reginald reached out and took one of her feet into his hands and began kneading it softly. The act brought tears to Berlin's eyes. Never before had she been treated to such tender foreplay. In his hands, she felt like a delicate piece of art.

From her toes he massaged his way along her ankles to her calves, pausing along the way to give each area extra attention. By the time he reached her thighs, Berlin was moaning. Unaware of the sounds coming from her lips, she was conscious of his warm skillful hands creeping where she needed to feel him most.

Berlin fought to stay still and to keep from begging him to touch her there between her parted thighs. His hands slid beneath her T-shirt, caressing the feminine curves of her tummy. When he cupped her bare breasts, she cried out his name.

"Yes, baby?"

"Please!"

"Please what?"

Before she could answer, he leaned down and suckled her breasts, worshipping each equally. She cried out as he kissed her so thoroughly that she yearned for him to slide down her pants and lay between her thighs.

He must have read her mind, because his lips traveled down to her belly button.

"Slide your pants down," he ordered.

She immediately lifted her hips and did as he requested. As soon as her legs were spread invitingly, Reginald slid two fingers inside and fingered her until she was dripping wet.

"Please, make love to me."

"I won't be second best, Berlin. Either you want Cameron or you want me."

Damn him! Why did they have to have this discussion now? All she wanted was for him to slide inside her aching sex and satisfy her needs. "I want you now, isn't that enough?"

"You can't have it both ways." His lips curled into a frown. "What's it gonna be, Berlin?"

She sat up on the table, staring at him. She couldn't think straight, let alone have a serious conversation, yet Reginald wanted to know where he stood before he made love to her. She was offering him her stuff for the night, what more did he need to hear? Apparently, he wanted to know if she still wanted Cameron. She didn't think so, especially not at this particular time.

Berlin was prepared to ask him to follow her up to her room, when her phone rang.

"Hold that thought," she said as she climbed off the table and reached for a throw from the couch and covered her body before moving into the kitchen.

"Hello."

"Hey, sweetheart."

She shuddered at the sound of Cameron's voice.

"I've been thinking about you all day and wanted to know if you wanted to have dinner with me Monday night at Landry's down at Union Station?"

She closed her eyes, realizing she had been seconds away from sleeping with Reginald before the phone had rang. If she had, she would have ruined any chance of ever being with Cameron.

"Sure, dinner sounds great."

By the time she ended the call and returned to the family room, Reginald was packing up the table. She stood close by, watching him and wishing things could be different. With the table tucked under his arm, he gazed up at her for a long moment.

"Have you decided what you wanted to do?"

She swallowed and hoped since he had come from the same place she had, he understood. "I can't."

He nodded. "I'll see you at work on Monday."

A Delight Before Christmas

The minute Reginald stepped through his door; he moved into the master bath and took a cold shower.

The girl had managed to wiggle her way into his mind and his heart. And he didn't like it. He wasn't ready yet to admit how much she had come to mean to him. All he knew was that right now no one would satisfy his need but her.

Chapter Eleven

Cameron was a nice man and would be an excellent provider, if their relationship ever reached that point. But there would never be any of the passion—that she knew. His kiss had been mild and unresponsive, not at all like the way Reginald made her feel. Reginald had a way of making her toes curl and gave her a hot run-and-tell feeling that singed her insides.

Sighing, Berlin leaned back in the chair and closed her eyes. Saturday night had taken all the strength she had to turn down Reginald's offer. He'd had her so tempted, and so damn horny she didn't know how much longer she could go without the real thing. Yesterday he had barely said three words to her. She knew something had to give real soon. She didn't know how much longer she could go without sex. Her nipples constantly yearned for attention while her sex begged for release.

Berlin forced herself to get back to work. It was Monday and her last official day until after the holiday season. Reaching for her mouse, she opened another final report and tried to concentrate. Instead, her mind kept wandering down Reginald's pants. Yummy was the best way to describe him. What he had she could easy lick like an ice cream cone.

She was sitting, staring at her computer screen still, thinking about him when Arianna entered. Forcing herself to reach for her mouse, she tried her best not to look distracted. Glancing up over at the door, she raised an eyebrow in question. "What?"

"Uh," she hesitated, then shrugged her shoulders. "Reggie and I were talking, and we both agree you shouldn't go out with Dr. Clarke. He isn't right for you."

Stunned, didn't even begin to describe how she felt. She couldn't believe what she was hearing. "How in the world," she began, but Arianna interrupted.

"Girl, are you crazy! Reginald is crazy about you."

Her face heated. "Did he tell you that?"

"Well, not in so many words, but I realize he'd probably never ever admit his feelings either because, guess what, he's as stubborn as you are."

She frowned as Arianna slid back out the door before she could give her a piece of her mind. She was upset that her dear friend was once again meddling in her life. True, Cameron was self-centered and boring as all get out. While with Reginald she was guaranteed, laughter and passion. She was certain if they slept together she would receive sexual satisfaction from that man. However, weeks…okay, maybe months…all right, years from now after she had filled her sexual appetite, she would come down from cloud nine and find once again she had settled for less than she had dreamed of living. Berlin groaned and swung around in her chair and stared out at the snow falling lightly from the sky. Why were the two of them trying to push her into a corner?

Angrily, she swung around and reached for the phone. She immediately punched in Reggie's cellular phone number.

"Hey, boo, if you were missing me, all you had to do was walk around to the playroom and come see me."

She ignored the vibrant sound of his voice and took a deep breath. "Look, you and Arianna need to mind your own business. I'm a grown woman and don't need you telling me who I can and can not see. If I want to date Cameron, then that is my business, not yours. Besides, I really doubt your boy would appreciate knowing you are meddling in his business."

There was a long pause. "Are you finished?"

"Yep."

"Good. I won't be over tonight because I've got plans. But don't worry, I'll still get the work finished on time."

The fact that he acted like he didn't care bothered her. "That's fine. Cameron and I are going to Landry's for dinner tonight."

"Sounds like a boring evening. I hope you get everything you're looking for." He abruptly ended the call. For the longest time she sat there holding the receiver, then placed it in its cradle. Why did she suddenly feel so sad?

Snap out of it!

She slumped back in the chair, wearing a confused look. She was losing too much sleep over that man, which was exactly why he was not the right man for her. She didn't need an emotional attachment. Her whole reason for dating Cameron was for the prestige and security a doctor could provide her. She wasn't interested in love. Feeling confident again that she was making the right choice, she reached for her keyboard and resumed working on the proposal.

Later that evening, Berlin waited until she was certain Reginald had left before leaving for the night. She then hurried home to get ready for her date with Cameron. As she stepped through the door, she was tempted to cancel. She didn't want to admit it, but she would rather spend the evening helping Reggie paint.

That's why you need to go.

True, the only way she would get over him was to start focusing on her relationship with Cameron. Reluctantly, she moved to her room, made her way to the bathroom and started the shower. She covered her hair with a shower cap, then stripped off her clothes, dropped them onto the floor and stepped under the spray of water. Within minutes she forgot about how torn she was about her feelings. She forgot about how angry she had been this afternoon. What she couldn't forget was the way Reginald's hands had felt on her body. The water beat against her nipples that were aching and begging for Reginald's touch. She cupped her breasts and thumbed her nipples, pretending it was him. Closing her eyes, she fantasized he was in the shower with her. She pressed a palm to her belly and slowly inched her hand lower past the nest of curly hair. Reaching the hood covering her clit, she unveiled its throbbing head and a soft moan escaped her as the hot water beat against it. Her breathing became ragged as she imagined it was his hand exploring the deep apex between her thighs. Her fingers traveled lower, and she spread her legs, allowing plenty of room to explore her heat. When she reached her engorged folds, she pushed two fingers between them. She drove long and deep, speeding up the tempo as she pretended it was his ten working her over until she felt her muscles tighten. Squeezing her thighs together, she released a loud moan as her body was shook by an orgasm.

While trying to catch her breath, Berlin screamed with frustration. Boy was she in trouble! Reginald controlled her mind and her body. She had never been considered easy; however, maybe if she slept with Cameron she would forget about Reginald once and for all. If Cameron made a pass tonight, she would invite him to share her bed.

Berlin accepted the apple martini from the bartender and smiled. "Thank you," she replied as she raised the glass to her lips.

"Did I tell you how fabulous you look tonight?"

She glanced across the table at Cameron and forced a smile. "Yes, I think at least three times."

"Sorry, I can't resist. If I don't say so myself, you and I are the hottest looking couple in here tonight. You in your slamming dress and me in my black slacks and dress shirt with cuff links and tiepin. Did I mention I was wearing Brooke Brothers?"

Three damn times. "No, I don't remember you mentioning that." She rolled her eyes and took another sip from her glass. What in the world was she thinking that tonight would be better than the last? Instead, it was worse. Cameron was so full of himself. How in the world had she thought he was everything she wanted? The sooner the evening was over the better. The idea of the two of them sleeping together was now a faded memory.

During the course of the meal, she questioned why the hell she'd agreed to go out with him again. He had gotten on her last nerve the last time they had gone out together. There was no connection between them. Despite the fact that he was a doctor and was good looking, he didn't make her juices flow or her panties wet. Yet she had agreed because she needed a distraction from the one man who had the ability to make her come in her panties just by saying her name.

Reginald was the reason why she had agreed to a second date. She needed something to take her mind off him.

Now she wished she could take it all back. She wished she had never answered that phone on Saturday. And that she had agreed to his offer to make love to her. Just thinking about Reginald made her want to sprint out the restaurant and run home and invite him over to her house. But she couldn't do that because then he would know he had been right all along.

"My parents are spending Christmas in Jamaica."

Berlin looked across the table and smiled. "That sounds nice. I've never been to Jamaica."

He gave her a cocky smile, then reached across the table and touched her hand. "If you play your cards right, I just might take you after my surgical rotation," he concluded with a wink.

Tempting offer. She wondered if she could stand all his yapping long enough to enjoy a vacation to the much-talked about island.

"I'm leaving tomorrow to hang out for the week with my parents, but I'll be back from Minneapolis on Sunday in time to spend Christmas with you and your family."

What? Her eyes locked with his. Cameron wanted to spend Christmas together. She saw the serious look in his brown eyes and her pulse jumped. Was he really planning to meet her family? *Oh my goodness.* Things were going exactly like she had hoped.

So why am I not happy?

She grew quiet, and Cameron didn't seem to notice since once again he started talking about himself and dominated the conversation.

Taking another sip, she looked over her shoulder and froze. Nothing moved, not even her eyes. She spotted Dr. Joyce Worley, a pediatrician at their clinic with her arm curled around a man who made her mouth water.

Reggie.

Her body went numb. *Is he here with her? What do you think?* Of course he was here with her. Surprise dissolved into anger and her hands clenched into fists when Reginald leaned forward and whispered something close to her ear that made her to laugh.

Dammit, it was bad enough to see him with Dr. Worley, but to see him leaning in close enough to kiss her was enough to make her sick to her stomach.

She had never seen him look so good in her life. He was wearing charcoal slacks with a black and gray sweater and matching knit hat.

She watched him standing at the front of the restaurant, smiling down at his date. It occurred to her that she hadn't seen his smile all today, and realized how much she'd missed it. She watched him help Joyce slip out of her coat. Jealousy brewed. Her red dress clung to every slender curve. She looked good and knew it.

Damn, she hated seeing him with such a beautiful woman. If she hadn't been so determined not to sleep with him, if she had been thinking with a little more sense, she wouldn't be sitting here right now feeling like a fool. Damn, she hoped he didn't see them.

His gaze lifted then, almost as if he had read her thoughts. Even from across the room, she could see that sexy smile curve his mouth.

Before she could prepare herself, the two of them walked over to their table.

"Cameron, man, what's up?"

He rose, looked from one to the other appearing surprised, then grinned sheepishly. "Reggie, Joyce, well, well, well. I would have never guessed the two of you had anything in common," he said, leaning toward her to give her a quick hug.

Reggie reached over and gave him a pound. "You'd be surprised," he said before he turned and trained his eyes on Berlin. "Joyce, you know Berlin, right?"

The beautiful doctor glanced over and gave her a sincere smile. "Sure I do. How are you?"

Berlin forced a smile. There was no way she would let either of them know how much it bothered her to see them together. "Fine, and yourself?"

She looked up at Reggie. "Wonderful," she purred seductively.

It took everything she had not to say something she would regret later. It was killing her to see Joyce gawking at Reggie like he was a new pair of shoes.

"Why don't you join us?" Cameron gestured at the two empty chairs.

"No thank you," Joyce jumped in. "I want this man all to myself," she added, her tone making it clear she wanted what was in his pants as well. With that she took his arm and escorted him to the front where the maître d' was ready to escort them to their own table.

Berlin reached for her glass and finished it with one gulp.

"Would you like another drink?" Cameron asked.

She nodded as she looked over again at the couple. "Matter of fact, make that two."

Berlin might have kissed him and allowed him to taste her in the most intimate way, but Reggie had obviously been wrong in believing that showing up with a date would make her think twice about her decision. His own plan had backfired on him, and as much as he wanted to tell his boy Cameron to keep his hands off her, he couldn't.

From across the room he continued to watch her. God, she was beautiful. He couldn't look away. The short, black dress clung to every feminine curve and dipped low enough in the front to cause an erection in every man in the restaurant. Black stiletto boots made her legs appear even longer. He could barely breathe.

He turned abruptly and focused on his date. Dr. Worley had been trying to get his attention for the last couple of days. At first he had ignored her advances, but after realizing Berlin intended to follow through with her plans to date his boy, he decided to see what all of the hype was about. He managed to make it through the rest of the dinner and made a point of looking straight ahead, but he realized that he was only using Joyce. Although she was beautiful and looked sexy as hell in that dress, she didn't make his dick hard.

By dessert he glanced over to his right and noticed that they were gone. He couldn't help wondering if Berlin had taken Cameron back to her house with her.

A Delight Before Christmas

By the time they left the restaurant it was snowing again. He engaged in idle conversation, but it was obvious to both of them by the end of the evening that they had absolutely nothing in common. He walked Joyce to her door and, following a kiss to her cheek, climbed back into his Escalade and headed toward home.

As he drove he tried hard not to think about Berlin, but it was almost impossible. He wanted her as he had never wanted any woman before. His feelings were beyond sex. He cared for Berlin. From the very first time he'd laid eyes on her, she'd stirred a response in him he never felt for anyone else. As he stared out in front of him, he realized that he was confused because he wasn't sure what he was feeling beyond overpowering desire. He only knew when he had vowed to never fall in love again, he had no idea such a wonderful woman would enter his life.

He white-knuckled the steering wheel as he zoomed up the road, trying to push aside the images of Berlin in that dress. The snow was coming down harder. He spotted several stranded cars on either sides of the road. He decided to slow down and pay attention and stop thinking about her, but he couldn't help it. Halfway home he made a sharp u-turn at the corner and headed toward Berlin's. He had to know if Cameron was there spending the night with her. He had to know where they stood. Not knowing would eat him up inside.

As he eased into her subdivision, he tried to talk himself out of pulling into her driveway. All he planned to do was drive by and see if Cameron's Jaguar was in the driveway. If it was, he would keep on going. But as he pulled up to her house, his shoulders sagged with relief to see the driveway was empty and a light upstairs in her bedroom was on.

Before he realized what he was doing, he had pulled into the driveway and climbed out of the SUV. He didn't even remember ringing the doorbell. Shortly after, he heard footsteps and the door swung open. He glanced down at Berlin's surprised face.

"I couldn't stay away," he admitted.

Her face softened. "I had hoped as much."

She stepped into his arms and tilted her face up for a kiss. He pressed his lips to hers, then pulled back and stared down in her face. He saw desire that mirrored his and he also saw fear.

"Come in." Berlin stepped aside so that he could enter, then she waited for what he had to say.

His eyes settled on her, and then she stepped closer. Gazing up at him, she licked her lips. Man, did she know how to turn a brotha on. His dick was screaming for release. She took another step closer. He could tell she had just gotten out of the shower. Her skin looked damp and her fragrance was fresh mixed with a floral body spray.

"So now that you're here, what are we going to do?" she whispered.

Reggie reached out and brushed a finger across her cheek. "As soon as I take your clothes off, I'm going to make love to you."

"Oh, really?" A slow inviting smile curled her lips, and then she allowed her robe to fall to the floor. "You think you can handle all this?"

Hell, yeah he could handle all that, he thought, as he took in every last curve in a short see-through nightie. She was sexy as hell. Her honey-colored skin glistened while her large breasts strained against the material. He needed to be inside of her as badly as he needed to take his next breath.

He reached for her at the same time she leaned toward him. "I sho in the hell gonna try." As he prepared to kiss her, Berlin turned her head. "What's wrong?"

She looked up at him. "Before we go any further, I need to make one thing clear. This can only be temporary. I still have an agenda, and that's to marry a doctor. So you have to agree after the holidays we'll both go our own separate ways."

Reggie smiled. "Deal. I leave for Memphis Christmas morning."

She swallowed, realizing she had finally decided to let Reginald Hodges make love to her. "Then Christmas it is." Slowly, she lifted her arms around his neck and pressed her breasts against his chest, then lifted her face to his.

"Tell me what you want," he said, his voice thick with need. Despite the throbbing of his dick, he wasn't going to touch her unless she asked him to.

"Kiss me," she ordered.

He hauled her into his arms and carried her into the living room. Moving over to the couch, he lifted her over, and she straddled his lap, then his mouth found hers.

The liquor on his breath caused her senses to spin. While his tongue invaded her mouth, his hands slowly slid down her side, fingertips teasing the sides of her breasts. Then his hands closed over her hips and he wiggled back and forth, tantalizing her with his hard dick thrust against her belly. Her nipples tightened beneath the thin material. She wanted him—*badly.*

Reginald slid one strap of her nightgown over her shoulder and cupped her breasts. Kneading and squeezing until she was moaning and moving restlessly against his lap. He leaned forward and circled the nipple with his tongue. Her head fell back with ecstasy. He licked and sucked slowly at first, then faster. Her nipples swelled and she moaned. The walls of her sex contracted and released.

"You like," he asked as he transferred his attention to her other breast.

"I like," she moaned as his tongue caused wetness to moisten her inner thighs.

Oh, hell yes. This was what she needed. She had been denying herself sexual release for too long, well the wait was finally over. She needed him, and she needed him now.

"Reggie, forget the foreplay, I need to feel you inside me right now."

He rose and began unbuttoning his jeans. They dropped to his ankles along with his underwear and he stepped free. *Oh my goodness.* Groaning, she took it all in. He was fine as hell. Her eyes traveled down. She thought it was only something she'd read about or seen in those x-rated magazines that she shouldn't have been sneaking and looking at. Even then she thought the camera had somehow enlarged it. Yet, here one was right in front of her, and there was nothing imaginary about what she saw. Reginald was hung. He would fill her to capacity. There was no denying that she wanted him. As he slipped on a condom, all she could do was watch. She couldn't find the words to speak. She was so caught up she couldn't move. He was lean and hard, and his dick was pointing right at her. She wanted so badly to touch him.

To suck him.

To demand he lay on his back so that she could slide all ten inches in and ride him. Instead, she moved over to a large area rug on the floor in front of the fireplace and parted her thighs, then signaled for him to join her. "Come here."

Reginald moved over, then lowered in front of her, his breathing audible even over the slithery sound of sleet pelting the windows. "The first time will be fast, but before this night is over, I plan on giving you everything until you beg me to stop."

"I'm ready," she said, spreading her legs wider.

"Tell me you want me," he demanded as the head rubbed against her inner thighs.

She swallowed hard. "I want you."

"What about Cameron?"

"It's you I want. Not him."

He smiled, obviously pleased at her answer. "Where do you want me?"

"Inside of me," she purred.

"I'll be gentle," he said as she removed his sweater over his head.

"Don't." She was so wet she didn't know how much longer she could wait. Her legs quivered as he slipped a finger inside her heat.

"You like that?"

"Yes," she whimpered. "But I want more, please."

"Tell me what you want," he asked while lightly stroking her clit.

"I want to feel you," she reached down between them and found his length and squeezed. "I want to feel this inside of me. *Now!*"

He pushed at the entrance, and she guided him inside. The room grew silent as they both took a moment to control themselves before he started the ride.

He pulled all the way out, and Berlin started to whimper. Then he pushed all ten inside of her again.

"Ooohhh!" she cried as he pumped a couple of long, hard strokes. She was surprised she could handle all of him at once, but as wet as she was her body quickly accommodated him. Only he didn't stay long. Reggie pulled out again and using his hand teased the swollen head of his dick along both folds and up to her clit where he pressed and teased some more. Damn him, he was going to make her beg.

And she had no problems whatsoever with that. "Please," she cried.

He ignored her request and traveled up to the patch of hair and stroked across, then down to her clit where he pressed and teased some more, then back up to her belly button. Her body was screaming for penetration, and he was taking his sweet time.

"Reggie, dammit! Give it to me."

"How bad do you want it?"

"So bad I feel like I'm going to explode! Please, I need to feel you inside of me."

On cue, he slammed deep inside her again, and she cried out at the overwhelming feeling building inside of her. Once he got started, this time he didn't quit. He plunged with deep, long strokes she felt all the way to her core. *Oh, yeah, now that's what I'm talking about.* Each time he would slide all the way out, and then drive back in hard, slapping his balls against her ass again.

He kept up the rhythm, and she knew it wouldn't be long before she reached an orgasm. It was inevitable after days of teasing and foreplay, she had known when she finally had sex an orgasm would come quick. Her back came off the floor when Reginald slipped his hand down between them and found her clit with his fingers. He stroked and teased until her hips were rocking and meeting the hard thrust of his dick. It wasn't long before she knew she was about to come. Her body grew hot and her walls contracted and her entire body shook, leaving her breathless and dizzy.

Reginald used both his hands to raise his body over her. In a push-up motion, he lowered and lifted, pounding all ten hard inside her. Her walls gripped him for dear life, and he grounded his hips and thrust even deeper. Flesh slapped against flesh. Everything was perfect. He knew how to give pleasure, and she was enjoying everything deep plunging minute. She could feel the pulsing of his dick, and knew he was losing control. He tried to slow down, to ease into her. Reaching between them, she stroked her clit and began to tremble around him, ready for another orgasm. She arched higher, panting, moaning, meeting each thrust. Her muscles tightened, and she cried out, "Ohhhh!" Her body shuddered, then climaxed.

Reginald increased the speed and pumped even harder until she felt his warm breath against her damp skin as he groaned then finally cried out victoriously, "Hell, yeah!" He came hard and shook. He collapsed on top of her, kissing her cheeks, neck and lips. Rolling over, he pulled her into his arms and closed his eyes as his breathing slowed.

Hours later when Berlin's breathing deepened into a sound of peaceful sleep, Reginald lay awake studying her. Smart, stubborn and downright sexy, she was unlike anyone he'd ever known. Despite her years of trying to reinvent herself and adapting a new lifestyle, she was a sweet and vulnerable woman that touched something so deep inside. He trembled as he kissed her lips. Reginald felt a pull at his heart as he watched her sleep.

Berlin said sex was overrated. But he intended to show her how good it could be. The dudes she'd been with had been weak in their game. He was more than happy to teach her. Just thinking about how good it felt being inside her, he felt himself growing hard again. A smile curled his lips. He was getting ready to teach her what it was like to wake up to a long hard dick buried deep inside of her.

Reaching down, he found her clit and circled. Her thighs collapsed and a moan escaped her lips.

"Wake up, Berlin," he whispered close to her ear.

165

She shifted slightly then grumbled, "Why?"

"Because I need to be inside of you again."

Her cries increased as his fingers worked. His thumb continued to tease her clit while he slid two fingers knuckle deep inside the welcoming wetness. He could feel the throbbing of her feminine muscles as she squeezed him tight.

"Ohhh?" she moaned, then opened her eyes and gazed up at him.

"You're beautiful." She rode his fingers while his thumb continued to work her clit. She lifted her hips off the floor and met each stroke. He slipped in a third finger, and he could feel her body tightening. Suddenly, he felt the need to taste her. He parted her thighs and leaned forward so he could explore her slick mound with his tongue, but instead she slipped her hand under his arm and pulled him up. Wrapping her legs around him, she rocked her heat against him, rubbing against his length. "I want you now," she insisted.

He was so hard he ached and was more than ready to give her what she wanted. As soon a he slipped on the condom, she arched and guided him inside. He gasped at the sudden heat.

"Yeah, baby," he hissed, then shifted his weight on top of her, plunging deeper. She rocked her hips intensifying the pleasure. Their rhythm started slowly, then built. She whimpered sweetly as her body trembled.

He buried his face into the sweet damp flesh of her neck, inhaling the scent of their bodies and heat as he pumped into her tight, hot body and fought the last of his fight.

Glistening with sweat, they clung to one another and rode out the explosion that rocked the world around them. Then together they both drifted away.

Hours later, Berlin found herself lying in her bed with the scent of sweat and cum lingering in the air. Her body was tired and her eyelids still heavy.

She had enjoyed their time together, but knew it to be only temporary. The sweet pain of heartache would come after the excitement of their lovemaking had faded. She wasn't sure if her heart could survive another heartbreak. In Reginald's arms, her body refused to allow her mind to override the passion between. Her body demanded no more than what the moment had to offer, and it had been much more than she had ever thought possible between a man and a woman.

She shifted on the bed, the walls of her sex were sore and wet with cum. She wasn't complaining. Nothing was better than waking up after sex and still feeling the man that had been between her legs.

Reginald stepped out of the bathroom, and she watched him move around the room, returning the covers to the bed and draping their clothes over a chair. For round three they had bounced around every corner of the room. They had started in the chair, then moved to her dresser and ended on the floor. Somewhere between rounds three and four, she discovered herself lying flat on her back in the bed with ten inches of satisfaction buried deep inside of her.

Berlin nibbled on her bottom lip as she admired Reginald's tight, firm ass. He had a fabulous butt for a man. She remembers grabbing onto his cheeks as he moved in and out of her honey vigorously. It was even better that he was confident about his nakedness. Something she'd probably never be.

Fresh white cream leaked between her thighs. She was ready for more. Reginald had spoiled her for sex with any other man. Damn, she loved his skill. Startled, she frowned. She could love his ability but she wouldn't fall in love with the man no matter how good he made her feel. She would simply enjoy the strong chemistry between them until they tired of each other.

"What are you lying there thinking about?" he asked as he reached for a book that had fallen from her dresser during their wild lovemaking.

"How good you look with your clothes off." Watching him was definitely a treat.

He looked over at her and grinned. "Keep that up and we're going to go for round five."

Berlin kicked a leg from beneath the sheet. "Promises, promises."

He turned and gazed down at her, causing her naked body to quiver. Her clit to tingle. "You should never tease a man."

Slowly, she removed the sheet covering her naked body, leaving her body exposed. "And you should never keep a horny woman waiting."

Reginald climbed onto the bed and crawled between her legs and lowered on top of her, molding his body with hers.

"You want some more of this?" He pressed his hard-on against her clit.

Her breath caught in her throat as he rubbed the top against her sensitive clit.

"Yes," she murmured as he kissed his way down her neck, sending heat pooling between her legs.

"Yes what?" he whispered near her ear.

Tremors of pleasure prickled her skin. "I want you to make love to me."

"I can't hear you," he teased.

He was driving her crazy. "Yes, I want some more of you," she wiggled her hips frantically, stroking her clit against his length. "Some more of that—now!"

Reginald chuckled. "Patience, boo." He touched his tongue to her skin again and slowly moved lower. Her nipples beaded with anticipation only seconds before he captured one between his lips. She threw her head back as he licked, nipped and suckled. All she could do was hold on and enjoy the ride—and what a ride it was going to be. She arched her back, wanted to make sure he didn't miss one corner of her breasts. She explored his body with her hands. Running her fingers across his back...which arched and rippled with muscles as he pressed against her. Traveling down, she gripped his buttocks and squeezed. Bolts of desire dashed down to her core. But even as he squeezed the two together and painted one nipple, and then the other with his hot tongue, she decided it was not enough. She desperately needed his lips somewhere else. Her body was ready for so much more. It hungered for his touch. For his tongue at her lower region.

She pushed on his shoulders, desperate to feel his tongue on her clit. He released her breasts, and his tongue traveled down the center of her stomach to her belly button. He licked the dip of her navel, and she jerked at the contact.

"I need to feel—"

"Slow your roll. I got this." The look he gave her promised to fulfill her every need.

She relaxed her head against the pillow and lowered her eyelids. As he continued to paint a path across her belly, she found herself grinning. Reggie was so confident in his ability to please her that she felt comfortable letting him run it and following his lead.

He shifted lower and lower still.

"Spread your legs."

She immediately parted her thighs, and his tongue painted a path down to her knee and back up again. When his lips were within inches of her core, he breathed his warm breath against her, tickling the hairs and made her squirm. She wasn't sure how much more she could take. The tension was building at her core.

And then it happened.

He slid his tongue along the seam of her; the feeling was so good she was surprised she hadn't exploded on contact. His tongue delved deep, teasing and nipping. She couldn't hold still and rocked against his mouth as he continued to explore. Her body vibrated, and her feminine walls clenched and released. What he was doing felt so damn good! His tongue traveled up to her clit, she gripped the sheets and tried to hold on as one wave of pleasure after another flowed through her body. Not wanting him to move, she wrapped her legs around him. She tried to hold on and savor the feeling, but the pleasure was too good. When he captured her clit between his lips and suckled gently, she came undone and took a deep breath as the power of his mouth won out. A bolt of hot light caused her to shatter. She gasped as an orgasm rocked through her body. Reginald continued to work his magic until the last contraction ripped through and her hips stilled.

"How do you feel?" he asked, and then she heard him rip a package open.

She chuckled lightly. "Drained." The muscles of her legs relaxed, and he moved over her again and gazed down at her.

Reginald kissed the side of her neck and murmured, "That's too bad. Because I have something else for you."

She felt wicked as she curled her arms around his neck. She was tired, but it would take very little for her body to respond to him. "What's that?"

"This," he whispered against her lips as he thrust his hard dick sheathed in latex inside her.

Her head rocked back with a heavy breath.

"Look at me." She opened her eyes and gazed up at him. He had a dark serious glint in his eyes. "I want you to watch me as I make love to you."

His words sent heat pulsing through her body. He drew his hips back, then plunged forward again. Having him watch her as he penetrated her had Berlin so turned on that she couldn't think straight. There was no time for being bashful. She took deep breaths and nibbled lightly on her bottom lip as he thrust into her again.

"How does that feel, baby?" he asked, rhythmically stroking her wet heat.

She trembled. "Good."

His body stilled. "I'm sorry, I didn't hear that."

"I said good! Please, just don't stop."

The agonizing loss of him moving inside her was more than she could bear. He plunged into her again, and she tightened her walls around his dick.

He stared down at her with an intensity that made her head spin. "You look so beautiful lying beneath me."

He tweaked her nipple between his thumb and forefinger, then circled lightly. "And you feel good lying between my legs," she murmured.

"You want me to stop?"

Another hard thrust made her cry out, "No!"

"Then tell me what you want," he said with each deep thrust.

"I want you to come inside of me."

"I think that can be arranged." Reginald placed her legs over his shoulders and dug even deeper as he held her hips firmly in place. Her head rocked from side to side, and within minutes she convulsed with sweet cries and spasms. His release came shortly after, and she held on as she relished the way his body tensed and his muscles steeled.

He rolled over and guided her head onto his chest where he held her as their heart rates returned to normal. Soon their breathing slowed and the two drifted off to sleep.

Chapter Twelve

"**H**ot damn! I can't believe you finally gave Reginald some."

Flashes of memories flushed her cheeks as she looked over at her friend. For the last forty-eight hours, she had been on the ride of her life. When Arianna had called and asked her to join her for another shopping trip at the mall, she jumped at the chance to get out the house. She had barely said hello before giving her all of the juicy details.

"Well believe it," Berlin said as they walked past the long line of children waiting to get their chance on Santa Claus's lap. She couldn't stop smiling no matter how hard she tried. Reggie made her feel sexy, alive, and horny as hell. Her breasts yearned for his attention.

"And?" Arianna asked merrily.

"Girl, the brotha has got skills." She clutched the Victoria's Secret bag tightly in her hand. It had been five hours, and he still had her clit tingling. And she wanted more.

"See," Arianna emphasized the word with a light punch in the shoulder. "Didn't I tell you to leave Cameron's behind alone and hop on Reggie's fine ass? If you had listened y'all could have been knockin' boots a long time ago."

"It's all about timing," Berlin told her as they stepped around a group of teenagers out shopping. Yes indeed. Waiting had made her appreciate him more. If she had given Reggie some that evening in the closet, she would have still been interested in finding out what could have been between her and Cameron. Now there was no need to wonder because she already knew. He didn't come close to his boy. He had been a poor substitute.

She shook her head as Reggie's dimpled smile appeared. The brotha was in a class of his own with his magical tongue. She shivered. She could still feel the last climax in her gut.

Arianna looped her arm through hers, and they headed toward Famous Barr. "My girl finally got some ding-dong. I'm so happy for you."

She's happy? Shoot her body was screaming, *"Hallelujah!"* It had been too long since she'd last had some. Longer than anyone should have to go without. Now she felt like she had been born again. When Reggie slid all *that* inside of her, he made her feel whole. Just the memory of him down between her legs made her feel wet inside her panties.

The mall was busy for a Tuesday night. Five shopping days until Christmas and everybody and their grandmama was out trying to finish their list. She loved the holiday season, and for some reason this year was extra special. Christmas carolers in the food court, an abundance of decorations, a twelve-foot Christmas tree in the main lobby and shoppers moving swiftly through the halls with green and red bags. If you weren't in the mood, all it took was hanging out at the mall to get into the spirit.

"How about I invite the two of you over for dinner? Or we can have a couple's night out."

At the sound of Arianna's suggestion, Berlin halted in her tracks. "Wait, now don't get it twisted. We're not a couple."

Her friend looked confused. "You just said y'all—"

Her lips pursed. "We're screwing, that's it. It ends on Christmas. That's what we agreed to. He's going to Memphis to visit his family, and I'll be spending the holidays with my parents."

Arianna rolled her eyes and swung her purse strap up her shoulder. "I don't understand you. Why in the world would you let something like that slip away?"

Because he was never mine to begin with, that's why. "He doesn't believe in forever and neither do I, at least not with someone like him." Even as the words left her mouth, she knew she was lying. Someone like Reginald was just what she needed in her life. As much as she tried to hide her feelings, Reginald had become quite special to her. And if she thought for even a second he might be interested in a commitment, she would be more than willing to give him a chance. But without Reggie, she might as well stick to her original plan.

When the smell of cinnamon popcorn wafted to her nose, she started walking again. "I still plan to meet a doctor," she replied without the usual level of conviction. The thought of meeting and marrying a doctor no longer seemed important.

Arianna snorted rudely. "Well you better get all you can while you can."

Berlin's smile returned. "I plan on it." For the rest of the week, she planned to spend every second possible with Reggie. In fact, tonight she planned to turn the tables on Reggie and show him just how much he meant to her. He was a compassionate man and for once she was going to cater to his needs. Berlin knew she wasn't the most experienced woman in the world, but for Reggie she was willing to do whatever it took to try and please him. Her clit throbbed at the thought of what she planned to do for him.

Damn, she had never been this horny before. She had never before had such a strong need for sex either. Her blouse brushed against her breasts and her nipples tightened. Berlin reached up and discretely rubbed one, trying to soothe it. Instead, her body hummed for more. She needed to feel him between her legs as soon as possible. Glancing down at her watch, she was pleased to see it was going on four o'clock. Her body tingled with anticipation. Reginald was picking her up at seven.

An idea came to mind. "Come on, Arianna, I need you to help me find Reggie a Christmas present."

That evening, Reggie parked his SUV in front of a brownstone located in one of the areas in the city that had been renovated in the last five years. Wide streets with luxury cars parked on both sides. No liquor stores, no loud music. No thugs sitting on the porch drinking forty ounces. The neighborhood was not at all what she had imagined.

Berlin climbed out of the Escalade and followed him inside. She was startled at the beautiful surroundings. The house had to be worth at least a cool half a million.

She gazed over at him in awe. "You live here?"

Reggie dropped his keys on a mahogany table in the foyer and met her gaze with an amusing look. "My loan company seems to think so." She must have looked as surprised as she felt because he gave her a puzzled look and asked, "What's wrong?"

"You're not selling drugs are you?"

He tossed his head back and chuckled. "No, I don't sell drugs."

Berlin glanced around at the rich dark wood, the expensive crown molding and chair railing. The living room was decorated in dark greens with white and sage as accent colors. Pillows, upholstery, matching rugs and expensive pleated drapes. "I'm just curious how you can afford this on a painter's salary."

"Who's says I'm a painter?"

You. Wait a minute; hold up, he never actually told her he was a painter. Berlin swung around and gazed up at him eyes wide with curiosity. "Well isn't that what you do?"

Reginald rocked back on his heels. "I do a lot more than paint. You just assumed that's what I did."

He was right she had assumed his occupation, based on his collar. She had also assumed sex was overrated; however, Reggie, in a matter of days, had turned the sistah out.

"I own RDH Construction."

RH for Reginald Hodges. Stupid, girl. It had never dawned on her that he had used his initials. Suddenly she felt extremely stupid. All this time she thought she was attracted to another wannabe, and instead Reggie had quite a lot going for himself. Looking at the size and quality of his home, a helluva lot. Berlin was so embarrassed she wished the hardwood floorboards would pop loose just so she could fall in them.

She stepped away from the mantel and turned toward him. "I guess I owe you an apology."

He moved toward her. "Yes you do. And I hope in the future you don't be so quick to judge a book by its cover." Leaning forward, he kissed her lightly on her forehead.

He was right. She had read many books despite the reviews and the ugly covers on front and had truly enjoyed them. "You're right. I made a mistake." She clutched her purse close to her side. "Thanks for bringing me here. Now I'm ready to go home."

"Why?"

She shrugged.

He reached for her arm and pulled her against him. "Berlin, I asked you a question. Why do you want to go home?"

She couldn't even look at him as she spoke. "Because I feel foolish for misjudging you."

"You thought I was a thug from the hood?"

She nodded.

"Who sold drugs?" He looked amused.

She searched his eyes. "You forgive me?"

She could tell he was struggling to keep a straight face. "Depends on how good you are to me."

Before she could answer, Reggie scooped her up into his arms and carried her up to his room. Resisting was the last thing on her mind. She wanted Reggie. Shoot, she'd wanted him since he'd left her house this morning. Eight hours felt like eight months.

Reginald moved across plush desert-brown carpeting and lowered her onto a magnificently large bed, then started removing his clothes while she did the same. When he finally took a seat on the bed beside her, she straddled him.

"I'm driving this evening," she whispered against his lips.

"You'll get no objections from me." He traced the gentle curves of her body, delving his tongue deep into her mouth with every kiss. Her hands traveled down his chest to his hips and over his belly button. With each touch, need shot through his body.

Berlin pushed his back onto the bed, then rocked into him. He felt her swollen clit against his hard dick. She stroked her soft hands across his smooth chest as though she was memorizing every muscle. A short, quick breath escaped. Lust took over his body. She grinded against him in a seductive foreplay, and he could feel the damp heat of her sex. He wanted to be inside of her now, but he didn't want another quick round. This time he wanted the moment to last longer. He took a deep breath fighting for control.

He gazed up at her breasts jiggling with each move. They were crying out to him. *Suck me.* He planned to do just that. Needing to taste her, he leaned and closed his mouth over one dark pebble, nibbled, then suckled eagerly. Berlin moaned and arched her body, pressing her fold against him.

The taste of a warm hard nipple in his mouth turned him on. The way she tasted. Hell, the way she wiggled in his lap as she moaned his name, he was barely hanging on by a thread.

He eased her nipple from his mouth, and moved to give the other equal attention. He caught the pebble between his teeth and gently nibbled. His tongue swirled around in a circle between suckles.

"Oh, yesss," she moaned. "That feels so good you're going to make me come on myself."

"Good." Reggie was glad to know he wasn't the only one on the verge of exploding.

Reaching up, he cupped her other breasts, squeezing gently, then captured a rock-hard nipple between his two fingers and teased. She squirmed and wiggled some more, and he could feel the wet heat sliding across his dick, each time heightening his need. Goodness, he wanted to be inside of her while he was still conscious.

She reached between them and stroked down to his balls, then slowly worked her way up and back down again. He couldn't think straight. As he suckled hungrily at her breasts, all he could think about was being inside of her. *Now!*

"You ready?" he asked.

"Patience," she said in a breathless whisper.

Reginald tried to think straight, which wasn't easy to do when she had his rock hard dick in her hand. As she played with his length, he tried to think rational thoughts, but right now he was burning upwith desire. She stroked his dick in an even rhythm that caused cum to rise to the surface of his large head. She swirled it with her thumb.

"You ready for me baby?" she asked.

"You think you can handle it?" he challenged.

"I know I can." She stroked his dick some more. "Tell me you want it."

He leaned back on the bed and gazed down at her, watching her stroke and drawing more cum from the tip. "I want to feel your heat clamp around my dick." His eyes traveled up to meet hers, and she looked so serious, he trembled. "I need to be inside of you."

She stared at him for several torturing seconds, with a devilish glint in her eyes before she finally replied, "You know what? I've got something even better."

He gulped. "Yeah? What might that be?"

Berlin rolled off the bed and moved over to her purse, which was beneath the pile of clothes. Resting on his elbows, he watched as she reached inside and removed a small can and returned to the bed. His dick jerked. In her hand was a can of whipped cream.

"Roll back over," she ordered.

She didn't have to tell him twice. Reggie rolled onto his back and folded his arms beneath his head and watched in anticipation as she shook the can. She then removed the top and squeezed the trigger. She started at the head of his dick and swirled her way all around until she reached his balls. He was completely covered in the white cream. Berlin then lowered the can onto the nightstand and gave him a long sultry stare. He watched her lick her lips. His dick jerked. Oh, shit, he was in trouble. He barely had a chance to catch his breath before she dropped down and swallowed the head in her mouth.

"Hell, yeahhhhh!" he hissed on contact. "That's what I'm talkin' 'bout."

She licked and teased the tip, then her mouth closed around the head and swallowed as much as she could manage. Her lips were pure torture yet there was no way he was asking her to stop, not when they felt that good.

Berlin traveled down to his balls where she licked first one and then the other, lapping up all the white cream in her path. She then grabbed the base of his dick and squeezed while she slid her tongue up one side and back down the other. Tension built and he tried to keep from coming, but he wasn't sure how long he would be able to last. His girl had skills. Removing his hands from behind his head, he brought them to her head where he caressed and tried to focus on how good her other lips would feel wrapped around his dick if he could just hold on a little longer. He groaned. She was making him feel so good.

Damn her lips are magical!

When she swallowed him again and moved up and down, making love to him with her mouth, Reggie rocked his hips lightly, meeting each downward stroke. She drew him in deeper, accepting more of his length in her mouth and he gritted his teeth as the tension increased.

"I'm ready for you to come inside and play," she cooed.

Hell, he wasn't one to argue. Not when he wanted her just as bad. She released him, then wiggled her clit along his length. "Then come on and ride this dick."

"Let me get a condom."

Never had a second seemed like forever, while she ripped open the foil package. He then held his dick while she worked the latex over his length. When she finally had it on, Berlin eased up on her knees, and it took everything Reggie had not to slam up inside of her. He was so hard, he was in pain, but he grit his teeth and took several deep breaths. Wiggling her hips, she slowly lowered a little at a time, teasing him when what he wanted to do was to thrust hard and plunge all ten inside.

She lowered another inch, her tight walls stretching to accommodate his package.

"Quit playing?" he groaned.

"Who's playing?" she purred. "I'm just taking my time." She lowered further. He was halfway home.

Leaning forward as she rocked her hips, she licked the side of his neck with her wet tongue. *Enough!* He grabbed her hips and thrust all the way in with a rush that had her crying out. He stilled and buried his face between her breasts. She then began moving again.

"Damn baby, you got skills," he hissed as she rocked her hips against his.

"You ain't seen nothing yet." Lifting her hips, he slipped all the way out. Then she dropped back down, taking all ten at once. Before he could catch his breath, she released him then swallowed him again. He gritted his teeth trying to hold on.

"You like that?" she teased.

"Do you?" he asked as he palmed her breasts and brought a nipple to his lips.

"Oh, yeeesss," she moaned, then found a rhythm and rode his dick with long thrusts. He suckled until all he could do was pay attention to what she was doing. He grabbed firmly onto her ass, causing her to drop even deeper onto his dick. He lifted her, then slammed her down onto his lap, making her buttocks slap. Her breathing became increased and changed into moans that could be heard in the next room. Luckily, no one was there. Not that he would have cared. He was enjoying himself too much to stop.

"Harder, dammit!"

He rocked his hips, meeting her downward thrusts faster, harder and she cried out his name. Berlin rode him harder and held onto his shoulders. He groaned. Reggie wanted everything she had to offer. This was the moment he had been waiting for, and it surpassed anything he had imagined. Heat built at his balls and he knew he was seconds away from exploding. He tried to slow her down and make the moment last forever, but he could not. It was too late. His body was on fire. Her sex was wet and hot around his dick.

Breathless, she asked, "Does that feel good?"

"Hell, yeah!" Absolutely perfect. He couldn't ask for anything more. Except maybe to come, and that was only a minute away. He kissed her shoulder along her neck and finally her breasts until his breathing became labored. Berlin's eyes were closed and she was panting heavily; he knew she was about to come as well. That was fine with him. They could come together. He could feel her as she squeezed her muscles around his length then deepened her strokes. Oh, yeah, it was right there. He was about three seconds from coming, when in one quick motion, he rolled her onto her back. She cried out, in desperation.

"Shhh. I got you, boo," he whispered as he rolled on top of her and slid back inside. She screamed. He howled. Nothing came close to feeling this good. He moved in and out of her, teasing her with little strokes, then thrusting himself home hard. He whispered her name against her cheek, his deep voice passionate as he drew closer to the finish line. She arched off the bed and released wild cries of passion. He was giving her everything he had. He felt her come. She trembled, then her body shook and climaxed. The final thrust sent him over the edge as well.

"Oh, yeahhh!" he grounded out between his teeth. A handful of quick strokes, he came hard inside of her. His dick pulsed. His body shook and he called out her name. One, two, three more long strokes, and then he collapsed on top of her.

A few seconds later, he rolled over onto his side, taking her with him. His skin was slick with sweat. His thighs wet with cum. He was completely satisfied…for now.

Berlin woke to the smell of bacon frying. She smiled to herself at the kind gesture. Besides her father, no man had ever bothered to make her breakfast before. Reginald was proving to be an exceptional man in and out of the bedroom.

Snuggling deeper in the covers, she took a few minutes to revel in last night's sexual experience. The encounter had earned its spot at the top of her list. She was proud of herself. Last night she didn't hide behind any inhibitions; instead, she had followed her heart and in doing so, willingly gave as good as she got, and enjoyed every minute. Last night, the world seemed to extend no further than Reginald's bedroom. Nothing had ever come close to the explosive union that had sent her dangling over the edge. Just thinking about it caused her feminine fold to pulsate. Damn, she wished things could always be this way, but she was smart enough to know what Reggie had to offer was temporary. After time the physical intensity and the mind-boggling feelings would gradually fade and their relationship would eventually end. Berlin released a heavy sigh and pushed the dooming thoughts away. Right now she would go with the flow and enjoy the moment, even if it was just a fairytale. If she thought there was even the slightest chance of things between them continuing past the holidays, she would jump at the opportunity, but Reggie wasn't interested. He made it clear he wasn't looking for a commitment. Berlin released a strangled laugh. It was ironic. Reggie had convinced her to have a relationship that originally she didn't think she wanted. In fact, she was the one who decided their relationship ended on Christmas. And now she wanted the relationship to continue.

She rolled over onto the pillow beside her and took a deep breath. The masculine scent reminded her that Reginald was definitely real and for the present time, although temporary, he was hers. She loved the smell of his Prada cologne mixed with his natural scent. Prada didn't smell right on everyone. She would know since she had bought the same brand for her ex, and it stunk on him. Drawing the pillow closer to her, she took another deep breath and wished she could bottle the mingled fragrances. At least that way once the holidays were over and they both went their separate ways, she would still have something to remember him by.

Covering her mouth with the pillow, she released a frustrated scream. Why did things always have to happen this way? She had found the ideal man who wasn't a doctor, but who was everything she wanted; and unfortunately, he didn't believe in commitments.

At least he's been honest.

Yes, that was one thing she could say about Reggie. He never tried to lie or mislead her into thinking their relationship would last. Only her heart had refused to cooperate, and now she faced heartbreak.

I love this man, she thought.

"Oh, God!" Stunned by the realization, Berlin rolled over and groaned. What in the world had she been thinking? She punched the pillow in an attempt to ease some of her frustration. It didn't work. She had allowed herself to fall in love. How stupid she had been to think that falling in love was a choice, but now she realized she had been so wrong. Love was an emotion that one couldn't control. It just happened whether you wanted to or not. Now that she was in love with Reginald, what did she plan to do about it? A minute passed before she decided for now she would do absolutely nothing. Regardless of how she felt about him, she would enjoy their relationship for what it was meant to only be—sexual satisfaction.

"Hey, babe, you hungry yet?"

Startled, she sat up in the bed and stared at the handsome man standing in the doorway. The sexy smile tempted her to invite him back between her legs. "Yes, very." She allowed the sheet to fall away. "However, I am very fickle. You think you might have something to satisfy my hunger?"

"It depends on what you want," he answered with a silly grin.

"Something hot and satisfying," she cooed as she leaned back against the pillow and spread her thighs. Reaching down, she fingered her clit. Reginald stood and watched, licking his lips. She was feeling quite naughty, and considering Reginald's reaction, she needed to behave this way more often. "You think maybe you might have what I'm looking for?"

"No doubt. This brotha got everything you need right here." Reginald stepped out of his boxers and dived onto the bed, causing Berlin to giggle. "The question is, how hungry are you?"

"Very hungry," she whispered

He kissed the inside of her thigh. "I hope you're open to trying new things."

"Yes, definitely."

"Good." Rising, he flipped her on her stomach. "Then I got a meal guaranteed to fill you up." As soon as he suited up, with one push he thrust firmly inside her, filling her completely.

The more time they spent together, and the more they got to know each other, the more her protective layers began to fade away. Berlin had not known it was possible to feel so comfortable and fulfilled in a relationship.

And she was terrified.

She spent the next two days in the company of a man who made her laugh one minute and cry out with ecstasy the next. Reginald Hodges was the most exciting man she had ever met, and she was thrilled to be along for the ride. He taught her things in the bed she had

A Delight Before Christmas

only read about in erotic novels. Each time he made her feel like the sexiest woman alive. His compassionate ways extended beyond the bedroom. During the day they worked together to complete the project. Reginald had even showed her how to cut and put up crown molding in the living room. Tears had sprung to the surface as she looked at the end result. Her house was shaping up to be everything she had hoped it to be. She just wished she could say the same about her heart. Deep down she never wanted this wonderful feeling to end. Even though he spent every night beside her, Reginald never mentioned a commitment or life after the holidays. Berlin tried to convince herself to live for the moment, and she would worry about the rest when it happened.

She thought about spending the rest of her life with someone like him. Every time those thoughts surfaced, she would push them away.

Thursday evening, Reginald took her downtown to see the decorations. Walking hand and hand with Reginald through the busy streets the sunset faded. The sky was clear and diamond-studded stars sparkled overhead. It was considerably warm for December, and a clear indication a snowstorm was on its way. If not for the slight breeze from the river on the banks of the St. Louis Arch, the evening would have been perfect.

They decided to have dinner at the Adams Mark Hotel and afterward, they walked over to the cobblestone streets to enjoy a romantic carriage ride.

They climbed into a white horse-drawn carriage and snuggled together under a thick wool blanket.

"You enjoying yourself?"

"Yes. I can't remember the last time I've had this much fun."

"I can," he teased as he reached inside her coat and caressed her nipple through her shirt. "Last night on the kitchen table, this morning in the shower."

"Don't," she hissed under her breath as his fingers continued to work. "You're not playing fair."

He unfastened the middle button and slipped his hand inside her bra. "So sue me."

Determined to get him back, she reached over and undid his zipper. The thought of being naughty under the stars with the driver a few feet away turned her on.

She flicked the top button of his jeans open, then freed his dick from his boxer shorts. She grabbed the thick base and glided her fist up to the throbbing tip and back down again. Her breasts were quickly forgotten as Reginald released her, then threw his head back with a groan.

"Shhh," she warned between giggles as she continued to stroke him. "The driver will hear us."

Reggie ground his teeth together. "Let him hear. Just keep doing what you're doing."

She stopped to tease his large head that was now wet with pre-cum before dropping her fist down again.

"Damn, baby, you got skills." His hips bucked against her hand, meeting each of her thrust as she continued to please her man. By the time their driver had come to a complete stop, the two raced from the carriage back to his SUV. Once there, Reginald climbed in on the passenger's side, dropped his pants and ordered Berlin to straddle him. She quickly shed her jeans while he retrieved a condom from his wallet and protected them. Before she could remove her panties, Reginald ripped them out of the way and slammed her down on top of him.

"Ride me," he ordered with a hiss.

Slowly, she moved up and down on his lap.

His eyes fluttered shut as he kissed her along her neck and jaw. "How do you feel?" he asked.

Looking in the face of the man who made her feel so desirable, Berlin felt a surge of hope maybe there might be a "we" after all. "Alive. You're so crazy."

"Yeah, I am. Crazy about you," he said while stroking her cheek tenderly.

Her heart swelled. But while she rode his heavy dick, she told herself not to get her hopes up. He hadn't said anything about being in love. They were two people enjoying a brief fling. Experience taught her that. Her ex had said the same thing, and she had interpreted it to mean something totally different and it had resulted in pain. She was so willing to give love a second chance, and yet she had fallen in love with the wrong man. She loved Reginald, and because of that, she didn't want him to feel pressured into giving her anything more than he was offering now.

His head was tilted back, and she drank in the sight of his face. He was so fine, and she loved looking at him. She watched him as she slowly eased herself up and down over his length. She loved the way he whispered her name and the groans of pleasure that escaped from his lips. The long, hot breath that stirred her skin. She loved the way he felt filling her. They were a perfect fit, and she wanted this to last forever.

Reginald opened his eyes, and she found that she liked him watching her. He brought his hands to her hips and guided himself in and out while she moved along with him. The pleasure built within her to a feverish point, and she cried out with pleasure. Reginald watching her only increased the excitement. The rhythm increased. She heard laughter and noticed a couple moving across the parking lot to their car nearby. Berlin was sure they could hear her loud cries. Hell, she didn't care. There was no way she was stopping.

"Come with me, now," he demanded, grabbed her hips and drove into her.

She gladly obliged him. Closing her eyes, she was hit by a powerful explosion. She screamed out his name as his long hard thrusts continued. The orgasm went on and on until he finally joined her with one final thrust.

As her heart returned to normal, she watched his face. She loved the control she had over him, but she loved him more. She would give anything to have his heart. Collapsing against him, she rested her head on his shoulder and listened to the sound of his heartbeat. Her eyes burned with tears and a shiver raced through her. She didn't know if she'd be able to bear losing him. Eventually it would happen.

"Berlin," he murmured as he kissed the side of her neck. "You okay?"

She forced back a sob. "Yes." As his length stirred inside her, she braced herself for round two. "I couldn't be better."

Berlin spent the following afternoon getting the last of the Christmas decorations from the attic. She hung a wreath on the front door, then merrily wrapped red and gold garland around the banister. Afterward, she strung Christmas lights along the windows in the living room and dining room so they could be seen from the curb. While she used the staple gun, she glanced out at the blanket of fresh white snow at the mechanical reindeers Reginald had placed out in her yard yesterday after he had strung the bushes in front with lights. Then he had plugged it all in, and while standing together they watched the lights dance and the deer and doe move their heads.

She was just finishing up when she heard Reginald calling for her to come in the family room. Tossing the staple gun back in the box, she moved down the hall, anxious to see what he had done. He had been locked in the room since the wee hours of the morning wanting to surprise her with an idea he had. Pushing open the double doors, she found him standing patiently in the center of the room waiting for her arrival.

"Whadda you think?"

Berlin gazed in amazement. Reggie had completed the walls in the family room with a brilliant burnt orange that contrasted gradually until it blended perfectly with a yellow textured ceiling. It reminded her of a summer sunrise.

"I love it." A smile curled her lips as she moved into the room. "I can't believe how wonderful this room has turned out." She swung around and threw herself into his arms. "Thank you!"

He brushed his lips hungrily against hers. "Merry Christmas, boo. I wanted to do something extra special."

Tears burned the back of her eyes. Reggie was so thoughtful. And she loved him for it. If only she could tell him. "It's the best present ever. Thank you so much," she said around the lump in her throat.

He kissed her again, then released her. "There is still one thing missing."

She gave him a puzzled look. "What's that?"

"A Christmas tree."

Berlin playfully swatted his arm for teasing her, then glanced over at the perfect spot in the far left corner of the room near a built-in bookshelf she had filled with books.

"I was hoping you would help me bring down my tree from the attic as soon as you have a few moments."

He frowned. "What's wrong with a real tree?"

"Who has time to go and pick out a tree and have it delivered?"

"Anything is better than an artificial tree."

Berlin's reply was a shrug. Her mother always believed in buying an evergreen every year, even if there were barely any presents under the tree. "My mother likes the smell of fresh cut trees."

"So do I." Reaching out, Reginald caressed her arm. "I know a place up the road that's selling Christmas trees."

Her face lit up. "Oh wonderful! You know if they deliver?"

He pulled her against him. "How about I take you?"

"I couldn't ask you to do that."

"I didn't ask you that. I asked if you want to go."

Her smile widened. "Yes. I would like that."

"Good, then grab your coat."

She bounced on her heels and found that she was excited about going shopping for a Christmas tree for the holiday.

It was snowing again. Blankets would cover the ground by morning. Reginald rocked back on his heels and mumbled under his breath. It had been over an hour since Berlin first began picking out a tree, and she still hadn't found one. Digging that white artificial tree from the attic didn't sound like a bad idea.

His uncle had told him to never go shopping with a woman. He had no idea that included shopping for trees. The trees were either too tall, too wide or not enough branches.

He was seconds away from tossing her over his shoulder and carrying her back to his SUV when she shouted, "I want this one!" *Finally!* Reginald practically ran over to where she was standing.

"Isn't she a beauty?" Berlin asked.

He thought the tree looked like a dozen others they had looked at. "I think she's a beauty."

Berlin beaming like a kid in a candy store made the trip to the tree lot worth it.

After they tied the tree down, they climbed into the SUV, and Berlin insisted they drop by the craft store for ornaments. It was almost sundown by the time he pulled his Escalade into her driveway. She climbed out and moved around back to give him a hand.

"Berlin?"

She turned around, and her right cheek was hit with an ice-cold snowball.

She screamed at the shock of the freezing cold. "Oh! It's on now!"

Reaching down, she cupped a ball of snow and swung it at his head. Reginald ducked and caught her with another at the side of her head. Hollering and screaming, she raced around the truck. She ducked down low and grabbed a glove full of snow. As soon as he came around the side, she jumped up, reached inside his jacket and dropped the snow. She took off running and laughed as he came after her, then she stumbled and fell into the wet snow. Reginald landed on top of her and covered her face with snow.

"Okay, I give up!" she screamed.

"Who's the man?" he shouted.

"You are. You are. You win. Now quit!"

"Okay. I'll give you a break."

He rolled over. Giggling, Berlin spread her arms and legs wide, then fanned them, making snow angels. "I remember when my sister and I couldn't wait for the snow to start so we could make angels in the yard."

She started to laugh again, but Reginald leaned over and covered her mouth with his. When their lips met, her laughter stuttered into a moan. He pulled back and felt a shudder run through him as he saw the impact of the kiss reflected in the shimmering depths of her eyes. Tilting her face, she pressed her lips against temptation. Her lips parted inviting a deeper sharing of intimacy. She melted against him. "We better get in before we freeze to death."

She nodded at his suggestion and took his hand as he helped her from the ground. They carried the tree into the living room and decided to set it up later.

Berlin disappeared up to the room where she peeled off her wet clothes and dried off, then slipped into a pair of sweatpants. Her teeth were chattering. It wasn't because she was wet from head to toe. It was all because of Reginald.

As she showered, she caught herself giggling. She couldn't believe how much she enjoyed spending time with Reginald. How could she have ever thought he was a pain in the butt?

She changed into a short yellow nightie and warm fuzzy slippers. Reaching for her robe on the back of the door, she slipped it on, then headed downstairs to make them both a cup of hot chocolate. As she moved past the thermostat, she paused, then moved over to it. She hesitated for a moment, then reached up and moved the dial to seventy-two degrees. Now that her house was painted, she could afford to splurge just a little on heat until after her parents' visit. With a giggle, she moved into the kitchen and reached for the hot chocolate mix.

"Need some help?"

Slowly, she turned around. Her eyes widened. Reginald had pulled off his faded jeans and stood in the entrance of the kitchen damn near naked in a pair of boxers that hung low on his hips. Her gaze moved to his chest, bare and glistening with two perfectly flat chocolate nipples that enhanced his sculpted pecs. She followed the trail of silky damp hair that spread over his chest, then narrowed and plunged down a muscular abdomen only to disappear behind the elastic waistband. Berlin gulped. Her eyes locked on the swell of an erection, tenting the left side of his boxers.

Her nipples tightened. Wetness generated between her thighs. A needy whimper slipped past her lips. Unable to tear her eyes from his luscious body, she licked her suddenly dry lips, then whispered, "You're gonna catch a cold!"

He smiled a slow sexy smile that deepened his dimples while turning up one corner of his mouth. "Not if I have you to warm me up," he replied thickly. In one fluid motion, Reginald scooped her into his arms and carried her down the hall toward the stairs.

"Wait!" she cried between giggles. "I was getting ready to make us some hot chocolate."

"Boo, I got all the chocolate I could possibly need right here in my arms," he said as he hurried up the stairs.

Early the next morning, Berlin laid in his arms after another round of love making. Reginald pulled her close, his hand running up and down her back.

"Berlin, we need to talk."

Reginald was leaving for Memphis tomorrow. That day would also signify the end of their relationship.

She swallowed the lump in her throat "About what?"

"I want to talk about us."

She dropped her gaze to his chest so he wouldn't read the disappointment. The comforting strokes did nothing to ease the sadness sitting in her chest. He was getting ready to remind her he wasn't looking for a commitment. Well neither was she, or was she? Maybe, maybe not. She didn't know anymore, but one thing for sure she wasn't allowing him to end it first.

Taking a deep breath, she lifted her eyes to him, then scrambled up to a sitting position, determined to say what she had to say before he did. "Before you say anything, I just want you to know I have enjoyed these last two weeks together. I have experienced things I have never felt before, and I thank you for it. But now it is time to get back to the real world. I'm not looking for a commitment or anything more than right now."

He gave her a long hard stare. "Is that really how you feel?"

Somehow she managed to swallow the lump in her throat. "Yes. I hope we can remain friends."

It took him a long time to speak. Reginald squeezed her tightly in his arms. "No doubt. Maybe we can still get together from time to time if you like?"

She forced the tears from her voice. "We'll see."

Long after she had drifted off to sleep, Reginald held her in his arms. He never wanted to let her go. The conversation didn't go anywhere like he had planned. He had intended to tell her he was feeling something he had never felt before and that he wanted time to explore it further. Instead, Berlin had put the brakes on things and quickly reminded him their relationship was nothing more than a brief fling that ended on Christmas.

He should have felt pleased by her words. So many women in the past cried and behaved like he had used them when he had been honest from the start. But Berlin made it clear that their relationship had run its course, and it was time to get back to their own separate lives. He should have felt pleased by her decision. Yet, instead, he felt like he had been sucker punched. Even though he was holding her, he suddenly felt all alone.

They must have slept, because the next thing he knew the doorbell rang.

Reginald rolled over onto his back when he felt her leave. He glanced at the clock on the nightstand. It was eleven o'clock in the morning. He thought about getting up, but lacked the energy. Last night's activity had left him drained.

He heard the doorbell ring again and shortly after, what he heard Berlin say made him sit up straight in the bed.

"Mom, Dad, what are you doing here?"

Chapter Thirteen

B erlin," her father boomed as he stepped through the door. He pulled her into his arms and hugged her tightly. "I missed you, dear." He drew back and gave her a thorough appraisal.

"I missed you, too, Daddy." She kissed his cheek, then moved over to hug her mom while her dad went back out to his Eldorado to retrieve the rest of their bags.

"Hello, Lil' Bit," she greeted.

For once she didn't mind hearing the nickname. Her sister had started calling her that when she was six, and after a while the name stuck.

"What are you doing here so early? I wasn't expecting you until this evening."

"Your father wanted to get here early enough to watch some football game. So I didn't bother arguing with him." She paused and gave her a long curious look. "I see you're still in your pajamas. I hope we didn't interrupt anything."

At her mother's suggestive smirk, Berlin pulled her robe tightly around her and remembered that Reggie was still up in her bed sleep. Yeah, like she was going to tell her mom she was seconds away from getting her some more. "Uh, no, I was just—"

"Whose Escalade's parked in your yard?" her father asked as he stepped through the door carrying two suitcases.

Oh, damn. She had forgotten about the SUV. "Um…" *Quick! Think of something.*

"It's mine, sir."

All heads turned as Reggie came downstairs. Berlin's shoulders sagged with relief. At least he had enough sense to put his clothes on first. Although…what in the world was he doing holding her plunger?

"Berlin called me this morning to tell me her toilet was over-flowing. So I rushed over to fix it. All done," Reginald said, then passed her the wooden handle.

She looked at him in time to see him wink. That brotha was not only good in bed, but he was also fast on his feet. She definitely liked that about him.

"Daddy, I'd like you to meet Reginald." She turned to him, willing her smile to remain grounded.

Her father lowered their suitcases to the wooden floor and grabbed Reginald's hand, giving it one quick but firm shake. He then slipped his arm around Berlin's shoulders and hugged her to his side once more. "It's nice to know my daughter has friends around to look after her," he said, then gave his daughter a swift peck on the forehead. "I worry about her."

"Daddy," she warned.

Her mother moved to her defense. "Dear, don't embarrass her."

Berlin gave her parents a tour of her house. She was proud to show off the bedrooms, now painted in vibrant colors of tangerine, lettuce green and lemon. Each ooh and aah validated her decision to have her house painted. Reginald carried their bags up to the guest room, then the four retreated to the family room. Her parents were truly impressed with her comfortable leather furniture, royal blue Persian rugs and roaring fireplace. She could tell her parents took an instant liking to Reginald. While he and her father discussed football, she found herself staring at his strong profile and prominent dimples when he smiled. What wasn't there to like about him?

When Reginald announced he was going to head home, Berlin nodded, realizing it was for the best. The last thing she needed was for her parents to get the wrong impression about their relationship. It was bad enough they had arrived only hours after they had finished making love.

"Are you guys hungry?" her eyes traveled from her dad to her mom.

Hattie Dupree, sixty, petite and recently retired after forty years as a head cook for the Chicago Public Schools, shook her head. "We stopped and got lunch on the way, but I can help make dinner." She rose from the couch. "I brought a pot of your Aunt Tot's pole beans and potatoes."

"Mmm, that brings back memories," Reginald said as he rose from the chair in one fluid motion.

"Why don't you come back and have dinner with us?" Hattie suggested.

Berlin glanced over at Reginald in time to find him staring and waiting for some indication it was okay. Okay? Goodness, she didn't want him to leave.

She shrugged. "Yeah, why don't you come back this evening and eat with us?"

His lips curled with laughter. "Only if you're also having fried chicken and homemade cornbread."

Bart slapped his knee and cackled. "Reggie, you're gonna fit in quite well."

Fit in? Berlin felt a moment of uneasiness, then let it go. As much as she didn't want to give her parents the wrong impression, she was glad he was returning. As she followed her mother into the kitchen, Berlin realized she was starting to become quite attached, which wasn't the smart thing to do considering today was supposed to be their last day together. She sighed deeply. Her body was so used to him being inside of her. Now what in the world would she do?

Berlin pressed the glass of eggnog to her heated cheek, and glanced beneath slightly lowered eyelids to watch Reginald, who looked delectable. He had returned in time for dinner. Showered, shaved and dressed to impressed, and she was definitely liking everything she saw. He looked at her, a smile tilting the corner of her mouth. Everyone at the table faded out, leaving her exposed under his seductive gaze. Her heart banged in her chest, pulses of heat spread through her. She licked her lip. So badly she wanted him to reach beneath the table and touch her. Unfortunately, her mother was sitting to her right and her father to her left.

"So, Reginald, how long have you been painting?"

"For over ten years, sir."

While he told her parents about the contracting business he had started, Berlin leaned back in her chair and half-listened. She stared at his thick lips and couldn't help wishing they were down between her legs nibbling on her clit. She didn't know why she had even gone there. Discreetly, she reached down between her thighs and pressed her hand firmly against her crotch and tried to calm the excitement she had caused. Her clit was pulsing and shouting, "More, I want more!" Too bad she hadn't worn a skirt. If she had, she would have slipped her fingers inside her panties and spent the next few minutes caressing her clit. It was screaming for attention she couldn't give it in a pair of denim jeans. As soon as she had a chance, she was going to drop her panties and stroke her—

"Berlin?"

At the sound of her mother's voice, she snatched her hand away. "Yes?"

Her mother gave her a worried look. "You okay? You look like you got caught with your hand in the cookie jar."

She swallowed. Her mother had no idea how close she was. If she could have managed it, she definitely would have been playing with her cookies. "No, I was thinking about something."

"Why don't you go get that banana pudding out the refrigerator?'

She scooted away from the table and escaped into the kitchen. What in the world was she doing thinking about playing with her clit while having dinner with her parents? She definitely needed her head examined.

Reaching inside the refrigerator, she removed the bowl and carried it back to the table. While her mother served, Berlin glanced across the table at Reginald and found him watching her. He licked his thick lips, and she had to resist the urge to squirm. Instead, she reached for her spoon and took a taste of her mother's infamous banana pudding.

"Mmmm," she moaned as her eyes locked on the fine brotha across the table. He brought his spoon to his mouth as well. Watching his tongue made her nipples bead. The last time they'd had dessert, it had been at Lula's when Reggie had his hand between her legs.

As soon as they ate dessert and drank their coffee, Reginald raised an eyebrow then carried his plate into the kitchen.

Berlin waited a moment then rose. "Mom, Dad, why don't you go on into the family room and watch the game while we take care of the dishes?"

Her mother's eyes sparkled. "You sure you don't want some help?"

"Oh no!" Berlin said almost fast enough to make her suspicious. Although she had a sneaky feeling her mother was more hip than she thought. "No, we can handle it." She reached for her plate and cup and dashed into the kitchen. As soon as she saw him, Berlin smiled at Reginald, who was standing in front of the window with his hands in his pockets, staring out at the soft white snow falling heavily from the sky. Berlin lowered the dishes on the counter, then moved up behind him and wrapped her arms around him.

"What are you in here thinking about?" she asked, running her hands across the tight ripples of his chest and arms.

"You." His voice was so low she had barely heard him.

"Me?" she snuggled her cheek against his back. "What about me?"

"You are truly something else."

"Thank you," she said, then stroked his chest. One of her hands traveled down his chest and disappeared inside his pants and grabbed his semi-hard dick. Instantly, she felt his body stiffen.

"Don't do that." She heard the sound of his breath and knew that he was holding it.

Feeling wicked at the effect she had over him, Berlin giggled. "Why?" she asked, even though she knew good and well what she was doing. She began teasing the head, and he didn't show any further signs of resistance. She continued to stroke his hardened length, traveling back and forth from his moist tip.

"Afraid my parents might walk in here?" she purred, as she gently squeezed his balls. He pulsated in her hand, then a groan escaped his lips.

"Damn it, Berlin," he hissed. "You're starting something."

"Good, then finish it." She knew he wouldn't pass up a challenge.

He reached for her hand and withdrew it from his pants, then in one swift move swung around, and then his lips were on hers, demanding, fiery and as stormy and fierce as the night outside. Grabbing her by the waist, he hauled her off her feet. Berlin wrapped her legs around his hips, pressing her heat against his erection. She stared up into his eyes, dark with unhidden desire as he squeezed her buttocks. He pressed her closer to him, and her breathing increased.

"I want you now," she cooed, then pointed to the laundry room.

"You sure?"

"More certain than I've been about a lot of things lately."

Once in the tiny laundry room, Reginald pushed the door shut with his hip, then planted her on top of the washing machine. Berlin quickly wiggled out of her jeans while he unfastened his pants and allowed them to fall to the floor. Reaching inside his wallet, he removed a condom and quickly slid it on. As soon as it was in place, Reggie crushed his mouth to hers in a heated kiss that she felt all the way down to her toes. His lips traveled down to her throat. She was on fire down there, and dammit, she wanted him to do something about it. He caressed the inside of her thigh, then slid two fingers in her, and she felt herself dripping wet around his fingers. Reginald recaptured her mouth in another kiss.

"Now," she moaned, clenching his waist.

Reginald removed his hand, then wrapped her legs around him as she slid off the machine and leaned against it.

"How bad do you want it?" he teased, grinding his length against her wet heat.

"Bad, real bad. I need you inside me right now."

He cupped her buttocks, then pushed inside her until his full length was with her. Instantly, an orgasm hit her. She rocked against him, and then when it eased, Reginald withdrew and entered her again. Each thrust in and out and in again was so filled with pleasure that she sank her teeth into the side of his neck to keep from crying out and her parents hearing them. She held on tight and rocked with him, wanting to feel him deeper inside her. As if he'd known what she wanted, he thrust harder and faster. She cried against his shoulder, never wanting him to stop. Nothing could come close to feeling this good. The rhythm ran on without control as Reginald whispered against her skin, his deep voice passionate.

"Kiss me," he demanded.

Returning to his lips, she covered his mouth with hers and with one final thrust his hot semen filled her as she cried out with pleasure of her own.

Moments later, Berlin surfaced slowly, her legs still around his waist, holding him tight. With her head resting on his shoulder, his arms around her, she tried to understand what was happening between them but could not. Instead, she heard the slow beat of his heart and the wild winter wind stirring outside. At that very moment, Berlin knew that their time together was officially over. She was the first to speak.

"Thank you."

He looked puzzled. "For what?"

"For everything. It's been fun." She dropped her eyes so he wouldn't see the tears that were seconds away from breaking through.

"It was my pleasure," he replied, then planted light kisses along her face and neck.

Thirty minutes later, Berlin stood in the door and watched as he pulled out the driveway. Snow was still falling. She was tempted to ask him to stay, but knew that Reginald was more than capable of taking care of himself. Closing the door, she stepped away and felt a feeling of emptiness that he was gone.

She moved into the kitchen and decided to make herself a cup of peppermint tea. Setting the timer of the microwave, she folded her arms and waited. Her mind traveled over the last couple of weeks. It was not at all how she had planned it. Here she was finally getting everything she thought she wanted, and now she wasn't sure she did. She was in love with Reginald.

Lowering her head to her hand, she finally allowed herself to admit what she had been denying. She was head over heels in love with Reginald and wanted to spend the rest of her life showing him how much.

"Want some company?"

She glanced up to find her mother's smiling face standing inside the doorway. Forcing a smile on her face, she nodded. "Sure. Would you like some tea?"

"Yes, but I'll fix it myself."

She watched her mom in a red flannel robe and Christmas slippers move over to the cabinet and remove another mug. Quietly, she took a seat at the table, then openly admired her mother's trim figure and her smooth mocha complexion. She had seen numerous pictures of her mother when she was a teenager. Even then she had been a beautiful woman.

"Mom, when did you know you were in love with Dad?"

Hattie dropped a tea bag in the water, then gave a dreamy smile. "At first I couldn't stand your dad."

"Really? You never told me that story."

She laughed, then moved over to the microwave and removed the piping hot mug, then placed hers inside and set the timer. "I was working at the elementary school and had just gotten the supervisor position. Your dad was the custodian. Every day he asked me to dinner, and every day I told him no. He'd bring flowers, lunch, wait after work and walk me to my car. He drove me so crazy that I finally went out with him just so he would leave me alone." She paused as she carried Berlin's mug over to the table and passed her the sugar bowl. "After then we were inseparable. I fell in love, and no matter how much I tried to deny it, he wasn't going away."

"That's a wonderful story."

Her mother moved and retrieved a spoon from the middle drawer and handed it to her. "Chile, I wanted a teacher. Refused to settle for less. I even dated one or two, but nothing ever came of it. And when your father told me he was going to make me fall in love with him, I fought the attraction to the end." She smiled at the fond memories. "But we can't pick and choose who we fall in love with. It just doesn't work that way. You can't fight love."

Dropping her eyes, she put two spoons of sugar in her tea and stirred all the while thinking about what her mother had just said. "But what if they don't love you back?"

"Have you asked?"

She simply shook her head.

She snorted. "Well you won't know unless you find out. Right?"

Her mother was right. That night Berlin went to bed and knew what she had to do. Find a way to let Reginald know exactly how she felt about him.

Chapter Fourteen

Reginald rolled over in bed with a serious hard-on. Man, he couldn't believe how quickly he had grown accustomed to Berlin lying beside him. Now their relationship was over, he would have to find a way to forget about her and quick.

Glancing out the window, he saw over four inches of snow that fell through the night. If he got rolling by noon, he could make it to Memphis by dinner. At least he would have company. His brother was traveling with him. There was no rush. Since his mother hadn't known he was coming, she was spending the holiday with her brother in Little Rock and wouldn't be home until tomorrow evening. He couldn't wait to see her, he thought with a smile. And he might as well get ready for a lecture. His mother believed it was time for him to settle down and start a Christmas tradition of his own.

Tossing the covers aside, he took a seat on the edge of the bed. A month ago, the thought of spending the rest of his life with one woman would have sent him running for cover, but not anymore.

Oh shit!

He had allowed Berlin to get in his head, and his heart. He didn't like it. He didn't like that at all, especially since she would never be interested in anything other than sex.

Isn't that what you want?

Dropping his head, he took a moment to think. He wasn't sure what he wanted anymore. All he knew was not having her in his life was going to be a hard pill to swallow.

He heard the doorbell ring. Frowning, he rose and reached for his jeans and slipped them on. Last thing he needed was for someone to see how hard his dick was.

He moved downstairs and walked over to the door. Peeking through the peephole, he spotted Cameron and frowned. What did he want this early in the morning, he wondered, although he knew it couldn't be anything good.

"Reggie, man, I need your help," he said the second the door was opened. He pushed past Reginald and moved toward the kitchen. Reggie followed behind him. His brow rose when he spotted Cameron rummaging through his refrigerator like he was at home.

"Can I help you with something?"

Cameron closed the door with a beer in his hand.

"Isn't it a little early for drinking?"

"Man, I'm stressed." Popping the tab, he took a seat at the small wooden table and waited for Reggie to lower in the chair across from him. "I'm sprung man."

"What?"

Nodding, he took a sip. "I know. It's still hard to believe, but I fell in love with a beautiful chick."

"You, in love?" Reggie started laughing.

"I know it sounds crazy, but I met Diane in high school and we dated, then I messed around on her and broke her heart. We saw each other at my parents' house this week. When we talked I felt something I never felt before. I don't know how to explain it."

He didn't need to explain it. Reginald knew exactly what he was talking about. He felt it every time he saw Berlin.

"Wow, dude. I can't believe after all these years someone has finally pegged your behind."

"I know, and that's why I need your help," Cameron said between sips.

Reggie remembered the last time he'd needed help it had been at the Christmas party. "What kind of help?"

Resting his elbows on the table, he finally said, "I need you to tell Berlin I won't be able to see her anymore."

"What?" Reginald tried to keep a straight face, especially since there was no way he would have allowed their relationship to have continued anyway. Not now after he had made love to Berlin. She didn't know it yet, but her body belonged to him. "You want me to end your relationship. Are you crazy?"

"I can't do it myself."

His eyes narrowed. "Why not?"

"Because Berlin is a really nice woman, but there is really no chemistry between us. I think she really likes me."

It took all he had not to set his boy straight. "She's a big girl. She can handle it."

"But since the two of you are such good friends, it would sound better coming from you."

He looked at his friend's somber face and shook his head. It looked like he would be joining the Duprees for Christmas dinner after all. And he couldn't be happier.

Berlin woke up to the smell of chit'lins' boiling on the stove. *Uugh!* She hated the smell, but they were one of her dad's favorites. And she'd do anything for him; even stand the smell in her house for the next several days.

Climbing out of bed, she felt like a child again, waking up on Christmas morning rushing down to open her presents. She slid her feet into her slippers, then traveled into the bathroom and took her robe from the back of the door and slipped into it. As soon as she washed her face and brushed her teeth, Berlin traveled down to the kitchen where she knew she would find a stack of pancakes straight off the griddle. Sure enough, she moved into the kitchen across the shining linoleum floor and found her father at the table reaching for a bottle of pure maple syrup.

"Good morning," she greeted. Berlin moved over to the stove and pressed a kiss to her mom's cheek.

She gave her daughter a loving hug. "Hello, Lil' Bit. I thought I would have to wake you up this morning."

"I haven't slept that good in a long time." Moving over to the table, she kissed her dad, then lowered in the seat beside him and reached for a strip of bacon. "I think having you guys around helps make this feel like home."

"Well, I'm glad to hear that."

Her dad patted her hand. "So am I."

Her mother reached for a plate in the cabinet and sat it down in front of Berlin, and then she watched and grinned as her father put a short stack on her plate, then reached for the butter.

"Dad, I can butter my own pancakes," she groaned playfully, then reached for the butter that he slid out of her reach.

"Now, now, let an old man have the pleasure of spoiling his baby girl."

"Yes, Daddy." She had always been a Daddy's girl. After twenty-seven years, nothing had changed.

"I've already got the greens cleaned and the turkey stuffed. All I have to do is cut the sweet potatoes and make the macaroni and cheese," her mother said as she reached for a large spoon and stirred the big pot.

"Mom," Berlin said between chews, "there is only the five of us. You're cooking like we're expecting an army."

"You never know. Maybe your friend will come to dinner."

"I already have a friend coming to dinner," she mumbled.

"So what? The more the merrier."

Berlin reached for the syrup and tried to hide the yearning in her eyes. She would love for Reginald to come and share the holiday with them, but she'd already invited Cameron. She groaned inwardly. He was sure to spend the afternoon talking about himself. Now that her parents had met Reggie and liked him, the chances of Cameron winning her parents over were next to none. That was all right with her. Even if she hadn't fallen in love with Reggie, she now knew Cameron was not the one for her.

"Mom, Reggie's heading to Memphis this morning."

"Too bad," she said, then reached for a smoked turkey leg and tossed it in the pot of greens. "I would have loved to have seen him again."

So would I. Already her body was yearning for another round.

Her dad reached for his cup of coffee and took a sip. "The way he was looking at you, I think he'll be around for a while."

Berlin blushed. "Daddy, Reggie and I are just friends."

A Delight Before Christmas

He reached across the table and patted her arm. "Lil' Bit, you need to pay close attention to what I'm about to tell you." Berlin shifted on her chair so that she could look directly at her father while he spoke. "That man of yours is a good man, and I should know. He's also in love with you."

She wished he was her man and that he did love her. All that time she had wasted, thinking she had wanted something else, only to discover what she needed was in front of her all along. She groaned and reached for her orange juice and took a sip.

"What kind of pie do you want? Sweet potato or apple?" Her mother asked, halting any thoughts of feeling sorry for herself.

"Mom, I said you're cooking too much."

She turned from the stove and waved the large wooden spoon in her direction. "Nonsense. There's no such thing."

The doorbell rang. Berlin jumped up from the table and moved to the door. Without bothering to look through the peephole, she swung it opened and was stunned.

There stood her pregnant sister with her daughter and husband.

"Merry Christmas!" they shouted in unisons.

"Oh my goodness!" she cried. "Come on in." As soon as they stepped into her foyer, she hugged her sister, then brother-in-law.

"Hey Berlin," Darryl said as he kissed her cheek, then moved to retrieve their suitcases from the porch.

Berlin looked from one to the other. "What are you doing here? I thought you were going to Paris?"

Eileen's amber eyes sparkled with amusement. "We decided to spend Christmas with the family instead."

"I can't believe it." Lowering her gaze, she stared down at her adorable niece who had grown since she'd last seen her. "Gabrielle, come give your auntie a hug."

The little girl raced over to her. Berlin scooped her up in her arms and smothered her with kisses. "How's my baby doing?"

She shook her head, swinging a long, thick ponytail. "I'm not a baby. My mommy has one in her stomach."

Glancing over at her sister, she winked. "Yes, I see that."

Her parents finally came out of the kitchen to see what all the commotion was.

"Merry Christmas! Well, it's about time you made it," her mother said as she moved over to her sister and dropped a kiss to her cheek.

"Hi, Mom, Dad."

Berlin dropped a hand to her waist. "You knew they were coming and didn't bother to tell me?"

Her sister gave her a guilty look. "I told Mom not to. I wanted to surprise you."

They giggled like little girls, then Berlin lowered her niece to the floor and draped her arm around her sister.

Eileen pulled back with a tear streaming down her cheek. "I'm so glad we came. I missed you, Little Bit."

Berlin's eyes watered with joy. "I missed you, too."

Arianna descended the stairs with Berlin right behind her. She moved into the family room and looked around, admiring the room a second time. "Berlin, your house looks awesome. I can't believe Reggie got all that done in one week.

That wasn't all he managed to do in a week. Damn, she missed him. "Thanks."

"Your parents are wonderful. I wish I had parents like them. My parents would have driven me crazy by now, but your parents are so laid back it's like something out of a movie."

Berlin grinned. She loved when people complimented her parents. "They are special."

"What time is Cameron coming?"

She glanced down at her watch. "He's supposed to be here around three, so he should be arriving soon." At least she thought so. It suddenly dawned on her, she hadn't heard from Cameron since he'd left for Minnesota.

Arianna glanced over and gave her a look. "I can't believe you didn't invite Reginald after all the work that he has done."

"I did invite him. He didn't want to come." It was probably for the best. The last thing she could do was look at both of them in the same room. Feeling the way she felt about him and having to be bothered with Cameron. Tonight she planned to break things off, and she didn't need an audience when she did it.

The doorbell rang, startling her.

Arianna rolled her eyes. "I guess that's your man."

Berlin stepped out into the hall and took a deep breath. *You can do this!* She opened the door and found Reginald standing on the other side. At the blank look on his face, she asked, "Is everything okay?"

He moved toward her. "It is now."

Reggie took her in his arms and claimed her mouth. She stood on her tiptoes, leaning into his body. He held her possessively in his arms, running his hands along her back and angled her face for a deeper kiss. Her entire body vibrated from the need to have him. She had allowed herself to get so wrapped up emotionally with him that she wanted him in a way that no other man could satisfy her but Reggie. She craved his taste on her tongue. A moan slipped from between her lips as he skimmed his mouth down the side of her cheek to her neck where a heavy pulse beat at her throat.

"Reggie," she whispered against his ear.

"Merry Christmas, boo." He suckled hungrily at her cheek, and she arched against him.

Finally, Berlin gave an exhilarating sigh, and pulled back from him. "What are you doing here?"

"Cameron's not coming. He asked me to fill in for him."

She raised both eyebrows at him. "I guess he makes a habit of that."

"It's a good thing. Otherwise, I would have had to tell him about us," he said as he stepped into the foyer.

Her breath caught. "What about us?"

"You belong to me."

He gazed down hungrily at her mouth. Kiss me, her lips screamed. And as if he had heard them, Reggie swooped down and pressed his mouth against her again. She took each stroke eagerly, loving the way he felt, he tasted. How could she have ever thought she preferred

Cameron to him? They were as different as catfish and salmon. And she loved her some catfish.

She considered sneaking upstairs to her bedroom for a little sumptin', sumptin' when she heard someone clear their throat. Berlin glanced over her shoulder to find her sister and Arianna watching and grinning.

"Mama told me to tell you, it's time for dinner. But it looks like you're already having dessert," Eileen said flirtatiously.

Berlin couldn't resist a grin. "Sis, let me introduce you to Reggie."

"The pleasure is all mine."

Her sister's eyes traveled from his head to his toes. "I can definitely see that."

Christmas dinner couldn't have been better. Reggie was an instant hit with her family. While they sat beside each other at the dining room table, he reached down and stroked her knee. He made her toes curls and her knees shake. The man made her feel alive and happy as never before.

After dinner the women moved to the kitchen. Sipping on a cup of coffee, Berlin listened to the men in the family room debate over football. She was beaming from ear to ear. She had her best friend, her family, and the man she loved. What could be better?

That he loved you back.

Arianna stepped into the room with her coat on. "I guess I better get home. My husband should be arriving shortly."

Her mother walked away from the counter and handed her a large brown paper bag. "There should be plenty of food for the two of you."

She smiled. Her eyes traveling from one to the other. "Thank you so much. I really enjoyed spending time with all of you."

"Anytime." Her mother leaned forward and embraced her like they had been long time friends. She turned and gave her sister a hug as well and exchanged goodbyes, then Berlin walked with her to the front door.

"Thanks for coming, girl."

"You know I wouldn't miss this opportunity for anything." Arianna reached for the door, then paused before opening it and swung around. "Reggie really likes you," she whispered. "And I know you like him, too. Tell that man how you feel."

Berlin pursed her lips. She should have known there was no way Arianna would leave without putting her two cents in. "We're friends, Arianna. That is not going to change."

"How can you be just friends with a brotha that turned you out? Every time you see him, you're going to want to drag his ass to the nearest bed."

She reached for the door handle and opened it. "Good night, Arianna."

Her friend shifted the bag in her arms and gave her a long hard stare. "Alright, don't listen. I guarantee by the time we get back to work you're gonna be saying, 'Arianna, girl, you were right.' "

Berlin laughed. "Girl, you're crazy. Bye."

Running his hand along his cornrows, Reginald closed his eyes and inhaled deeply before slowly letting out a breath. After a few seconds, he felt some of the anxiety ease. He couldn't believe he had allowed his emotions to race out of control.

Damn!

Why now? With the one woman who wasn't interested in anything but a fling that ended the minute the football game ended. He wanted more. He wanted a relationship. He wanted to go to movies, take her to dinner. He wanted to introduce her to his friends. He wanted to spend time with her and her parents as her man, not as her friend or the dude who painted her house. He wanted something with Berlin that he hadn't wanted with any other woman, and that was a relationship.

He released a frustrated breath. There was still one problem. Berlin didn't want any of those things. Was he crazy or what?

"You men ready for dessert?"

He swung around to see Berlin standing in the doorway with that sexy smile that made his body ache. His dick pulsed. He was ready for dessert all right.

"Might as well." Her father used his arms to pull himself up from the chair. "This isn't even a game. The Packers are down twenty points."

Darryl shook his head. "They already made the playoffs, so it really doesn't matter." As the two strolled toward the kitchen discussing the last play, Reggie sat frozen in his seat, staring over at her. There was so much he wanted to get off his chest and share. If only she would give him some kind of hint she was even interested in having a relationship with him.

"You coming or what?" she asked. "There's no guest in this house. Everybody's got to help themselves."

Reginald laughed out loud and watched her retreating back. It was nice to know that she considered him part of the family.

"Come here."

She stopped, then slowly turned around. "What?"

He rose from the couch. "I said come here."

"Who you think you're talking to?" she asked, obviously struggling to keep a straight face.

"You," he said with a wink.

Slowly, she moved toward him. He loved watching her hips wiggle. She stopped short of touching him, then gazed up at him with a wicked smile. "What do you want?"

"This." He pulled her against him, then slanted his head slightly and pressed his mouth against hers. He was certain she could feel his erection jerk in his pants against her stomach. To make sure that she did, he gripped her hip and rocked against her. She rewarded him with a moan, then wrapped her arms around him and deepened the kiss. He couldn't get enough of the way she tasted.

They heard voices coming from the other room, one of them calling Berlin's name, was the only reason he finally released her. She gave him a long seductive look, then turned and joined the others.

A *Delight Before Christmas*

She was definitely something else, he thought as he shook his head. He took a moment to get himself under control, and then followed.

While they demolished two sweet potato pies, he openly studied the woman he'd spent the last several weeks fantasizing about. She sat across from him looking sexy and sensual. He couldn't get enough of looking at her. Nor was there any way to stop his dick from growing hard again. All he could do was sit there until it went away, which wasn't easy to do. He could hardly think around her, let alone try to concentrate.

Around seven, Reginald decided it was time to call it an evening. He wanted to get an early start in the morning. Berlin didn't object when he took her hand and had her walk with him to the door. They walked slowly, hips brushing, in no rush for the evening to end.

"Thanks for letting me spend Christmas with you and your family."

"I'm glad you were here."

He smiled. "I'm glad Cameron asked me to come."

She laughed at his comment, then her eyes grew large. "Ooh! Hold on. Don't go anywhere." He watched as she dashed off into the family room. She came right back carrying a small white box and held it toward him. "Merry Christmas."

"You didn't have to get me anything."

She nodded. "Yes I did."

Taking it from her hand, he stared down at the bright red bow then back at her again. "I didn't get you anything."

"Yes you have," she said, pressing a palm against his chest. "You did all this work for me for practically nothing, and I truly appreciate it."

Heat seeped through his skin on contact. Gazing down at her parted lips, he thought about how good they had felt wrapped around his dick. Was their time together really over? He searched her eyes and saw nothing. "Thanks for the gift. Want me to open it now?"

Shaking her head, she answered, "No, open it later." Berlin then glanced over her shoulder and his heart sunk. She was ready for him to leave so she could get back to the others.

He put the small box in his coat pocket then laced their fingers together. "Enjoy the rest of your holiday." He shifted from one foot to the other uncertain what to say or do next. All he knew was that this would possibly be his last moment ever with her.

She nodded. "Have a safe trip to Memphis."

"I'll call when I arrive."

He pulled her to him, then and kissed her long and hard, hoping that she would say something about tonight, tomorrow or the next week. But by the time they pulled apart, she had reached for the door handle.

"Bye Reggie."

He tried to hide his disappointment as he nodded, and said, "Take care."

Reggie moved through the door and didn't bother to turn around. When he finally climbed into his SUV he looked up, the door was shut and she was gone. He slammed his hand against the steering wheel. He couldn't believe the relationship was over. He had hoped that they would have been able to spend one more night together. He wanted her to tell him she would be by his place tonight after her family settled in for the night.

Yeah, right.

Raking a frustrated hand across his face, he realized that a nice visit to his mother was just what the doctor ordered. Kia had things pretty much under control that he could dip out for a couple of days and be reachable by phone. His shoulders relaxed with relief. Getting away from the city was just what he needed to take his mind off Berlin and their uncertain future.

Putting the key in the ignition, he started it and allowed it a few minutes to warm up. Hopefully, the weather would be much better in Memphis.

It had been months since he'd seen his mother. It would only temporarily take Berlin off his mind, but at the moment he was willing to take what he could get. And by the time he drove back to Missouri, he would have decided what the next step would be in his life.

Two hours later, Reginald decided he was going crazy.

He was sitting at the kitchen table, drinking a shot of whiskey with an erection that only Berlin could ease. Only there was no more her because their relationship was officially ended. She hadn't called as he'd hoped.

Reginald gripped his throbbing dick through his jeans with his fist. This wouldn't work. He couldn't go on like this. He had just left her house. The smell of her still on his hands. The taste of her still on his lips, yet he could hardly think or focus on the television, because he couldn't stop thinking about her.

With his other hand, he reached for his beer, trying to do whatever it took to numb the feeling inside. When had everything between them change? Fun and sex—that was all it was supposed to have been. Instead, he yearned for her smile, the sight of her burned at his chest. Pacing around the room didn't help. Holding his own dick didn't do the trick.

He finally released it and rested his elbow on the table. Maybe being with a different female might work. Some wild hot sex might be the best way to cure what ailed him. Setting the can down, he moved over to the phone and dialed.

Berlin tucked her niece into her bed. Tonight she welcomed the small warm body beside her. After having Reggie for the last several days, sleep tonight wouldn't come easily alone.

Slipping her feet in her house shoes, she moved down to the kitchen where her mom and sister were loading the last dish in the dishwasher.

She frowned. "I told you I would do them later."

Her mother gave a dismissive wave. "Nonsense. Have a seat."

Obediently, she lowered into the seat across from her sister.

Eileen leaned across the table. "I really like your friend."

"So do I." *Too much. That's the problem.*

"Does he know you're in love with him?"

Her eyes grew wide as she looked from her sister to her mom and back again. *How did her sister know that?*

"It's written all over your face," she replied as if she could read her mind.

"She's right, Lil' Bit," her mother said as she wiped down the countertop. "That man couldn't take his eyes off you and neither could you take yours off him."

Was it that obvious?

Berlin no longer wanted to pretend. Dropping her eyes, she looked down at her hands. "He's not looking for a commitment."

Her mother snorted rudely. "That man loves you."

Berlin's head shot up. "You think so?"

"We know so," they replied in unisons.

She smiled. It would be so wonderful if he did love her.

"Why don't I go check on the men while y'all talk?" Her mother gave her shoulder a quick squeeze, then moved into the other room.

"Lil' Bit, you deserve to be happy." Her sister's face sobered. "You know, I've never said this before, but I've always been envious of you."

She was stunned by her admission. "You have?"

Eileen nodded, then leaned back in the chair and rubbed her belly. "You're smart and educated with a good head on your shoulders. I never had that. You don't need a man to be successful."

"Neither do you."

The look she gave said she disagreed. "Yes I do," Eileen whispered, then smiled. "You know I was never any good at school. All I have ever wanted was to be a wife and mother, and that is exactly what I am, and I'm happy. But you've always strived for more, and I admire that about you."

"I guess."

"Just keep in mind there is nothing wrong with being independent, but don't let it get in the way of your happiness."

Her brow rose. "What do you mean?"

Eileen's amber eyes darkened. "Put your pride aside and tell that man you love him before it's too late."

"I'll have to wait until after the holidays. He's leaving in the morning for Memphis."

"Girl, then I guess you better go and tell him tonight."

"I can't do that, I have company."

"Family, who can entertain themselves." Eileen stifled a yawn. "Beside, I'm getting ready to take my husband to bed. It isn't often that we get a night alone without your niece climbing under the covers with us."

"I can't leave Gabrielle alone."

Eileen rolled her eyes as she slowly pulled herself up from the chair. "That girl is out for the count. Now quit coming up with excuses and go."

Her sister was right. She had nothing to lose but quite a bit to gain.

Quietly, Berlin hurried up to her room where she changed into something warm then hurried to see Reggie. As she grabbed her coat and keys, she was bubbling with excitement and her body was on fire, anticipating having him inside of her again. Tonight she was going to tell him exactly how she felt about him.

She pulled onto his street and parked across the street so that he wouldn't see her headlights. She wanted to surprise him. Walking up the sidewalk, she admired a lovely white Mercedes parked behind his pick-up truck. She strolled up to his door and saw someone moving in his living room window. Not one to pry, however, something told her to take a look anyway. What she saw made her heart stop.

Reggie was lying on the couch and the woman from the restaurant, his ex, was standing over him in nothing but a thong. Music was playing, and she was dancing around in high heel red shoes and a sequins thong with her breasts jiggling freely.

Slowly she backed away, feeling hurt and disgusted that he had already moved on to the next woman. Berlin quickly climbed back into her car and headed it home.

He shouldn't have invited her over.

Reggie knew that now. Even having three more shots before Jasmine's arrival didn't help. He watched her dance around the room, thinking how her striptease used to turn him on. Tonight, however, it had an opposite effect.

He shifted on the couch, feeling like a heel. When he had invited Jasmine over it was because he thought he just needed a quick screw to alleviate his erection, but there was more to it than that. He admitted that now. It wasn't that he wasn't attracted to her. Jasmine was fine. Big succulent breasts. Wide hips and a narrow waist. She even had a tongue that she knew how to use. But as he watched her prance her naked body around his living room, he realized that with Berlin it was more than sex. He loved her mind and her soul.

With his limp dick in hand, Reggie watched Jasmine gyrate her hips to Mary J. Blige. He scowled inwardly. Poor Jasmine. She didn't even know it, but he had used her as a distraction to take his mind off Berlin.

Although he no longer had an erection, his plan to get Berlin off his mind hadn't worked at all. He hated hurting people's feelings. Releasing a heavy sigh, Reggie realized he would have to pretend to be interested, then let her down easily. If he couldn't have Berlin, then he didn't want anyone at all.

Chapter Fifteen

Berlin gazed out the window at the blankets of snow on the ground. Her parents and Eileen's family were long gone. She had enjoyed their company and the bond she and her sister had renewed. Now her sister was on her way back to sunny California, to her life as mother and wife. Her parents were returning to the life she had known as a child that for some reason she had spent years trying to escape for all the wrong reasons, and now she didn't even have a clue as to why. The last two weeks she had developed a deep appreciation for life for who she was, not who she wanted to be. She loved soul food and hanging out at juke joints, dancing to oldies but goodies. All of it had been a lot of fun, because she'd had Reggie by her side.

Turning away from the window, she gazed around at her formal living room, at the expensive royal blue furniture that she never sat on and frowned at how ridiculous the whole idea was. Why have a room you never use? Reggie was right; it was dumb. To prove that she had gotten past that stage, she flopped down onto the couch. Slipping off her house shoes, she curled her feet beneath her.

She had spent the last ten years governing her life by ten stupid rules. Buying clothes she could barely afford, living in a house she was afraid to heat, and searching for prestige instead of love. Only love had found her instead.

Berlin sank back against the couch as the strong ache returned to her middle section. She was head over heels in love with a man whom she had ruined ever having a chance with. Closing her eyes, she tried to push back the tears as she remembered telling Reggie that she could never love a man who wasn't rich. She had said it so many times that even she had started to believe it herself. She thought all she had to do was point out the man she wanted and everything else would come in time, only it didn't happen that way. Instead, she had learned you cannot pick and chose who you fall in love with. It just doesn't happen that way.

I know that now.

Why couldn't he be like other men? But then, that's why she loved him so much, because he wasn't like other men. She hated feeling out of control. For the last several years, she had been able to control every aspect of her life, but with Reginald, her world had been turned upside down.

A hot tear rolled down her cheek as she thought about what she had done. She had run Reggie away and into the arms of another woman. Dragging her legs to her chest, she rested her chin on her knee as she was hit by a strong emotional need. She already missed him.

For the last twenty days, Reginald had been a daily part of her life. She had looked forward to his calls. His presence. Now she was left feeling sorry for herself, yearning his taste, touch and smell. How in the world had she ever thought she wanted someone like Cameron? The conceited jackass. Not when she had such a caring man in her company. She was in love with a simple man who turned out to be quite successful.

Now there was no way he was going to believe how she felt.

She hadn't heard from him since he left, and she was dying inside.

How stupid I have been.

As she glanced around her home, she realized that even with a big house and a fancy car, none of that meant anything if she wasn't happy. And she was far from it. Her dream of marrying a doctor and being part of the elite medical community no longer mattered to her. Tears pushed to the surface that she allowed to flow freely. She had scraped and sacrificed so much over the years, and for what? She was no more happier now than she had been before. In fact, growing up in Chicago sharing ghost stories with her family around a room lit by candles after the lights had been cut off were some of her happiest moments. Her mother was right. Love got you through just about anything. One thing they'd always had in their house was love. Her parents were prime examples of that. Her parents could always be found cuddling in a corner with one another. Love. She hadn't believed love existed and all along it was right there in front of her face. How in the world had she ever come up with such ridiculous ideas?

Berlin leaned over and grabbed a tissue from an end table and blew her nose. She had met the most wonderful man in the world, and now he thought she was a gold digger. He thought she was interested in marrying rich and didn't believe in love, whereas, in the last week that was no longer true. She didn't care about money. She no longer cared about becoming Mrs. M.D. All she wanted was Reginald.

She curled her feet beneath her and stared off into the fire as she tried to think of a way to tell him. Now she knew that he was more than just a painter, he would never believe she fell in love with him long before she had known his true occupation. Reginald would think that she was now only interested in him because he was the owner of a successful business.

But none of that was true. She had fallen in love with him the first time he had ever kissed her. Only she had been too stubborn to admit it. Now that Cameron had ended their brief relationship, Reginald would think she was on the rebound and desperate.

Her doorbell rang, and she sprang to it hoping that it was Reginald. Her shoulders sagged with disappointment when she found her flamboyant friend standing on the other side.

"It's good to see you, too," she said with sarcasm as she followed her into the living room.

Glancing over her shoulder, she gave her friend an apologetic smile. "I'm sorry, Arianna. I was just hoping you were Reggie."

"Reggie? Isn't he still out of town?"

She nodded her head, then moved over to the couch and took a seat. Arianna took a seat in the chair across from her and kicked off her shoes and curled her legs beneath her.

"Yeah," she began with a sigh. "I was just hoping that he would be back by now."

"When was the last time you've spoken to him?"

"Not since the Christmas party. He told me he was going to go spend a couple of days with his mother, and he'd be back before New Years."

"Then he should be home soon." Her friend leaned forward and observed her for several long seconds before she asked, "Are you in love with Reggie?"

That was one question she didn't need a second to think about. "Yes."

"Oh my goodness!" Arianna jumped out of her seat and raced and draped her arms around her, practically knocking her from her chair. "I can't believe it. No, I take that back. I knew it would happen if you gave the man half a chance."

Berlin laughed lightly. "Can you please let me go?"

"Sorry, girlfriend." She released her and returned to her seat. Her eyes were still sparkling with excitement. "About time. The two of you make such a lovely couple. I can already see beautiful babies in your future."

She couldn't help chuckling as she groaned. Her dear friend had a wild and vivid imagination. "We haven't even got past the 'I love you' stage, and you're already marrying us off."

"It's just a matter of time."

I sure hope so. The thought of spending the rest of her life with Reggie made her feel warm and cuddly inside.

"And, as you can see, I know a good thing when I see it." She paused to clap her hands. "Have you told him how you feel?"

"No."

"Are you planning to tell him?"

"No."

Arianna's brow rose. "Why not?"

"Because he's not going to believe me."

"Ooh! I need some popcorn before I hear this." She raced into the kitchen.

Berlin followed, chuckling lightly at how quickly Arianna had grown comfortable in her house.

Arianna headed straight for the pantry.

Popcorn in the microwave, Arianna said, "Okay, now you sit down and give me all the juicy details." Arianna rubbed her hands together like she was about to get a pot of gold. She couldn't resist a smile before lowering in the chair across from her.

"Why don't you think he'll believe you?"

"Because I told him I was marrying for money. He thinks I am a gold digger, and I can't blame him. I told him he wasn't good enough and that I was only interested in men with money."

"But he does have money."

"I know that now. Before I thought he was a painter, and because of it he'll think I am only interested in him now because I found out he owns one of the largest contracting companies in the city."

"Well, is it?"

"No," she said defensively. "I realized I loved him long before I found out he was rich."

"Then tell him that."

"Like I said. He won't believe me." The timer went off and she rose and retrieved the bag. Reaching into the cabinet over the sink, she removed a large plastic bowl then ripped open the bag and poured it in.

"I think you're underestimating him. Reggie seems to be very understanding."

Berlin tossed the bag in the trash, then carried the bowl over to the table. "I don't think it would really matter. He's not interested in a committed relationship. We had an agreement. Sex until the holidays with no strings attached."

Arianna reached for a handful of popcorn and shook her head. "That may have been the beginning, but things changed. I saw the way the two of you looked at each other at your Christmas party. That man is crazy about you."

Then why the hell was that hoochie at his house? "You really think so?"

"I know so," she said between bites. "But because he is a man, you know he probably doesn't even realize it himself."

"Great." She reached for the bowl and grabbed some popcorn.

"Don't give up yet. You have to show that man how much you want to be with him. That you've changed."

"And how do I do that?"

"Throw it on him. The way I did Carlton."

She popped another kernel into her mouth. She loved hearing how the two of them met. Carlton was a cop who had no intentions of settling down. But Arianna had other plans. She seduced him until Carlton had no choice, but to pay attention. Before long, she had him eating out of the palm of her hands and proposing marriage.

Berlin gave her suggestion some thought. "It might work. He loved the way I looked in that leather skirt and red shirt."

Arianna's lips curled upward. "Then he is going to love you in something a little more revealing. Trust me."

"I hope you're right."

Reggie brought the beer to his mouth, then glanced up at the woman gyrating her hips around the stage to 50 Cents "Candy Shop." He shivered at the sight. The exotic dancer was overweight with more stretch marks than he ever wanted to see in one place. He didn't know why he let his brother talk him into going to Dreams—a small hole in the wall strip club in the hood.

Carrying an extra bottle of beer, Reginald moved to the end of the bar where Jay was putting a dollar bill in a thong attached to another chunky woman with breasts that hung almost to her knees. He shook his head, then tapped his brother on the shoulder.

Jay tapped her lightly on the behind as she sashayed away with a little extra *umph* in her step.

"Man, what's up with the honeys in here? They all look like they've been eating too many Krispy Kreme doughnuts."

Laughing, Jay took the beer from his hand. "Yo, man. I see you still got jokes." He took a sip, then shrugged. "Hey big girls gotta work, too."

"True, but do they all have to work in the same place?"

They shared a chuckle. "Hey we can always go down to Illusions and pick up a couple of honeys."

"Nah, I'll pass." He put his beer to his lips again, then glanced over at the stage again. Big Love was gone.

The music changed to Jagged Edge's "Good Luck Charm," and the deejay's voice flooded the room. "We got Cherish in the house. Brothas, y'all show her some love!"

A tall brown skin woman moved onto the stage in a nurse's uniform. Skin shining. Long auburn hair. Small waist. Large breasts. Everything about her reminded him of Berlin. Not everything. There was only one Berlin.

Jay howled like a dog. "Yo, boy. That's what I'm talking about up there!" He reached into his pocket for another dollar, then quickly moved over to stand at the stage. Reginald leaned back against the counter and shook his head. He remembered when he used to rush to strip clubs giving away his hard-earned dollars. He remembered the black book full of numbers he looked through every weekend. None of that seemed to matter to him anymore. He wanted one woman, and one woman only.

The last two weeks had changed him. Berlin was a beautiful woman with a fabulous personality. He once thought her to be a gold digger with a hidden agenda, but instead found her to be a compassionate and insecure woman who only wanted the best, and he couldn't be mad at her for that.

And he wanted to be the one to give it to her.

In the days that he had known her, she had become the most important person in his life. In the past, those feelings would have scared him away. Now the only thing that caused him real fear was the thought of losing her.

"Yo-Yo-Yo, Reggie. I need a favor."

He glanced at Jay as he moved to the bar stool beside him. He finished his beer, then spun and faced him. Reginald knew before he even opened his mouth that he was getting ready to ask him for some money. "Yeah, whassup, man?"

"I'm a little short on cash and was wondering if you could give a brother a loan."

Reginald gave him a firm look, then reached into his back pocket for his wallet. He never had been any good at saying no. "So, how the job hunting going?"

"Just a minor setback."

Reginald had to laugh at that one. "Minor? You've been unemployed almost six months."

Jay gave him a dismissive wave. "Dude, I don't know why they want to pay a brotha peanuts for a day's work."

Reginald removed two twenties and handed them to him. "Something is better than nothing. Then at least you won't have to ask your brother for a loan."

"It's gon' get better. I promise you. Hey, I might even come and work for you."

With his brother's track record, he would rather just keep giving him loans.

Chapter Sixteen

Reginald stepped into his mother's small kitchen that she decorated completely with apples.

"Good morning, dear," Margaret Hodges said as she set the table for breakfast. A short, round woman, she wore jeans and a pink turtleneck, her salt-and-pepper curls perfectly in place. She rose on her tiptoes to kiss her oldest son. "Sit."

Reginald frowned. "Mom, you don't have to serve me," he said as he took a seat.

"Yes, I do. I don't get to see my son enough." She carried over a plate of waffles and sugar-cured bacon.

"Mom, you're spoiling me."

"That's what mother's do." She pointed a scolding finger at him. "And as soon as you find a good woman, she can have the job."

"Oh, boy, here we go," he murmured around a slice of bacon.

She moved in the seat across from him. "I've been watching you mope around here for the last couple of days. Who is she?"

He snapped to her attention. "Who is who?"

She gave him a knowing look. "The woman you're in love with."

"I'm—"

"Boy, don't lie to me," she interrupted. "It's written all over your face. It's in your gestures. You're miserable."

"I guess I've never been able to put one over on you."

"No you haven't," she said as she reached for a strip of bacon. "Have you told this girl how you feel?"

"Not in so many words."

"I'll take that as a no," she replied between chews. "My advice to you is to tell that girl you love her before it's too late. I want grandchildren, but, most importantly, I want you to be happy."

He was silent, although her words rushed through him. Love? It was something he refused to think about. Something that had burned him before. But his mother was right. When he thought of Berlin, the emotion that overwhelmed him ran deeper than lust. It was deeper than sex.

He loved her. And damn it, he planned to tell her.

Berlin curled up in the bed and decided to spend the evening watching *Lifetime Television*. What a way to spend a Friday. She was single and didn't have a date or plans for the weekend, except for Arianna's New Year's party on Saturday. She hoped her current single status was not a sample of the upcoming year.

By eleven she started to doze off when the phone rang. She started not to answer because she knew it was Arianna calling to again invite her to join in on a slumber party with her and her sisters. She just wasn't in the mood for running around in pajamas and gossiping into the wee hours of the morning.

The telephone rang loudly. About the fourth ring, Berlin bolted upright in the bed when the sound finally filtered through her sleepy mind. She reached over to her bedside table and grabbed the phone before its sixth ring.

"Arianna, I was trying to sleep."

"What kind of way is that to spend your vacation?"

She sat up in the bed, suddenly wide-awake. "Reggie."

"Yeah, boo, it's me."

Her heart fluttered against her chest. "Hey. How is your family?"

"Good." There was a slight pause. "I miss you."

"I miss you, too," she heard herself confess as she lay back against the pillows again.

"Show me how much," he said, his voice soft, seductive.

"Show you?" she asked puzzled.

"Yes. I want to know what you're wearing."

Berlin brushed her hand across her flannel gown. Nothing sexy about that. She decided to tell him what he wanted to hear. "Oh, nothing. I decided to sleep in the nude."

He groaned through the phone. "Damn, why you got to tell me that?"

"You shouldn't have asked." She giggled, then there was a long pause.

"I wish I was lying beside you."

"I wish you were to because I am really horny right now," she cooed.

Reggie groaned. "You're starting something."

"Am I, baby?" she asked softly.

"Hell, yeah."

She giggled softly, then reached up and slipped her gown over her head so that she was lying there nude just like she said. Lying back comfortably on the pillows, she closed her eyes and moaned. "I missed your hands caressing my breasts."

"I love you breasts."

"They love you, too."

"Tell me what I would do to you if I was there."

"You'd run your hand down my neck, then travel from one nipple to the next." She ran her fingertips across her nipples as she spoke, her breathing had deepened, her voice dropping down to a whisper. "Mmm...that feels good."

"Oh yes, baby. I can feel your heart beating against my hand. I can smell the sweet scent of your skin." His low voice was seductive. "Where's my hand now?"

She had to swallow to get the words out. "Traveling down past my belly button, slipping into a patch of hair." Her sex began to throb, begging to be touched.

"Are you wet?"

Oh, God, was she. As she traveled past the sensitive numb, she parted the fold. "Yes, Reggie, I'm wet."

"How do my fingers feel sliding inside of you?"

As her fingers slipped inside, she inhaled deeply and released a shudder, "Slippery. Oh, yes." She moaned as she plunged deeper. "I wish you were here to make love to me." Her breath caught in her throat.

"I don't think you're ready yet."

"Oh, I'm ready," she said as she dove deeper. "I want you more than I should. All I think about is you no matter how hard I try not to."

"You sound like that's a bad thing."

She stroked her clit and released another moan before answering. "The bad thing is that I've gotten so used to being around you. I've gotten attached, and that was a mistake."

"Why is that a mistake?"

"Because I want you here. Instead, I'm lying here alone, wanting you inside of me."

"I am inside of you. I'm getting ready to make you come all over this fat dick."

"Yesss, baby." She pushed her fingers deep inside of her while her thumb caressed her nub. She imagined her legs spread wide, her thighs parted with Reginald lying between her thighs, thrusting deep inside her heat. "Reginald…" she cried his name as an orgasm exploded through her. Her entire body shuddered and her eyes rolled back. She could barely hold the phone and allowed it to rest on the pillow beside her ear. While her breathing slowed, she used her hands to pinch her nipples.

"Let's do that again," she heard whispered near her ear. Berlin thought it was through the receiver until she felt his warm breath.

She opened her eyes to find Reggie standing in front of her bed removing his clothes. She gasped. He was here. *Really here!* "When did you get back?"

"Now."

"How did you get…" the rest of her question was cut off by a long wet kiss.

He pulled back and licked his lips. "I know where you hide the spare key. Now I want you to come again, while I watch."

She slid two fingers into her heat, then her thumb found her clit and circled it. "I missed you." Her body trembled.

A Delight Before Christmas

"I missed you, too. Now I'm back and ready to be inside of you," he said while he removed a red piece of paper from his pants pocket and laid it on the nightstand. As soon as Berlin realized what it was, she started laughing.

"I see you opened my gift." She had given him a dozen sex coupons she had discovered in a lingerie shop. There were redeemable for kisses, blowjobs and mind-boggling sex. When she had given him the gift, Berlin had hoped Reggie would come back to her and redeem them. And now he had, she was going to do whatever she had to do to make sure he never left her again.

She continued to play with her clit while licking her lips and staring across the bed at him. Reggie grabbed his dick by the base and stroked upward in the same rhythm as her fingers.

"I'm getting ready to get all up in that."

It's yours and you don't even know it. Heat and anticipation built inside of her as she stared over at him. "I sure hope so." Her legs were spread, and her inner thighs dripping wet.

He caressed the head, releasing a drop or two of pre-cum he smeared across the tip. All the while, she watched and continued to finger herself. "Tell me how much you want me."

"I want you."

He flipped her over and pulled her hips back toward the edge of the bed, then ripped the small foil package open. She reached down and continued to play with herself, then withdrew her slick fingers when the condom was firmly in place. "And I want you now. Please."

"It's all yours." He pushed all the way in. Reginald growled and he pumped wild inside. Within seconds, another orgasm shattered through her. He held onto her waist and slammed into her. Then pulled out slightly and slid all the way back in until she screamed his name. His back arched. The next orgasm was so powerful they shared it, and she could only collapse on the bed and sob.

"What's wrong, babe?" he asked minutes later as he held her in his arms.

"Nothing. I'm just happy," she answered between pants.

He kissed her lips. "So am I."

When she woke up the next morning, Reggie was gone. However, he left a note on the pillow beside her that if she wanted him all she had to do was call.

Chapter Seventeen

She called Reggie and told him she wanted their third date. He agreed, and she invited him back to her house that evening, then spent the rest of the morning wracking her brain, trying to plan the perfect evening. She wanted to do something that he wouldn't expect, and that would show how much she truly loved him.

Hours later, she was ready, or at least she hoped she was. The phone rang, and she was glad to discover it was Reggie.

"Hey, boo."

At the sound of his voice, she felt her walls clench.

"We still on for tonight?"

"Yes."

"Anything I need to bring?"

"No, I think I got everything. I want tonight to be perfect."

He was quiet for a long minute, and she could hear him breathe deeply before saying. "As long as I'm with you, everything is perfect."

She hugged an arm around her waist and tried not to let the words settle around her heart, but they did. Her heart pumped wildly, and she felt the verge of tears. "You always know just the right thing to say."

"I'm just telling you the truth."

She smiled to herself and pushed aside the overwhelming need to tell him how much she loved him. She wanted to wait until tonight when the time was right.

Berlin glanced down at the white teddy she had found in the bottom of her dresser. The material was form-fitting and showed any imperfections. She knew she had them. She didn't exercise anywhere near enough. Not anymore. At one time she used to spend hours in front of the television, kicking and punching with Billy Blanks, but now those days were few and far between. Her thighs had softened over the years, and no matter how many stomach crunches she did, she still had a slight pouch in front. Still, even with a few strikes, she was relatively pleased with her shape. She had taken her body from her grandmother's side of the family. Small waist, big breasts and legs. She couldn't complain. It could have been a lot worse. Eileen had inherited the small chest and wide hips. Although even then her sister managed to be gorgeous.

She took a long hot bath in scented bubble bath, then rubbed a generous amount of *Lovely* body lotion on her body, followed by powder and perfume. By the time she heard a knock at the door, she was ready. He had arrived on time.

"Hey."

"Whassup, sexy?"

You in a few minutes. Berlin moved aside so that he could enter. As soon as she shut the door, she turned around and dropped the robe to the floor.

His jaw dropped in amazement, then his eyes traveled from the two pigtails in her head to the midriff sweater that showed off her firm belly to the short tweed skirt. He gazed down at her long legs in white thigh highs to a pair of four-inch white stilettos that made her look sexy as hell. She looked like a schoolgirl, although girls never looked like that while he was in school.

Yum. He licked his lips. She looked quite delectable. "Damn, baby. Can we skip dinner and go straight for dessert?" He moved forward to kiss her, but she pushed a hand to his chest and stopped him.

She gave him a stern look. "Nope. I'm in charge tonight. Not you."

She strolled past him, and he watched the sway of her hips and her sexy butt cheeks that peeked out the back of her skirt as she moved into the dining room. This was the woman he'd been fantasizing about. Tonight she appeared more sensual, more womanly than ever before. Like a puppy, he followed her.

Reginald walked into the room and stopped. Candlelight. Soft music. Fancy place settings. Berlin was planning to seduce him. A devilish smile turned his lips. He couldn't wait.

"Have a seat." She pointed to a chair to his left, and she lowered in the one across from him.

As soon as he was seated, she removed the covers from their plates.

"Wow!" he said as he gazed down at collard greens, black-eyed peas and fried chicken.

"Eat up. You're going to need your strength."

He definitely liked the sound of that.

They were silent as they enjoyed the food and the sounds of Jamie Foxx. The entire time he kept his eyes trained on her. She had unfastened two buttons at the top of her sweater, and the swells of her breasts were exposed. He could hardly think. He just wondered how fast they could eat so he could carry her up to her room and make love to her. Berlin seemed to be taking her time, moaning between bites. With her eyes closed, she ran her tongue slowly across her lips. His balls swelled. His erection pulsed in his pants. She was trying to torture him.

Finally, she opened her eyes and lowered her fork to the table. "Would you like dessert?"

"Only if you're on the menu," he replied, leaning forward over the table.

She gave him a seductive look, then rose from the chair. "I have a surprise for you. Put your hands behind your back and close your eyes."

Amused, he did as she said and felt her thigh brush across his arm. A second later, he heard a clicking sound and something tightened around his wrist.

"What the…" He opened his eyes and tried to move his hands and could not. Berlin had handcuffed them behind his back.

"I told you before I'm in charge tonight," she said with a wicked grin.

A groan escaped his lips. "Now how do you plan to make love without my help?"

Her gaze lowered to his crotch. "I don't think that will be a problem."

He didn't have to look down to understand her meaning. The very thought of her and his dick was standing to attention.

"What are you planning to do to me?"

"Just wait and see."

She walked over to a stereo in the corner, and Will Downing flooded the room. Reginald swallowed and waited. He expected her to slip out of her outfit and straddle him. Instead, she reached down and slowly unbuttoned her sweater, watching his face as she did. Once she reached the last button, she pushed it off her shoulders and allowed it to fall to the floor. With a wink, she grasped the hem of her tennis skirt and raised it and slowly turned around. Reginald licked his lips as her skirt slipped away next. She was left standing in a red lacey bra with the darks of her nipples peeking out the top of the lace and matching low-ride panties. Her eyes traveled back to his dick, and she nibbled on her bottom lip with her eyes sparkling mischief. She began to dance and slowly gyrate her hips. She moved to the beat of the music.

She then turned her back to him and leaned over with her thighs parted and touched her toes at the same time her butt cheeks clapped. Reginald swallowed as he realized her panties were crotchless. She had shaved her folds, and her clit was proudly on display. Standing up again with her back still to him, she unsnapped her bra. She allowed it to fall to the floor, then slowly turned around. Reginald felt his erection pulse as he gazed at her breasts. They were swollen with cinnamon nipples that were erect. She rubbed her chest and along her crotch, and he watched her eyes close and her lips quiver.

Her striptease apparently had her excited as well. As she moved, dropping and rolling her hips, he was discovering an adventurous side of her he never imagined. She squeezed and plucked at her breasts, and when she placed one of her nipples in her mouth, and suckled, he thought he was going to burst from his jeans.

Berlin squatted in front of him. Leaning forward, her hair brushed his chest, his abdominals contracted in response. She reached for his belt buckle.

"Boo, take these handcuffs off," he said harshly. He was tired of sitting watching and not being able to participate. To further his frustration, Berlin ignored him and released his zipper.

"Raise up."

Obediently, he lifted his hips and allowed her to slide his jeans down to his ankles followed by his boxers.

He watched her gaze down at his dick that was standing to attention, then she leaned forward and gently blew on the head, making him close his eyes in pleasure. Damn! She hadn't even touched it yet and already he was threatening to explode.

"Are you going to let me go?"

"No," she whispered before kissing his chest. She moved to one nipple, and then the other. She left a trail of kisses across his chest down across his stomach.

"What are you trying to do?" he hissed as she moved to his knee and up his inner thigh then over to the other.

"Make love to you," she responded between slow, wet kisses. "Now hush and enjoy it." She then moved in and closed her mouth over his tip and suckled like a newborn baby.

"Oh, God!" Reginald exclaimed.

Pausing, she looked up and grinned slightly. "Does that feel good?"

"Hell yes!" he gasped as his head fell back. She sucked him like a kitten at his mother's breasts. It was obvious she knew what she was doing. She sucked, then released and sucked again. She took the head into her mouth, then slowly pulled back and swallowed a little more.

She was driving him crazy at the slow, sedate pace. Opening his eyes, he gazed down at her to find her staring up at him while her tongue slid across the tip. After several long powerful minutes, he was squirming on the chair, ready to come hard down her throat. Only he didn't want to come. Not yet.

"Let me loose," he asked, desperately. "So I can slide all this inside of you and make you feel good."

Berlin paused to peer up at him questioningly. "No. I told you I'm running things tonight, not you."

She then stood and moved in front of him just enough for one of her nipples to brush his nose. Tilting his head, he kissed the side of her breasts before closing his mouth over a nipple.

Berlin moaned, then went completely still as he ravished her hungrily as if it were his last meal.

"You're not playing fair," she cooed.

"Neither are you."

He could feel her body trembling while he licked, nibbled, and sucked. Groaning, she eased away from him and shook her head. A groan of disappointment slipped from his lip.

"Nice try. Now be a good boy before I go get the duct tape."

He nearly laughed. "You wouldn't dare."

"Try me."

He watched as she took a step back to slide her panties seductively down her hips and kicked them away.

She then positioned herself over him. Greedily, he suckled at her breasts as she probed and rubbed herself over his swollen member. He groaned and she giggled, obviously enjoying her power over him. He tried to concentrate on sucking, but she had rested her hands onto his shoulders and was rocking her wet warmth folds along the length of his dick.

"How does that feel?" she purred.

"So good." He tugged at his handcuffs. "You going to let me go now?"

"Not yet."

He closed his eyes as she continued to rock her hips back and forth until finally she moved and retrieved a condom she had stashed in a drawer near the sink. He couldn't resist a grin. She had thought of everything. After sliding it over his length, Berlin lifted up and over and eased him into her warm passage. He moaned and groaned something fierce.

When he was ready to demand that she release him, she braced her hands on his shoulders and raised up sliding him halfway out before lowering again. She watched him, and he gazed at her as well until she closed her eyes and leaned her head back. As she rode him, he heard her breath hiss.

"Yes, baby. Ride this dick."

She continued to move in a slow up and down movement. In and out and after a while it started driving him crazy. He struggled in the handcuffs, wanting his hands free so that he could bury himself deep inside of her and thrust faster and harder.

"Dammit, Berlin, take these handcuffs off!" he yelled in frustration.

She glanced at him and frowned. "No."

"Please, I want to touch you," he begged. She stopped with him still buried inside of her and a wicked smile turning her mouth.

"Like this." She cupped her breasts, then closed her eyes. She squeezed them together and captured the nipples between her thumb and fingers. As she pinched and caressed, a moan slipped from between her lips. Reginald watched and felt his dick pulsate between her tight walls. She began to ride him again, raising and lowering in a relaxed rhythm as she continued to play with her breasts. She brought one nipple to her mouth and sucked like a newborn baby, then shifted to the other. Unable to hold still a minute longer he rocked his hips, lifting off the chair and thrusting deep inside her. Her lips parted slightly and her head fell backward. Reginald gritted his teeth as excitement overtook him. His body jerked, and then cried out exploding inside her with force. Heart pounding, eyes shut, she collapsed against him.

As soon as his breathing slowed, Reginald lowered his head and kissed her at the temple.

"Release me so I can hold you in my arms." She slowly rose. He watched the smile on her lips as she retrieved a small key from the table. As she moved toward him, she paused.

"Not until you tell me why that woman was at your house last week."

It took him a second to realize who she was talking about. Berlin seen Jasmine, which meant she had come to him after all. "That was a mistake. I swear I didn't sleep with her. I planned to, but I couldn't because the only person I want is you."

Pain etched her face, and he hated knowing he was the reason why it was there.

"How do I know you're telling me the truth?" she asked barely above a whisper.

Reginald looked up at her with sincerity in his eyes. "Because I love you Berlin."

Her mouth dropped open. "You love me?"

"I've loved you since that day you tried to get in Santa's pants. I was just too stupid and stubborn to admit it."

Berlin straddled his lap with tears streaming from her eyes. Reaching up, she cupped his face then kissed his lips. "Oh my God!" she gazed up at his handsome face. "You just don't know how badly I wanted to hear those words. I love you, too." Berlin laughed. She was so happy. "I want to spend the rest of my life showing you just how much you mean to me."

"For real?"

Nodding, she kissed him again.

"Can you let me go now, so I can make love to you properly?"

She gave him an amused look. "You promise to behave."

"Of course."

She slid from his lap and removed the key. The cuffs were barely off his wrists when he lifted her off the floor and tossed her over his shoulder. As he walked down the hall, he slapped a hand across her buttocks.

"Ow! That hurts."

"Good. You deserve it." He slapped her again.

Berlin woke up to find the sun peeping out from behind the curtain and a warm body beside her. Shifting on the bed, she realized something was wrong. Turning to the right, she found Reginald rolled onto his side, smiling down at her.

And then she tried to move her arm and realized what he was grinning about.

He had handcuffed her wrist to the headboard.

"What are you doing?" She couldn't resist a grin.

"Getting you back."

Reginald rose up on the bed and trailed an index finger down between her breasts. A shiver went through her. She swallowed and realized she was in trouble. He was getting ready to make her pay.

"You're mine."

He swooped down and captured her mouth. She was stunned by his claim and pleased to hear him say it. The idea of belonging to him made her heart swell and tears sting at the back of her eyes. She loved this man more than life itself.

She tangled her tongue with his, and heat flooded her body, hardening her nipples and stimulating her clit. The man had a power over her body that charged and made her want him with something as simple as one kiss.

While she continued to stroke his tongue with hers, his hand slid down across the tip of her breasts all the way down to her clit. On contact, she arched up and wanted his hand. She relaxed her hips and parted her thighs. He moved his fingers across her fold, teasing along the way.

No sooner than she was about to come, he removed his finger, slipped on a condom and rolled on top of her. He then pushed her legs apart and grinded his erection against her passage, but didn't come in. Instead, he placed one hand on either side of her head and stared down at her. She wiggled her hips trying to entice him in, but he pressed his weight into her hips and held her firmly in place, then slowly slid in barely an inch.

She groaned and tried unsuccessfully to push him all the way in. He was punishing her for last night. She wanted pleasure, but instead he had decided to torture her like she had done him. And she was helpless to do anything about it.

"Reggie, please—"

"Be patient," he whispered, then slid in another inch. Her body stretched, eagerly awaiting his return.

Her eyes fluttered shut as she released a sigh.

"Open your eyes."

She did as he said, and he slid in a little further.

"Good girl. I want you to look at the man you love as he gives you all of this."

She gazed up at him and the moment intensified. She tried to kiss him, but he held back. Damn him! Without the use of her hands, Reggie had complete control. He slid in a little more and another moan escaped her lips. Pleasure began to build quickly inside, and she wasn't sure how much longer she could wait for him to fill her completely.

"Quit playing and make love to me," she demanded.

"Who's running this?" he asked and to her frustration, his hips stilled.

"Please, Reggie. Make love to me," she whimpered. She wasn't too proud to beg—not when she knew *all* he had to offer.

He answered by sliding in a bit more, but he still had quite a bit to go. She tried to push him in even further, but he held back. She cried out with frustration, and Reggie kissed her pouting lips and laughed. When his face sobered, he grabbed her hips and drove home. Berlin arched off the bed as she felt him slide in completely and exhaled with pleasure.

"Whose is it?" he growled near her ear as he pumped deeply inside.

"Yours baby. It's yours!" She cried as her head rolled from side to side on the pillow. She was his and didn't care who knew it. She forgot about the rest of the world. All she cared about was that he was inside of her filling her again and again. Reginald set the rhythm that started out slow and eventually increased to a powerful speed she could no longer keep up. An orgasm exploded from her, and she cried and wrapped her legs around his waist.

After their breathing returned, Reginald carefully removed the handcuffs and held her in his arms.

"I love you, Lil' Bit," he whispered against her forehead.

Berlin giggled at his use of her pet name. "I love you, too."

"I love you more."

"No, I love you more." Teardrops rolled down her face. She wrapped her arms around him. Hearing those words released any apprehensions she'd had about their future together. The sweet words told her together they could face any obstacles that might stand in their way.

Group Discussion Questions:

1. After learning about Berlin's impoverished background, do you believe she was wrong for wanting to marry for money?

2. What do you think of her ten-step plan?

3. Reginald and Cameron's friendship went way back. As soon as he had learned Berlin was interested in Cameron do you think Reggie should have considered her off-limits? How about after Cameron and Berlin started dating?

4. If Cameron was a bit more appealing after their second date, do you think Berlin would have really invited him back to her place and slept with him like she had originally planned? And if she and Cameron had sex, do you think Berlin and Reginald still would have slept together?

5. After they had run into each other at the restaurant, Reginald went to Berlin's house and she told him she had been waiting for him. If he had had gone home instead do you think she would have called him and asked him to come over?

6. Before they'd had sex, Berlin made it clear that it was a temporary arrangement because she still had an agenda. If you were Reggie how would you have reacted to her you're-good-enough-to-screw-but-not-enough-to-marry statement?

7. Berlin said she enjoyed giving oral sex more than receiving, but yet she didn't bother giving him any head until after she had found out where he lived. Do you think that was just a coincidence? Do you feel that Berlin went down on Reginald only because she found out that he was successful?

8. If Cameron hadn't fallen in love with someone else, do you think Reginald would have told him the truth? What do you think would have happened?

9. Do you feel that Reginald and Berlin have a real chance at being happy?

About the Author

Angie Daniels is a chronic daydreamer who loves a page-turner. An avid reader since age seven, she knew early on that someday she wanted to create stories of love.

Angie Daniels began her writing career in 2000 and has sold eleven books to date. Born in Chicago, she considers Missouri home. You can visit her website at www.angiedaniels.com.